What Happened to Piper Archer?

By
K.J. RABANE

Copyright © 2015 K.J.Rabane
All rights reserved.

Dedication.
To the memory of my brother Alan Lloyd MBE who sadly passed away on the day this book was published.

Acknowledgements

Many thanks, for their continued support, to Frank Baker, Nona and Glyn Evans, Alan Lloyd MBE; *Tiny writers* - Pam Cockerill Bob Davies, Annie Jenkins Janet Marsh, Ron Powell, and Steve Hitchins our inspirational creative writing tutor.

My continued thanks to Rebecca Sian Photography for the cover image.

This book is a work of fiction and therefore any resemblance to persons living or dead is merely coincidental.

TABLE OF CONTENTS

Chapter 1	Chapter 33
Chapter 2	Chapter 34
Chapter 3	Chapter 35
Chapter 4	Chapter 36
Chapter 5	Chapter 37
Chapter 6	Chapter 38
Chapter 7	Chapter 39
Chapter 8	Chapter 40
Chapter 9	Chapter 41
Chapter 10	Chapter 42
Chapter 11	Chapter 43
Chapter 12	Chapter 44
Chapter 13	Chapter 45
Chapter 14	Chapter 46
Chapter 15	Chapter 47
Chapter 16	Chapter 48
Chapter 17	Chapter 49
Chapter 18	Chapter 50
Chapter 19	Chapter 51
Chapter 20	Chapter 52
Chapter 21	Chapter 53
Chapter 22	Chapter 54
Chapter 23	Chapter 55
Chapter 24	Chapter 56
Chapter 25	Chapter 57
Chapter 26	Chapter 58
Chapter 27	Chapter 59
Chapter 28	Chapter 60
Chapter 29	Chapter 61
Chapter 30	Chapter 62
Chapter 31	Chapter 63
Chapter 32	Chapter 64
Chapter 65	

- Chapter 66
- Chapter 67
- Chapter 68
- Chapter 69
- Chapter 70
- Chapter 71
- Chapter 72
- Chapter 73
- Chapter 74
- Chapter 75
- Chapter 76
- Chapter 77
- Chapter 78
- Chapter 79
- Chapter 80
- Chapter 81
- Chapter 82
- Chapter 83
- Chapter 84
- Chapter 85
- Chapter 86
- Chapter 87
- THE END

What happened to Piper Archer?.........K.J.Rabane

BERESFORD

Chapter 1

I still can't believe I've seen her, behaving as if the last two years have been a figment of my imagination. It's the reason I'm writing this – to save my sanity - to explain how it all began.

The day starts like any other. I go to work as usual and as the afternoon blurs into evening I look forward to going home where my wife will be waiting.

The last patient leaves my consulting room and my secretary asks if there are any more letters, as her husband is waiting in the car park. She's not unreasonable - it's her birthday and she needs to be home with her family, not stuck in hospital waiting for me to make up my mind.

"Thanks, Celia, nothing that won't wait until tomorrow. Have a great time."

She beams, "Thank you, Mr Archer, I will. See you in the morning then."

It's been an unremarkable day; one Polypectomy, one delivery of Sally Watson's baby, which her mother was convinced was a cyst, and the successful outcome of a C-Section resulting in triplets for the Maynard couple to whom IVF has been a last ditch attempt to have a family.

I pick up the phone on my desk, our house phone rings twice before I put it down and leave the hospital. Driving towards the ring road I imagine Piper in the kitchen. My signal call will prompt her to begin to set the dining-room table and warm the plates in preparation for our evening meal. I'm one of the lucky ones, I've been told often enough, a successful career and a beautiful, young wife.

Our house is in the suburbs of Lockford, a small town on the south coast of England within easy driving distance of London. It's large and comfortable. We have all we need.

I pull into the driveway as evening shadows lengthen, park in the garage, and enter the house calling out my usual greeting, "I'm home, Piper, kick out the milkman."

There's no reply, no smell of cooking, no sound of her favourite radio station playing rock music – nothing. Perhaps she's gone to the shops, called to see a friend, her sister? But why didn't she text or ring to let me know? It's not like her.

After a while, I wander around the house like a lost soul, looking for a note, checking to see if her clothes are missing, looking for something, anything, which might give a clue as to her whereabouts, but as the hours pass my fear increases. Eventually, after phone calls to her sister and friends, I ring the police and report her missing.

This is how it begins; I arrive home to find my wife gone, with no note of explanation.

What happened to Piper Archer?.........K.J.Rabane

Chapter 2

Serena doesn't seem too bothered. She stands in our kitchen, makes a cup of tea and slides it across the worktop towards me.

"She'll be back. Have a tiff did you? Mike and me are always at each other's throats. It's part of marriage. We love each other, of course we do. But he's like you, high-powered job, bound to get a bit fraught from time to time. I said to him, only the other day, time we had a holiday, I said...."

They are nothing alike, Piper and her sister. I find it difficult to tolerate the garrulous Serena and her 'high-powered' husband at the best of times. He is an inspector on the South Eastern Railway with delusions of grandeur. But they are her family and hers and mine were always poles apart. I only wish mine were still here; there are times when I miss them as intensely as if the accident had only just happened. But I've inherited Serena and her family and it's better than nothing.

"Gone up to London to cool her heels, make you suffer, I expect," Serena is still talking. "She'll be back, mark my words."

But she doesn't come back, not then, and the weeks turn into months and the police investigate her disappearance, put her name on the missing persons register, and eventually forget about her. They stop looking when an expert from the police IT department finds Piper's 'hidden' computer diary file and discovers she's been regularly meeting someone called Rowland Green; they assume they were planning to go away together. Why would she keep the diary hidden, they asked, if it wasn't some sort of liaison? Besides which, a woman had recognised her from the newspaper photo

What happened to Piper Archer?.........K.J.Rabane

and had seen someone fitting her description in a motorway service station with a man; they were enjoying a meal together – like lovers – she said. When they tell me I want to laugh – it has to be a joke, this man, this lover who sounds like a bowling green - I am sure Piper didn't intend leaving me for him, she'd have more sense.

Life continues with little change to my daily routine. I get up, shower, make breakfast and drive to Lockford General just as before but underneath it all I merely exist, going through the motions. Women still have babies, still develop gynaecological problems and still need me to make things better, whilst the fabric of my life unravels thread by thread.

Celia sympathises at first, so do my colleagues. I am the topic of conversation amongst the secretaries until Celia's youngest becomes involved with a married man and their focus shifts, and as far as the medical staff is concerned the daily dose of dramas experienced in a busy teaching hospital soon puts the story of Piper leaving me into the past.

As time goes by and the first year passes, I start to look for her everywhere. I bore her friends, her family and acquaintances, constantly asking if they've seen her or heard anything. Gradually it becomes clear that I have no alternative but to come to terms with the fact that she's left me and get on with my life. And to a degree I succeed, work is my panacea during the day; I spend long hours when I don't think about her. But the nights are a different matter. Dreams punctuate my sleep; her face haunts me, together with her smell, and her smile until I wake up to an empty bed and reality.

What happened to Piper Archer?.........K.J.Rabane

"You should find someone else," Jeff Hughes says, seeing me staring into my coffee cup in the canteen, "it's been long enough. Plenty more fish in the sea, old boy."

Jeff is testament to the fact. He is an orthopaedic surgeon, larger than life and twice as promiscuous. He would never understand the concept of fidelity.

"I don't think so," I mutter.

"Come to *Bruno's* with me on Saturday night, paint the town red."

"I don't...." The sudden prospect of yet another Saturday night waiting for the phone to ring, eating a take-away meal for one, makes me hesitate and it's true what they say, he who hesitates is definitely lost.

"Good, that's fixed then. I'll get a cab and pick you up about nine, we'll sink a few in the wine bar on the High Street and walk to Bruno's from there."

I suppose it could be the start of a new life but I'm not really ready to cast off the old one. Meeting Katrina is fun, she is good company and it helps that she looks nothing like Piper. I take her home, kiss her goodnight and say I'll ring, because I don't know what else to say – dating is a foreign concept to me. Of course I don't plan to ring her or anyone else, my head is too full of my wife and what has happened to her. I don't go along with the version that she's left me for this Rowland Green – there is no way she'd leave like that, not without a word of explanation.

Six months later I'm driving home from the hospital when some fool bumps into the back of me. Luckily I'm stopped at the traffic lights on the junction of Manor Road and Westbourne Road and the car behind isn't travelling at speed. I look in my mirror and see a red Nissan driven by a woman with a mop of curly black hair. I drive into Manor Road and pull in at the kerb followed by the red car. In the mirror I see the driver leaving her car and hurrying towards me.

"I'm most dreadfully sorry," she says. "I wasn't concentrating. Are you OK?"

I would say she is in her late twenties, early thirties, attractive, slim and tall with broad shoulders and obviously in a hurry. I get out of the car and inspect the rear bumper, which is slightly scratched but nothing of any importance.

"I'm fine and the car seems to have suffered no more than minor injuries." I smile reassuringly. "How are you? Are *you* OK?"

"Thank goodness! Me? Annoyed with myself. I wasn't concentrating, my mind was elsewhere; here's my address and telephone number. If you find there's more damage than you think, give me a ring." She hands me a card then hurries back to her car, calling over her shoulder. "I really am most terribly sorry, you know."

"No problem, take care, " I reply.

Glancing at the card I see she is a freelance IT consultant. Her name is Isobel Myers. At the time I think nothing more of it. But I often find it's strange how inconsequential meetings can have far reaching consequences.

Chapter 3

Choosing holiday times from work rotas mean nothing to me now, not after Piper left. Previous hectic rushes to make sure my operating lists were kept to a minimum, as the holiday period approached, are no longer an option. I could cheerfully work through but recognise that I owe it to my patients to be on top of things, besides everyone needs a break from work to return refreshed. So I fit in with the plans of others and book an early spring break.

Nostalgia prompts me to visit Careg Wen, a small village near the coast of South Wales. Piper and I spent some time there when we were first together. We'd stayed at a pub in the village I seem to remember. Logging into my laptop I search for holiday cottages in the area and soon find what I'm looking for, a two up two down overlooking the harbour.

Without much enthusiasm, I pack my things in a small suitcase and drive towards South Wales. The weather is temperamental and throughout my journey I'm subjected to torrential rain, high winds, blindingly bright sunshine and light breezes. It's as if I've crossed some invisible meteorological fault line once I drive over the Severn Bridge, leaving the rain and rough weather behind on the English side; contrary to expectations the rain clouds have disappeared, as the lush, green Welsh hills appear in the distance.

Stopping a while later at a service station, I park the car, use the facilities, and then buy a polystyrene mug of coffee to take-away.

I'm balancing the hot coffee in one hand, and trying to press the car remote key with the other, when a voice behind me says, "Hello again, here let me."

What happened to Piper Archer?.........K.J.Rabane

It's the woman who'd bumped into the back of my car a while back. She takes the remote from my outstretched hand and presses it.

"There. You don't remember me do you?"

I shake my head. "Er, yes, of course. Miss Myers," I reply.

"Isobel. Fancy seeing you again so far from Lockford."

"Yes; quite a coincidence. Are you driving to the coast?"

"Yes. I'm visiting a friend actually. It's nice to see you again. So glad I didn't do too much damage the other day."

"No problem. Have a good journey."

I watch her pulling out of the parking area, feeling it might be wiser to drive behind rather than in front of her, if our last meeting was anything to go by, and soon lose sight of her in the motorway traffic.

A while later I'm travelling along minor roads, which twist and turn towards the coast and see the sign for Gareg Wen. As I draw nearer to the village memories, of the time Piper and I last visited, resurface and once more a powerful feeling of loss sweeps over me, making me wonder whether it is such a good idea to spend time here after all. I come to the conclusion that whatever destination I chose Piper will still be in my thoughts, so Careg Wen is a good place as any.

Driving past the Anchor pub I glance at my Sat Nav and drive in the direction indicated, which is towards the harbour. The air filtering through the car's vents smells of salt.

"*You have arrived at your destination,*" The disembodied voice announces as I park outside the cottage and remove my case from the boot. I'd been told

What happened to Piper Archer?.........K.J.Rabane

the key would be in the adjacent house and an elderly gentleman opens the door to my knock, hands me the key and wishes me a pleasant stay.

The cottage smells of polish and is, to my relief, clean and tidy; the bed linen is crisp and obviously freshly laundered, the kitchen surfaces shiny and the sink smelling of bleach. I put my case in the front bedroom and look out over the harbour. The tide is full and sparkles in the late afternoon sunlight. I open the window and inhale the salt-tinged air with something akin to pleasure. It is an emotion I hardly recognise.

After I've settled in, I stroll to the pub for a snack and a drink. Piper loved staying at the Anchor. She used to say it was like stepping back in time. The village is fairly quiet, the children having gone back to school after their Easter holidays. But the warm spring weather has encouraged local families to linger on the harbour wall and shopkeepers to stay open well past their usual closing time. Three young girls and a thickset boy are watching a football game through the window of a shop selling televisions.

Outside the Anchor there are two men drinking in the last of the evening's sunshine, along with their pints, and a couple sitting on a bench, oblivious of the weather, are concentrating so hard on each other it seems to the exclusion of all else.

Inside, as I'd anticipated, the bar is quiet. The landlord's daughter is talking to a woman who has her back to me but I can hear their laughter as I order a steak sandwich and a pint of lager from a waitress who has one eye on the T.V screen as she takes my order.

Finding a seat at a table near the window, I wait for my food to arrive whilst glancing at the clientele. Our eyes meet at exactly the same time, she having turned away from her conversation with the landlord's daughter to look out of the window.

Isobel Myers smiles and raises her hand and it does cross my mind to think two coincidental meetings in one day are a little unusual. But, it is nothing compared with what is to come.

What happened to Piper Archer?.........K.J.Rabane

Chapter 4

Isobel Myers says something to the landlord's daughter and then walks towards me. "Who's following who?" she asks.

"Now, that *is* the question," I reply.

"Are you staying in Gareg Wen?"

"I am, I've rented a cottage near the harbour. And you?"

"The friend I've come to visit is Lorna. Her father owns this place.

"I see. So we are likely to go on meeting like this." It isn't really a question; Gareg Wen is little more than a hamlet thrown against a hillside boasting a harbour and a few shops.

"Quite possibly. Have a nice holiday. I must get back to Lorna, we have so much news to catch up on."

"I will, you too."

Two weeks of bumping into Isobel Myers not literally I hope, is not appealing. Although she seems pleasant enough, I'm in no mood for a diversion. My intention is to relax, not have to make small talk, to forget about work and the fact that nearly two years ago my wife left me.

Three days later I decide to drive the short distance around the coast to Aberglas, a small town near an estuary. The last time we'd visited, Piper and I had picnicked on the banks watching the sailing boats making their way to the open water and my wife had said we must come back as she'd enjoyed the day so much. So I suppose this is a pilgrimage even though I don't want to acknowledge the fact. Every road I drive along, every sight and sound, a painful memory of the happy times we'd spent. Why am I putting myself

What happened to Piper Archer?.........K.J.Rabane

through it? It's a question I've asked on more than one occasion since Piper left but one for which there is no succinct answer, other than to say that in doing so I'm trying to hold on to the threads of my life before my wife disappears completely and I forget her face.

Of course it isn't the same; how can it be? I've picked up some food in a supermarket on my way to Aberglas, intending to re-create our picnic but the essential ingredient is missing. I sit alone on the banks of the estuary and have no appetite for the food, which I feed to the gulls, cawing and squawking above my head.

"Good heavens, I don't believe it. This is crazy." Isobel Myers stands between the sun and me.

Blinking, her image appearing dark around the edges, I see her sit beside me and watch her stretch out her long legs as she says, "We're obviously two people with a single mind. Oh this is just perfect; it's like a summer's day."

"Not with Lorna today?" I ask, when my vision has returned to normal and I can see she is wearing a blue and white cotton sundress and strappy sandals.

"No, she's had to work in the bar. Holidaymakers or something, they are just too busy apparently. Actually it was she who told me about this place, as there's a great little clothes store in the centre of town. But I thought I'd take in the view before I started the serious task of shopping for clothes."

"A wise decision."

"So I see."

We chat amiably enough and I become unaware of the passage of time. She doesn't seem in a hurry to catch the store before it closes and for the first time in ages I haven't thought about Piper.

What happened to Piper Archer?………K.J.Rabane

"Well, it looks like I'll have to come back again if I want to buy clothes. It's gone six. I must say I've enjoyed our chat, and the view. It's been good to relax." She stands up. "I'm sure we'll meet again, Gareg Wen isn't exactly London, is it? Enjoy the rest of your holiday."

I get to my feet. "I'll try and I must say I've enjoyed this afternoon more than I thought possible."

She is about to reply but just smiles and walks back to her car as I pack the remains of my picnic into a plastic bag, drop it into a waste bin and walk towards the town. There is someone I need to see, someone who knew Piper before I met her.

He is sitting on the sea wall outside his cottage, puffing on his pipe. His face is weather-beaten and his grey hair is thick and worn longer than when I'd last met him.

"Hello, Evan."

He squints up at me. "Beresford?" He leans forward. "Pip not with you then?"

"No. I thought you'd have heard."

"Heard what, lad?"

I sit down beside him and cough as the smoke from his pipe drifts towards me.

"Sorry," he taps the pipe out on the wall. "Filthy habit I know, don't need no doctor to tell me that. Now what's this about Pip?"

"She left me, nearly two years ago now. I got home from work to find her gone - no note, nothing, and I haven't seen her since. The police think she left me for another man."

"Never! And what do you think?"

"I'm sure she didn't. But it isn't like her not to have at least written a note of explanation or a phone call, text message, something to let me know she's still alive. I just wondered, as I'm in the area, whether you'd heard anything."

"Me? No. Not a word."

"You knew her when she was young. Do you think it's like her not to let me know?"

He scratches the back of his head and stares out to sea. "It's true I knew her and Serena when they were kids and were staying at the *Seabank* in Gareg Wen with their parents. They spent hours sitting on the wall here, helping me mend my nets, always asking questions. Serena was a chatterbox but Piper was the one I took to. She was a beaut. Quiet like, serious on times, but as straight as an arrow. Now I come to think of it, lad, You're right, she would never have skipped off without letting you know – not the Pip I knew."

I breathe a sigh of relief. "Thanks Evan. I knew I could count on you for an answer."

"Them English police don't know what they're talking about. Why don't you come with me to *The Ship* and you can tell me all about it?"

So I follow Evan down the cobbles to the pub and we talk about my wife. It helps to have confirmation, from someone who knew her as a child, that my opinion of her is correct. But it doesn't make any real difference Piper is still missing and neither Evan nor I have the slightest idea what can have happened to her. The thought that she is no longer alive is something I refuse to contemplate.

What happened to Piper Archer?.........K.J.Rabane

Chapter 5

My holiday is drawing to a close when I next see Isobel. She is knocking on my door when I return from a walk along the cliffs.

"Isobel?"

"I'm so glad to see you. I've got a problem."

"Come in." I turn the key in the lock and hold the door open for her.

Inside, I open the windows in the living room to let in a welcoming cool breeze on which floats the scents of the harbour.

"It's my car. It's finally given up the ghost. The guy in the garage said it will take at least a week to get the part but I need to get back to work for Monday and you did mention you'd be travelling back to Lockford tomorrow. Could I ...?"

"Of course, no problem. I'll be leaving about eleven – that do you?"

"Excellent. Thanks a million." She looks relieved, her curly black hair seeming even curlier this evening. "Can I buy you a drink in the Anchor to thank you?"

"No need. I've a good bottle of red waiting and I'd rather share it than drink the lot myself."

"That sounds great, if you're sure you don't mind?"

"Not at all. I'd enjoy the company."

It's a pleasant evening. She's good company and I walk her back to the Anchor at half past ten as she has some packing to do.

When I awake it's earlier than usual and I decide to have an early morning stroll along the cliff path before picking up Isobel. The air is cool, the sky the sort of blue you usually see in the Mediterranean. I've been walking for about five, maybe ten, minutes when I hear a dog bark followed by, "Scamp, here boy." It's Lorna from the pub chasing a brown and white spaniel cross.

"Lovely morning," I say.

"Yeah but this dog is giving me the run around. I'm bloody-well worn out already, I am."

"You're Isobel's friend from the Anchor, aren't you?"

"I'm the landlord's daughter, that's right. But I don't have a friend called Isobel."

"Miss Myers? I saw you talking to her at the bar the other night."

"Oh, yeah, now I know who you mean. She's on holiday, nice person, I often pass the time of day with our visitors but I've never seen her before she came to stay. Scamp! Sorry I got to go." She hurries away leaving me confused.

I'm quite certain Isobel told me the friend she was visiting was Lorna – absolutely sure of it. Why would she lie?

I think about asking her on the way home, saying something like, why did you lie about your friendship with the landlord's daughter, but decide I don't care one way or another.

Picking her up at eleven I place her bag in the boot of my car and we drive home. We have lunch in a service station along the way, make inconsequential conversation, comments about work, the weather, the holiday and finally I drop her off at her house in Westbourne Avenue at twenty to six.

"Thanks so much, you must let me take you out for dinner to repay your kindness, what about Wednesday?"

"No, really, it was a pleasure, goodbye Miss Myers."

What happened to Piper Archer?.........K.J.Rabane

I decide the Miss Myers bit will help her get the message and when I reach my car I don't turn around but drive out of the avenue with a sigh of relief.

The following morning, I'm awake at seven, tidy the bedroom a bit and put my holiday washing in the machine. Mrs Dawes will see to the housework tomorrow when I'll be back at work, attending to my clinics, arranging operation lists and catching up on what has happened during my absence.

At half ten the telephone rings. It's Serena.

"Did you have a good holiday, Berry love?"

"Yes, thank you."

"Good, that's the ticket."

She carries on talking, inconsequential titbits about her friends and neighbours, what Mike is doing, how well Mike is doing; but I've learned to switch off, to think about other things. I've been doing it for years and she is content as long as I add the occasional comment, hoping it's appropriate.

The summer months pass without significance for me. The flowers blossom, the trees bloom and the leaves finally fall in the autumn winds. Then Serena rings.

"I was wondering if you fancied coming over next Sunday, it being yours and Piper's anniversary, and no doubt you wouldn't relish spending it on your own. It's our Ellie's eighteenth too and we're having a few friends over. Not that Ellie will be around though. No, she wouldn't want to spend her birthday with the wrinklies, as she's taken to calling us the little devil. What'd'you say, Berry?"

I wish she wouldn't call me Berry. Can I stand Saturday night at Serena and Mike's place? Mike is OK.

What happened to Piper Archer?.........K.J.Rabane

It isn't his fault that his wife has given him delusions of grandeur. There is nothing wrong with being an inspector on the trains – far from it but it isn't exactly brain surgery. I hesitate, aware that Piper would have called me an old snob for even thinking that way.

"Well?"

"Er, I'll be glad to pop in for an hour but I won't be able to stay long, if that's OK?" I am hedging my bets and besides I owe it to Piper to keep in touch with her sister. The thought makes me wonder why I bother, in view of the fact she's left me.

"Good, see you on Saturday then, Berry."

The week passes in a flash and without too many dramas. When Saturday arrives, I think of ringing my sister-in-law with an excuse not to attend her party but can't quite do it.

So at nine o'clock I press the door bell of the nineteen thirties semi, on the edge of the Cranmore estate, which Serena refuses to acknowledge is there, insisting that they live off Manor Road, and wait until Mike lets me in.

The party is in full swing. The living room is crowded, but the French doors leading to the garden are open as we are having what the weather forecasters call an Indian summer.

"What'll you have, Beresford?" Mike asks. "I see you came by taxi, sensible move.

"My car's in for a service, won't be ready until Monday," I raise my voice above the music blaring from Mike's oversized speakers, which are strategically placed near the window. "Beer'll be fine, thanks."

I've met some of their friends before, some are distant relatives; no one asks about Piper. I chat with Mike for a while until Serena drifts in from the garden wearing a flowing green maxi dress which clings like a second skin and makes her look bigger than she is.

"Berry! Come into the garden, it's stuffy in here. Who would have thought the weather would be so good at this time of the year. It's global warming I expect. I said to Mike, he'll have to get rid of that gas-guzzling car of his if he wants to save the planet."

I shouldn't have come. I don't know whether I can stand Serena tonight. She's still talking, "There's someone I want you to meet. A friend of mine; she's moved into a house nearby since her Mum died, big house on Westbourne Avenue. Izzie, come and meet Berry." She giggles and I realise she's been celebrating for quite some time before I arrived.

"Hello again." Isobel Myers, looking very seductive in a strappy yellow dress, looks up at me, and smiles.

What happened to Piper Archer?.........K.J.Rabane

Chapter 6

Serena is on the phone before I've had a chance to shower.

"I wanted to catch you before you went to work. You and Izzie have a good night then? Are you seeing her again?"

Trust my sister-in-law to get straight to the point - no beating about the bush – no finesse.

"I am as a matter of fact." It's no use trying to avoid the question she'll only eat away at it until she finds the answer.

"I knew it! I said to Mike, they look as if they're hitting it off. Good luck to him, Mike said, it's far too long to keep thinking Piper is going to pop up any day soon."

"I'm only meeting her for a drink after work tomorrow, nothing more."

"Yeah right," I can hear disbelief in her tone. "Well anyway, whatever happens, I wish you all the best."

"Well nice of you to ring, Serena but I've a busy day ahead. I'll be in touch."

Throughout the day I concentrate on my patients as usual but something has changed. I no longer spend hours thinking about Piper and it's as if a cloud has cleared from my mind. During the drive home I find I'm hoping Isobel will ring and am looking forward to our get-together the following day.

As it turns out, she rings to cancel – a problem at work she says. I am unaccountably disappointed. She tells me she'll ring and re-schedule once things have calmed down a bit. I can see a brush off, a mile away. It is the sort of thing I might have said in similar circumstances. I suppose I must get used to this, if I'm to start again, although the thought terrifies me. I'm in my forties; I don't want to start again. I was quite happy with my life before my wife suddenly disappeared.

Serena rings to find out how our 'date' went and I take great pleasure in having nothing to tell her. She sympathises and assures me I'll meet someone soon. I've tried telling her before that I'm not looking but it has fallen on deaf ears, so just I keep silent and listen.

I've almost forgotten about Isobel Myers. It must be a month since the party at Serena's, when suddenly she rings me. "Hi, Beresford. I'm so sorry I haven't been in touch before. Work has been manic. How are you fixed for Saturday night? I thought we could go out somewhere."

I don't want to sound too eager so pretend to consider the question, and eventually say, "That should be fine. Where would you like to go?"

"What about Vellucio's?"

"Italian? Great by me."

"I'll get a taxi and call for you. That way we can enjoy the very best Chianti Giovanni Vellucio has to offer, without any worries."

I agree and it is only after I've put down the phone that I realise she doesn't know my address.

When Saturday arrives there is no sign of the Indian summer, it's disappeared like Piper and I awaken to grey clouds and the patter of raindrops on my bedroom window.

I spend most of the day reading and I'm ready and waiting when a taxi draws up at eight on the dot. I slide into the back seat alongside Isobel who looks lovely. She's immaculate, shining hair, beautifully made up face and wearing an emerald green dress that reveals just enough of her figure to entice without appearing tarty.

"I had to ring Serena to get your address," she explains.

"Yes, she told me. I should have your telephone number I suppose," I say, and I'm aware that I sound less than enthusiastic. I try to make amends but she doesn't seem to notice so I end up listening to her chatting about the weather and her frustration with work problems until we reach the restaurant. Then, dodging the rain, we hurry to the entrance and wait to be shown to our table.

I'd like to say I've entertained her with sparkling repartee but in truth I remember very little of our conversation after I see Piper standing in the rain on the pavement opposite.

Isobel is looking at the menu in order to choose a dessert and I have my glass raised to my lips savouring the Chianti, which is, as she's led me to believe, excellent. Looking over the top of my glass into the street I see a figure, her hair is hidden by a knitted hat and she is wearing a mackintosh, which I've never seen her wear before. She is looking straight at us. I blink believing my eyes are deceiving me but when I look again she is still there. Our eyes meet and she turns away.

"What is it?" Isobel looks up from the menu.

"Er," I shake my head in disbelieve. "Do you see that woman standing in the rain on the other side of the road? Try not to stare."

She glances out of the window, not making it too obvious. "Er, where?"

"There – opposite – on the pavement."

"What? I don't understand."

I look again and she's right – there's no one there.
"Who have you seen?" Isobel asks
"Piper."
She looks at me as if I've grown two heads.
"Your wife?"
I nod.
"Yes my wife."

Chapter 7

Isobel suggests I go over to her, she can't have gone far, and ask her what is going on. I think about it but decide not to. I've spent too much time worrying that she might be dead in a ditch somewhere so I turn away from the window, order another bottle of red and concentrate on my companion. When I eventually risk looking again, I see only rain sliding down the glass. And in spite of, or perhaps because of, seeing Piper, I enjoy the evening immensely. It is obvious the police were right all along, she has a lover and left me for him. I decide I must do something about arranging a divorce.

"So," Serena says, one Sunday morning when Christmas was approaching faster than a steam train. She's just 'called in' to see how I am. "So, I gather you and Izzie are an item?"

We've decided not to tell Serena about me seeing Piper, just in case I've made a mistake. We don't want to upset her unnecessarily because she'll be wondering why Piper hadn't rung her, or visited her, if she was in Lockford. Serena prefers to think she's gone abroad than face the fact that she might be living somewhere nearby and hasn't made any attempt to contact her.

"Let's say we are just good friends."

"If that's what you want to call it." Serena sighs. "Anyway, Berry, I'm pleased for you."

But her expression doesn't match her words, especially when I tell her about the divorce.

As the last patient of the day closes the door behind her, I scribble some details on a notepad and attach it to the hospital folder thanking heavens for Celia who has no

What happened to Piper Archer?.........K.J.Rabane

trouble deciphering my scrawl. Isobel is in London but she promises to catch up on Friday after work and that she'll ring me every night before bed. It feels good to have someone who cares.

The drive home is uneventful. I stop at the mini-market off Manor Road and buy a microwave meal and a bottle of Merlot – or what passes for it, as Isobel and I diminished my stock of red wine at the weekend. It is chilly and there is a hint of snow in the air. Last weekend we spent Saturday and Sunday afternoons relaxing by the fire and drinking wine before falling into bed pleasantly tipsy.

Parking in the garage I close the door with the remote and put my key in the lock of the front door. Isobel has decorated it with a holly wreath, its berries plentiful and a rich red, the thorny leaves pluck at my coat sleeves as I open the door. Then I hear rock music coming from the back of the house. My heart begins to race it's Razorback – Piper's favourite band.

Once inside, I follow the sound to the kitchen.

The carrots are peeled and sit in a saucepan alongside ones containing potatoes and broccoli.

"What the? Piper?" My voice echoes around the empty kitchen. Then she comes in from the conservatory and acts as if she's never been away.

I sit on the stool and wipe my forehead with my handkerchief in stunned silence. I can smell her perfume. It's everywhere.

"There's a pie in the oven. I'll just put on the veg. Go into the living room and I'll bring you a whiskey and soda."

It's what she would usually say. I wonder if she's had amnesia and try to coax an explanation out of her but she just smiles and says, "Did you have a busy day?"

What happened to Piper Archer?.........K.J.Rabane

Her hair looks odd – it's shorter and a different colour.

In a dream, I walk into the living room. She's acting as if the past two years haven't occurred.

"Piper?" The word comes out in a croak, as I wait in the living room for the ghost of my wife to appear.

I shake my head knowing this is ridiculous. The music is loud - it swirls around me like a whirlpool, sucking me under. I reach out and switch off the IPad dock then go back into the kitchen as anger sweeps over me in a wave. I am determined to get the answers to the questions, which have plagued me for the past two years.

But there is no one waiting for me – the house is empty. I shake my head in disbelief – someone was here – someone who has a key – someone I spoke to.

Feeling as if I am in the middle of some ghastly dream, I tip the vegetables, my imaginary wife has prepared, into the bin, turn off the oven and remove the pie, which follows the vegetables into the re-cycling container then open the bottle of wine. It's warm and sour tasting but if I drink enough of it, it will help me to ignore the fact that Piper has been in the house whilst I was at work. Am I going mad? Why would she prepare a meal and disappear again? It's inconceivable but then everything concerning Piper, since she left, is a mystery and one, which I have little inclination to solve. After she left I'd spend months trying to understand why, and now I no longer care.

When I awake, my head is pounding and my tongue feels thick and coated. I'm almost afraid to open my eyes in case I see further evidence of her. I reach out a hand and find a reassuringly empty space at my side; the sheets are cold and unwrinkled. I breathe a sigh of relief.

What happened to Piper Archer?.........K.J.Rabane

My dreams linger and I call out, "Piper?" But the house is as silent as it is most mornings since she left. After using the bathroom, I go downstairs and into the kitchen. The remains of my supermarket meal stand on the worktop alongside a glass and an empty bottle of wine.

Picking up the phone in the hall I ring Austin Banks, my senior registrar.

"Austin, sorry to ring so early. I seem to have picked up a tummy bug. Could you see to everything for a day or two?"

"Of course, no problem. Hope you'll be feeling better soon, sir."

I've tried to stop him calling me sir but to no avail so I've given up trying.

"Thanks Austin. I'll be in touch."

The events of the previous evening have shaken me more than I would have thought possible. As if in a waking nightmare I search every room for signs of her, go into the garden in my dressing gown scanning every bush, tree, and shrub for some trace of Piper and, finding nothing, finally sink to my knees on the lawn, which is covered with frost and pray I'm not going mad.

Isobel

Chapter 8

My first impression of Beresford Archer was of a George Clooney lookalike – younger of course but like George the greying hair added to his attraction. I'd been preoccupied, thinking about ditching Phil because he was far too interested in sport for my liking. He'd cancel our dates, if fixtures coincided, without a thought of how I was feeling and I wanted more from a relationship.

Bumping into Beresford, literally, had shocked me into concentrating on my driving rather than my lover. He was gracious, considering my lack of awareness. Meeting him later, on his way to Careg Wen, had seemed like fate. At least I thought so. It was a mistake to lie to him but I was cornered and I made up my friendship with the landlord's daughter in case he thought I was stalking him and knew at some point I would have some explaining to do. But I couldn't tell him the whole truth because that would have spoiled my plans.

Although he didn't question me about it, maybe lying about Lorna had blown any chance of us getting together in the near future. I could tell he didn't want us to meet again during the journey to home to Lockford. He'd cooled – gone into himself – didn't even turn to wave to me when he dropped me off at the house. So I had to think again. Serena was a walk over. I'd met her through a friend on one or two occasions and it wasn't really difficult to cultivate a friendship with her. Being invited

What happened to Piper Archer?.........K.J.Rabane

to a party at her place was just what I needed. I was sure her brother-in-law would be there, which suited me just fine. She was basically a kind person and wanted to help him get over her sister. The trouble with Serena was she had verbal diarrhoea and her consistently drawn out conversations were tiresome in the extreme. However, I soon found the ability to switch her off quite effectively and just nodded or responded with some vague interjections where appropriate, which seemed to satisfy her, thus solving any problems on that score.

I was right. He *was* at the party and afterwards, one thing led to another. Beresford understood when my work took me away from time to time. He had a high-powered career himself and his patients relied upon his dependability. I think it was part of what made him such a caring individual. It did cross my mind, on more than one occasion, to wonder why Piper left him when she had it all. But then who knows why people do things, which to others seem inconceivable? I suppose I envied her, having a husband like Beresford, a beautiful house, an active social life. It was something I'd always dreamed of having but had never been lucky enough to find that special someone who could give it to me. Before meeting Beresford, I mean.

Serena insisted on calling him Berry, like he was some kind of overripe fruit. It grated on me every time. But that was typical of Serena and it was another facet of her personality, which I chose to ignore.

I'd almost begun to believe that we were heading towards something more lasting in our relationship. I'd begun to dream of having Piper's life, of him coming home to *me* at the end of the day in that beautiful house and of him kissing *my* cheek and asking me how my day had gone.

What happened to Piper Archer?.........K.J.Rabane

Then Piper came back. At least he *said* she'd come back. It was odd. The whole thing - it was very odd. He was sure she'd been at the house and had even prepared a meal for him. I was concerned about his state of mind. Had he seen her or was it wishful thinking?

He was definitely shaken up. I thought I was getting to know Beresford but I was beginning to wonder if I knew him at all. First he called in sick at work. Then he kept waiting for Piper to return. A couple of days later he told Serena he'd had a phone call from her saying she'd be back later. Serena went around to their place to wait for her but she never turned up. I could see she doubted her brother-in-law's sanity, as she was sure Piper would have phoned her or come to see her if she was in Lockford.

I know it sounds a bit over the top to suggest he was delusional. He was an intelligent man, a man with a flourishing career, looked up to, revered, it wasn't the sort of reaction you'd expect from him. He didn't want to see me either. I could tell it was the end of the line. I told him to ring me if I could help in any way. It was no good making a nuisance of myself. He'd come around, once he realised she wasn't coming back and that he'd had some sort of breakdown, I was sure of it. In the meantime I kept in contact with Serena. She was my way in. The only hope I had of getting to Beresford.

What happened to Piper Archer?.........K.J.Rabane

Serena

Chapter 9

Mike was snoring fit to burst when the phone rang. I'd been up for over an hour, put on the washing, cleaned the kitchen and was making a shopping list. It was half nine. Mike was off on the sick, man-flu, chest infection, the lot. He always suffered in the winter when the weather turned.

"Serena?" It was Berry and he sounded rough. If I didn't know Izzie was in London, I'd have thought they'd had a session last night. I recognised the hoarse voice from too many late night parties when I was young, and a few since. "Has Piper been in touch, she's not there with you this morning, is she?"

I could hardly believe my ears. "Berry? Are you OK?"

"Sorry, I should have explained. Yesterday I arrived home from work to find a meal prepared in the kitchen, her favourite band playing on the IPad and there she was standing in the kitchen as large as life, as if nothing had happened. She told me to go to go into the living room and she'd bring me a drink. I was so shocked I went along with it. When I came to my senses and went to find her, she'd gone."

I didn't know what to say, was he on something? I'd heard of hallucinatory drugs, like what they took in the sixties, and Berry *was* a doctor, he could get his hands on anything I shouldn't wonder. "You're sure you didn't dream it, Berry love – one too many glasses?"

"Er, no; as I said, I'd just come home from work."

What happened to Piper Archer?.........K.J.Rabane

"Look, I'll come over if you like." I was expecting him to say, no, there was no need and he'd obviously been dreaming the whole thing, after a session on the booze, but he said thanks he'd appreciate it. Really shocked me that did, the great Beresford Archer wanting my help, well I had no illusions on that score, he must have been desperate.

I must admit I felt sorry for him then. Berry was all right, bit of a stuffed shirt, old for his age, well no, he *was* old actually; I said to Piper on more than one occasion *before* they'd married – he's too old for you – Mike had agreed. I said, fifteen-year age gaps might be OK when you're in your twenties, my girl, but think, when you're fifty-nine he'll be seventy-four! But she'd just smiled that self-satisfied smile of hers and said they loved each other and nothing else mattered.

If our dad had been around he'd have had something to say on the matter but Mum was impressed with Berry's job and he was always sucking up to her before mum's decline. Alzheimer's the doctors said but I wasn't so sure, she was confused that was all. They found her in the park one night; it was freezing, it was in the middle of January, when we had the snow - hypothermia, they said. She died on the way to hospital.

I think she's dead – Piper I mean. Someone's taken her, someone she met on the net, that Rowland Green bloke if you ask me. If she'd been alive she'd have rung me – she wouldn't have let Ellie's eighteenth pass without sending a card. I know we've had our differences but she *is* my sister and I know she would have rung, if she *was* alive, I mean.

Berry saying she'd just turned up out of the blue was rubbish. I was sure of it. But he did sound awful on the phone and when I went round there I could see for myself.

He let me in and I noticed the kitchen was in a bit of a mess, not at all like when Piper was around. There was a half-eaten carton of food on the worktop, empty bottle of wine and a glass near the microwave. Breakfast dishes in the sink; he hadn't even bothered to put them in the dishwasher.

"I thought you said she'd prepared a meal – her chicken-pie wasn't it?" I said.

He looked bewildered, rubbed his hands over his forehead. "I threw it all in the re-cycling bin. But I suppose it's gone now. I heard the bin men earlier, before I rang you."

"Look, sit down, I'll make us a cup of tea," I said.

He didn't argue, didn't say he preferred Lapsang something or other, or filtered coffee, just plonked himself down at their fancy breakfast island and waited for me to put the kettle on.

"I wonder if she'll come back today?" he said, looking out of the window to where the lawn was white with frost.

"I wouldn't bank on it, Berry love. Drink this, have a shower and go for a brisk walk up on the Heath, blow away the cobwebs." I began stacking the dishwasher and putting the food from the carton into the re-cycling container.

"You don't believe me. There's no reason why you should. I don't believe me." He ran his fingers through his hair, which seemed to be much greyer than before.

"Would you like me to give Izzie a ring?"

He looked up. "Er, no, thanks, Serena. She's in London and besides I've nothing to tell her that makes any sense."

"Yeah, perhaps not. I tell you what, come over to ours later and I'll cook us a nice meal. You and Mike can watch the rugby and you could stay over if you feel like it. Ellie's in Spain with her mates so the house will be quiet for once."

He tried to smile. It wasn't much of one though. "That's very sweet of you but I think I'll stay, just in case she comes back."

Oh my Lord, I thought. I've seen this sort of thing before. I hoped he wasn't going to follow Mum down that particular road. "Right you are then. You know we are just a phone-call away. And we *are* still your family after all." I picked up my handbag from the chair. "Don't forget that walk, it will do you good."

"I won't, I promise." He came towards me and kissed my cheek. "And thanks again, Serena."

The front door closed behind me before I realised I'd smelled, amongst other things, the distinctive odour of Piper's special chicken-pie sauce, spiced with garlic and chillies, when I'd emptied the contents of the fast food carton into the re-cycling. I shook my head. I was at it too now. The power of the imagination is such a dangerous thing, I always find.

What happened to Piper Archer?.........K.J.Rabane

Chapter 10

A few days later I was shopping in town when I bumped into Izzie.

"I didn't know you were back from London," I said.

She looked confused for a moment then smiled. "Serena! Er yes, came back the day before yesterday. I'm glad I've seen you; I was going to ring. Have you time for a coffee?"

I could tell there was something wrong - it didn't take a mind reader. She was usually so composed but something had ruffled her feathers.

In the coffee shop we ordered our drinks and sat down. We talked about the weather, her London trip and Ellie's university choices until the drinks arrived. She was avoiding the subject bothering her so I had to take the reins. "OK - out with it," I said.

She sighed. "It's difficult."

"Has this got anything to do with Berry, by any chance?"

She looked relieved. "Yes, yes, you've heard he's convinced Piper has come back?"

"Thinks she has. I'm surprised he told you. I thought he'd forgotten all about it."

"You don't believe him? A while back he told me he'd seen her standing outside a restaurant when we were having a meal and now this."

"Of course not. I don't know what he told you but he'd had quite a bit to drink at some point. The empty wine bottle was on the worktop in the kitchen when I arrived. I think he dreamt the whole thing. As for seeing her, wishful thinking, if you ask me."

"He seemed so sure, even told me she'd prepared a meal for him." She picked up her cup.

"Oh yeah, the food, all trace of which disappeared by the time I appeared. The re-cycling bin men had come, before I arrived, apparently. Did he tell you the remains of his supermarket meal for one were still on the worktop when I arrived?"

"No, not exactly."

"So he's still insisting she's been to the house? It doesn't make any sense. If Piper had come back she'd have rung me and why would she have disappeared again? Think about it, Izzie. He's confused, love."

"I have been. I can't get it out of my head. It's such a relief to talk about it. He seems so sure."

That was the bit I thought odd at the time but I didn't let on to Izzie, nor did I tell her about the smell of Piper's 'special' sauce coming from the unwashed re-cycling bin. Berry was no fool, OK perhaps it was the drink making him a bit confused but sense would normally have returned with the hangover. I couldn't understand why he was still insisting she'd come back.

"My advice would be to try to help him to forget about it. You are more than capable of getting his mind off it, I'm sure." I patted her hand.

"Yes, you're right. I'll certainly try."

My conversation with Izzie buzzed around in my head all day. When I told Mike, he said we were typical women – looking for trouble where none existed. I asked him to explain but he put on the telly and the next thing he was lost in the rugby and I knew he'd be useless to talk to for the next two or three hours at least.

The weeks passed. There was no mention of Berry seeing my sister again and winter turned into spring. One morning just as I was making a cup of tea Ellie rang from Spain where she was spending a holiday with a

What happened to Piper Archer?.........K.J.Rabane

friend and said she'd met a girl who was working in a bar who asked if she'd like to stay on for a bit, do a couple of weeks' work, as they were desperate for help what with the season starting and being short-staffed. I told her to be careful and to have a word with them out there to see if it was legal. Anyway she said she'd looked into it and it was OK she'd got the relevant documents signed and she was going to stay on with her friend in the apartment she was renting with another girl. Oh to be young and fancy-free I thought. It would all change for Ellie next year. Having a gap year couldn't last forever.

Afterwards, I felt a bit low to tell you the truth. I'd got used to Piper not being around and it had been hard when she left. It wasn't as if we were terribly close but we did talk quite a bit on the telephone and we'd meet up for coffee in town every now and then, so for a while I missed her like mad. But I'd had to move on, you couldn't keep expecting her to turn up, not as the months passed and then a year and the months sped towards another anniversary of her disappearance. But, although I was sure Berry had imagined the other night, I don't mind saying it disturbed me more than a bit. What if she was close by? Did she need me? What if she was like mother? Alzheimer's can be hereditary or so I've heard. It was when I had time on my hands that the question bothered me most.

I suppose I would have put it all to the back of my mind if Izzie hadn't phoned me the following week and said, "He says she's rung him."

"Piper?"

"Yes. He'd stopped off at the supermarket on his way home. We were going to have a night in and he said he'd cook. He said his phone started to ring as he was getting into his car in the car park. He said she didn't speak but he knew it was Piper. I don't mind telling you, Serena, I'm beginning to think Beresford is delusional to say the least."

I tried to laugh it off. "You're sure he's not pulling your leg because he feels embarrassed about believing he'd seen her the other night?"

"I don't think so. He was really spooked."

"How exactly?"

"His hands were shaking and when he answered the door to me he was as white as a sheet. He looked scared stiff, Serena. He doesn't want to see me at the moment – he asked if we could leave it for a while."

"I see. I'll pop over this evening, after he comes home from the hospital."

"He hasn't gone into work."

When I put the phone down I told Mike I was going to the shops. I didn't mention my conversation with Izzie. How could I? He'd have thought we were both making a mountain out of a molehill. But I knew my brother-in-law would never have missed going to work without a good reason, so soon after the last time. He was too conscientious where his patients were concerned.

The curtains were drawn in the living room. All the windows were closed even though I could feel the sun on the back of my neck as I waited for Berry to open the door. I shouted through the letterbox but when he still didn't answer I used my key and let myself in.

I must admit it was quite a shock. He looked as if he'd aged ten years since I last saw him. I followed him into the kitchen. It didn't escape my notice that there was another empty bottle of wine on the worktop.

What happened to Piper Archer?.........K.J.Rabane

"Now what's all this about, Berry?" I said, "You look terrible." I don't believe in beating about the bush. "I've heard from Izzie."

"So you know she's rung me."

"Izzie said the person didn't speak. It could have been anyone. Was it her phone?"

He put his head in his hands. "No. I didn't recognise the number but I could hear her breathing. I know it was her."

I felt as if someone was walking over my grave. I shivered. He meant it – he was sure he'd seen my sister the other day and sure she'd phoned him – it was obvious. The fact that she was nowhere to be seen and no one else had seen her was worrying. But whatever I thought about it, I knew without a doubt Berry was certain he was telling me the truth.

I sat down on the kitchen chair opposite him and reached out for his hand. "Why? What do you think she wants to achieve by doing this?"

"I don't know. That's the problem."

His grey hair was curling around his collar. I always thought his dark hair was natural but as I looked at him now it occurred to me that he might have been colouring it for a while before Piper left. Some faded patches of colour still remained but most of it was now as grey as a badger's backside.

"I suggest, the next time you think you see or hear from her, you give me a ring and I'll come over. Have you thought someone might be playing in sick joke by pretending to be Piper? Perhaps someone who looks like her. After all, it's surprising what a change of hairstyle will do. People are always telling me I look like that woman who does the cooking programme on a Monday evening when I've had a bob cut and colour."

What happened to Piper Archer?.........K.J.Rabane

He was looking at me as if I'd suddenly grown two heads. "Do you honestly think I wouldn't recognise my own wife?"

"No, not really, it was just a thought."

He stood up and walked to the window whilst rubbing his hand over his chin, which had sprouted a growth of grey stubble.

"The agonising part of all this is I have absolutely no idea whether I'll see her again or when. Why, is something I can't fathom? It's not like the Piper I knew to be so cruel."

"Perhaps she's sick, in the head I mean?" I suggested.

He turned towards me then. "That's it, of course, you must be right, something happened to make her leave without a word of explanation all those months ago and it must have something to do with her state of mind. I don't know why it hadn't occurred to me before, except that she's always been so grounded, so sensible, not given to flights of fancy." He sounded relieved at the prospect. "Thank-you, Serena. You've made me feel a lot better. And I promise I will ring you, if I see her again, although I can't say when that's likely to be."

"Good. Now I'll get this place cleaned up and open some windows, whilst you get in the shower"

"Excellent, thanks."

The fact that my brother-in-law, who always gave the impression he was above the likes of Mike and me, had thanked me twice in as many minutes made me think he was more shaken up by recent events than I could ever have imagined.

So, if he was sure he'd seen Piper, what if he was right? My head spun with questions for which I had no answers. I thought I knew my sister - game playing was not her thing. She was an open book, what you saw was

What happened to Piper Archer?.........K.J.Rabane

what you got. At least that's what I'd always thought. But for now I could only sit back and hope Berry would be true to his word and would ring or text me next time he saw her then perhaps I'd have a chance to get to the bottom of what was happening. I didn't want to dwell on her having mental problems – it was too close to home for me to even contemplate.

What happened to Piper Archer?.........K.J.Rabane

Chapter 11

The following day Mike said he was being sent to London for a two-week training session. There were new rules to learn and team building exercises for all senior staff. He didn't want to go, naturally. Mike likes his home comforts too much. He didn't fancy what he called rubbish hostel food and fancy-pants instructors teaching their granny to suck eggs. But I told him it would be good for his career – a step up the ladder. He said he was quite happy with the rung he was standing on thank you very much, but I didn't take any notice, just packed his case and drove him to Lockford station to meet the early morning London train

The thought of not having to make his meals and watch endless sport on the TV made me light-hearted but deep down I knew I'd miss him moaning about the state of the country and his work colleagues, amongst other things, after all two weeks was the most we'd been parted since we got married.

Mike didn't care much for Piper, though he didn't show it. Said she was up herself and as for Beresford, he thought he was the giddy limit. He couldn't understand why my sister, who was considered to be beautiful, had nailed her colours to his mast and married a man old enough to be her father. I pointed out that he'd have been fifteen at the time for that to be the case but he wasn't listening.

Driving back from the station, I could see it was going to be a nice day so once inside the house, I opened all the windows, cleaned the place, washed the bed linen and hung it out to dry on the line in the garden.

"It's going to be another good drying day, Mrs Platt."

What happened to Piper Archer?.........K.J.Rabane

Julie from next door, almost nine-months gone, was standing on her decking, her head just visible over our fence.

"Looks like it, love. How are you feeling? Any day now, is it?"

"I'm OK, Mrs P. But I said to my Ben, I'll be glad when I can get into something pretty instead of feeling like a beached whale. I went to the hospital for my antenatal check up yesterday but I didn't see Mr Archer. They said he was off sick. All right is he?"

"Bit of a tummy bug I think. Can't take any chances when he's dealing with pregnant women and young babies."

"I s'pose. I don't like that Austin Banks though, creepy bloke, smiling all the time when he's looking down below. Not a bit like Mr Archer. Pity about his wife going off."

She suddenly realised what she was saying and tried to cover it up.

"I mean, sorry, I forgot she was your sister."

"It was a long time ago. People have to move on. And I must move on and get this washing out," I said, not wanting to go over old ground.

Everyone I knew thought like Julie - that Piper had gone off with some man or other. I'd thought it myself at the time, her being so much younger than Berry. But now I wasn't so sure. Maybe there was something else going on. Maybe Berry wasn't seeing things after all.

Later that evening, I was about to have an early night as it was too warm to do the ironing and I couldn't settle to watch TV, I picked up my magazine from the table and was walking into the hall when the phone rang.

"She's just rung to tell me she was sorry she was late, the film went on longer than she'd anticipated but she'd pick up a takeaway for us on the way home. She should be here any minute," Berry sounded anxious.

"I'll be there in ten to fifteen depending on the traffic," I said, picking up my car keys from the hall table.

What happened to Piper Archer?………K.J.Rabane

Chapter 12

My hands were shaking and my palms were wet as I pressed the doorbell. I'd forgotten my key. Berry let me in.

"Come in."

"She hasn't come home yet?"

"No. Any minute though, I'm sure. Let's go into the living room." He ran his fingers through his hair, which was nearly white now. It would have suited him if he hadn't looked so haggard.

"How did she seem when she called you?" I asked.

"OK, nothing odd, although the line wasn't good. She sounded far away or as if she had a cold."

"You're sure it was her. Recognise the number did you?"

He shook his head. "Some sort of trauma might account for it. I've spoken to a friend of mine in Neurology and put the scenario to him, not mentioning Piper of course, just a hypothetical query, and he did suggest something of the kind. When she arrives, we should insist that she has both a psychological and neurological evaluation."

"I'll go along with anything you say. If she comes home. I just want to see her."

We sat discussing my sister and how we should proceed as the minutes ticked by and the sun sank lower in the sky. At ten o'clock we knew she wasn't going to come.

"Perhaps she saw my car and couldn't face the two of us together?" I suggested.

"Possibly, but I don't mind telling you, Serena, this is getting to me. It's driving me up the wall. Who is going to believe I'm not making it up? No one has seen her except me." He put his head in his hands. "If I were you I'd seriously begin to think it was I who needed a psychiatric evaluation." He gave a harsh laugh, rubbed his eyes and looked at me waiting for my reaction.

"Yeah, well, what I think doesn't matter, Berry. You're the doctor, you tell me." I hadn't meant it to sound so harsh but what could I say? Trying to soften my words, I said, "Look, I can stay the night, if you like. Mike and Ellie are away. If you think it would help?"

He hesitated. I thought he might even be considering my suggestion. Then he smiled and patted my hand.

"Thanks for the offer but I'll be OK. I promise I'll ring you the moment I hear anything more from her."

"Well, if you're sure."

Driving home, I thought about how the future might pan out. Would Berry keep thinking about her and would he try to find her? More questions without answers; I wanted to help him find my sister but didn't know where to start.

Both Izzie and Mike finished working in London at the weekend and I had other fish to fry than thinking about Berry and what he was going to do. Mike settled down for a summer of sport, as the weather was settled. He'd taken up membership of the golf and cricket clubs, when he'd had his promotion so what with watching it and playing it I saw little of him. I didn't see much of Izzie either. She was working flat out in the IT department of a large insurance firm, which had sprung up on the High Street and who desperately needed some technical help. However, she did call me at the weekend and said she was terribly worried about Berry.

"He's completely obsessed with this Piper thing. I can't understand any of it. Why does he only see her when no one else is around? And what about these phone calls?"

She was just repeating the questions I'd asked myself over and over again. Why had she turned up at Elm Tree house and not contacted me? "I can't answer that one, Izzie love. All we can do is support him and hope things get sorted soon."

She sighed. "You're right. I'm just a bit stressed at the moment. It's hectic at work and I just don't have the time to help him look for an imaginary lost wife."

"You think he's making it up?"

"Oh, I don't know. Don't take any notice of me. As I said, I'm a bit stressed myself at the moment."

After I put down the phone, I thought over what Izzie had said. It might be that she would get fed up of hanging around for him to stop thinking about Piper. But I had to admit he did look as if he was going through hell – he looked as bad as he did during those weeks after Piper first left. I felt sorry about seeing him like that.

When Monday arrived and Mike had gone to play golf for the day I ambled around the house like a lost soul. I needed some help to sort this mess out - to find Piper - and the sooner the better. The previous evening I'd been watching a drama on BBC1 and it was about a woman who was convinced she was seeing her dead husband. She'd enlisted the help of Morgan Reynard, the Private Investigator.

In the den, I sat behind the desk and opened the laptop. Then I searched for the telephone numbers of Private Investigators in the Lockford area. There were a couple on the outskirts of town but there was one in Hastings Buildings, five minutes away from Primark. I could kill two birds with one stone, I thought, picking up

What happened to Piper Archer?.........K.J.Rabane

the phone and ringing the offices of Richard Stevens Private Investigator.

Isobel

Chapter 13

I'd decided to take a week's holiday out of my allocation. The office can spare me. I'd made sure everything was up to date before I left. The weather was settled so a holiday in the UK wasn't such a dismal proposition. Nevertheless, I was acutely aware that to leave Lockford now would mean I wouldn't be able to keep tabs on Beresford.

My attempts at trying to replace his wife in his affections had ground to a miserable halt. He was sinking further into depression and I could do nothing about it. Serena kept me informed as to his state of mind and I'd ring him occasionally but always with a less than satisfactory result. So I had a decision to make. Should I look on the Internet for a hotel at a coastal resort, perhaps somewhere in Wales, Careg Wen was uppermost in my mind, or should I stay and see what I could do on the Beresford front? Maybe there was a third choice. Would it be possible to suggest to Beresford that he could do with a holiday? I didn't hold out much hope there but I always worked on the assumption that if you didn't ask you didn't get.

So with this thought it mind I drove to Elm Tree house on a bright sunny morning, with just the faintest trace of apprehension lowering my optimistic mood.

Leaving my car parked out of sight of the front door, I pressed the bell and waited. It seemed like an age before I heard the sound of footsteps in the hall followed by the unlocking of the door.

"Beresford? Are you OK?" I asked. He looked terrible. His hair was too long, dark shadows ringed his eyes and he appeared to have slept in his clothes. If I thought he looked bad the last time I saw him, this was infinitely worse.

"Did you want something?" His voice was thick and I wondered if he'd been drinking.

"Can I come in?"

He stood aside without answering. The house smelled; the windows were closed and the kitchen stank of unwashed dishes and stale food.

"I'm worried about you. Serena told me she hasn't seen you in weeks and that you won't answer the phone or the door."

"I let you in."

"I see. So you thought I was Piper?"

Again he didn't answer me.

"May I open the windows? Clean the place up a bit?"

He looked around as if unaware of his surroundings. "If you like."

I'd expected a fight, and argument or at least a polite no thank-you and to be shown the door. But there was no fight in him and I desperately wanted to make it better, to heal the hurt. I hadn't expected the feeling to be so strong. In the ordinary scheme of things, I don't do emotional responses to situations; it surprised me.

I spent the next couple of hours tidying up whilst I ran a bath and insisted he relax. In his wardrobe I found some clean clothes and in a chest of drawers, his underclothes. To my astonishment I saw that Piper's clothes were still there as if waiting for her to return.

What happened to Piper Archer?.........K.J.Rabane

Later, when he was dressed, I suggested I make an appointment for him at his hairdressers. Again he didn't argue and I drove him into town and waited in the car park until he returned. Finding him in such an acquiescent mood, I said. "I think you could do with a holiday, just a few days, perhaps a week. I've decided to go back to Gareg Wen in a day or two. Shall I book you into the Anchor? I don't mind driving us down."

As if in a daze, he nodded. "OK," he said, staring out of the window.

Why I thought I could deal with his obvious mental instability myself is a mystery, but I was so confident in my ability to make things better.

Careg Wen hadn't changed since our last visit, in fact I always felt as though I'd slipped back in time once I'd driven into the village. The pace of life was slower than in Lockford and a million miles away from the maelstrom in the city of London.

Beresford talked little on the journey. I'd chatted away like a train unable to stop. Eventually we arrived at the Anchor, were shown up to our rooms by Lorna and left to our own devices. I told Beresford I'd give him a knock at half past six and we'd take a stroll down to the harbour. Again he didn't protest. It was like taking a well-behaved child out for the day. I was seriously worried about his state of mind and was determined to get him to have a chat with his doctor, if his condition didn't improve by the end of our holiday. I'd persuaded him to stay the week and hoped by that time I'd see a change in him, especially as he wouldn't be looking for Piper around every corner.

At first he was uncommunicative and I left him much to his own devices. On the third day I suggested we take

What happened to Piper Archer?.........K.J.Rabane

a boat trip around the coast to a cove to do some sunbathing and maybe to swim. As before, he let me lead him figuratively by the hand like a young child.

It was early when we reached the harbour and queued up for the first trip of the day. We stood behind an elderly couple, who were chatting to each other as if they'd only just met. After a while, a teenager carrying a fishing rod and his father holding a fold-up stool under one arm and carrying a cool bag joined the rest of us waiting for the boat to arrive.

Before long we saw a converted fishing boat pulling in alongside and a red-faced man wearing a navy Guernsey sweater and shorts who smiled up at us, saying, "Right then, folks, climb aboard."

From the cabin someone said, "Is that all there is?" and was answered by the red-faced man, presumably his father, "Quality not quantity my boy. Now everyone's siting comfortably why don't you get us out to sea and keep your chat down, there's a good sort?"

When we reached Honeywell cove we left the boat; the others were staying aboard. "We'll pick you up at four then?" the captain said, removing his sweater and giving us the dubious pleasure of seeing his beer-belly.

We walked over the soft sand and made for the shade underneath a rocky overhang, as the sun was already hot on our backs. Beresford talked little as we unrolled our towels, spread them out on the sand, and changed into our bathing costumes.

"Just the place to relax and forget our troubles," I said.

Beresford gave a rueful smile. "Thanks for trying, Isobel, I know I'm not much fun to be with."

"Fun can be overrated."

What happened to Piper Archer?………K.J.Rabane

I saw the ghost of a smile cross his face and wondered if today might be a bit different. Watching him stretching out on his towel face downwards, I removed a paperback from my beach bag and began to read. After a while Beresford stirred at my side. "I think I'll take a dip to cool off."

Hiding my surprise that he'd instigated an event of any kind without prompting from me, I replied. "Great, I'll just finish this chapter and join you."

I suppose that was the start of the change in him. For the rest of the week he seemed to enjoy the holiday. He chatted about friends he'd made in his youth and about his childhood growing up in a large house overlooking an estuary on the Devonshire coast, which had been used as a setting for a popular television soap opera. Neither of us mentioned Piper and gradually I saw him relax and become more like his old self.

When Saturday arrived and we drove out of Gareg Wen, I wondered if the change in him would continue once we returned to Lockford. All I could do was hope. However, I could never have imagined what would be waiting for us when we returned.

What happened to Piper Archer?.........K.J.Rabane

Serena

Chapter 14

Beresford and Piper had given me a key to their house years ago. I didn't use it much, only when they went away and they wanted me to water the plants - when old Maynard, their gardener, was getting frail. So when Izzie rang to tell us they were on they way home from Gareg Wen, I thought it might be a nice gesture to stock up the fridge and open some of the windows for Berry. I knew Izzie had tidied up the place before they left.

Mike was playing golf. It was Saturday morning and the local shops were busy but I managed to get to the house before lunch. I didn't expect them to arrive home much before teatime. Parking outside the front door I began by entering the house and opening the windows. I looked around and couldn't see Izzie's car.

"Anyone home?" I called out, just in case. I could hear the sound of the radio coming from the back of the house so I walked towards the kitchen door and sniffed. Definitely cooking smells – bacon, toast and something stronger – chilli sauce?

"Izzie? Berry?" I called out just to cover myself – what if they were upstairs - in bed? With my hand poised on the kitchen door, I hesitated. Then taking a deep breath, I pushed it open.

The oven light was on and I could see Piper's French casserole dish standing on the worktop. There were vegetables sliced and diced, waiting in salted water in the steamer Mike and I bought them for their first wedding anniversary.

What happened to Piper Archer?.........K.J.Rabane

I breathed a sigh of relief. Passing the window, I saw the garden furniture on the decking. I knew he'd always insisted stacking it away when Piper and he went on holiday – he said it was asking for trouble if you left it out for every Tom, Dick, and Harry to pinch. Then I saw the table.

I walked towards the back door. There was a jug of lemonade, two glasses and a plate of sandwiches, left out in the sun for the flies and wasps to attack.

Perhaps I should have rung the police. It might seem odd that I didn't. It took me a while to pluck up the courage to go upstairs, just in case someone was up there – waiting. But eventually, I decided I was being stupid and climbed the stairs calling out, "Hello? Anyone home?" Mrs Wooley, our drama teacher in Lockford High, once told me I should have been an actress.

Why two people without any children would want five bedrooms had always been a mystery to me. Mike, Ellie and I lived in a three – bedroom semi and it had always been perfectly big enough for us.

First, I looked in the guest rooms, which were, as they always were, except for a layer of dust, which would never have been there in Piper's day. I checked the guest bathrooms, and then walked towards the master bedroom. As I opened the door, I saw the French windows to the balcony were open, the bedcover thrown back, Piper's nightdress lay across the bed and the door to the en suite was open. Piper's perfume filled the air. It made me smile.

There was no mistake; it definitely looked as if someone had recently taken a shower in the en-suite. The mirror was steamed up. The soap in the dish was still wet, used towels were draped over the edge of the bath and in the shower cubicle I saw three long black strands of hair near the drain hole. Satisfied, I left things as they were, walked out of the house and saw a car driving towards me.

What happened to Piper Archer?.........K.J.Rabane

Beresford.

Chapter 15

I've almost begun to feel normal. The numb sensation is receding the longer I stay away from the house. Isobel is good company but I know I can't give her what she wants, what she needs, not until this business with Piper is sorted.

She drives us back to Lockford on the Saturday morning and we stop off for lunch in a coastal town. Its proximity to Cardiff makes me shiver as I remember the reason I left the city all those years ago. It's too awful to think about now as I have enough on my plate.

We eventually reach the Severn Bridge and drive into England heading across country then south towards Lockford. My mood is relatively light-hearted; there is no hint of a premonition, nothing pulling at my sleeve to disturb my mood. Maybe it will be OK. Maybe I won't see her again. Perhaps I'm getting better. Who knows?

After lunch, Isobel asks me whether I'd like her to stay for a while, just to see to things until I feel able to cope – maybe think about getting back to work. But I can't think about work – not at the moment - it's a step too far. I need to come to terms with seeing Piper around every corner. I'm starting to think it might be a psychological problem. I've wanted her to come back so much in the past and now, at least, I want to know why she left. I need to talk to her about it. So perhaps wanting it so much has made me imagine all the things that have been occurring lately. The mind is unknown territory to me medically speaking but I do know I'm not in a hurry to have my psychological condition assessed and to be found in need of an admission. I know enough about the situation in Lockford General, overcrowded wards with basic facilities for dealing with mental health patients, to go down that route. Of course I could book myself into the Burbridge Centre, a private clinic ten miles away but I'm not ready for that yet either. I should be able to deal with this without intervention. I'm feeling more positive than I've been for weeks.

Isobel switches on the sound system and I hear the strains of Bruch's Violin concerto filling the car.

"Joshua Bell?" I ask.

She nods.

"We have similar tastes in music I think." I hum along and she smiles.

"We are similar in many ways, but perhaps you are only now beginning to see it."

I wonder if she's right and I've been ignoring what's under my nose.

By the time we reach the outskirts of Lockford, I'm feeling ready to face the future. Whatever lies ahead I will deal with it.

"The answer to your earlier question is – yes please – stay for a while – I'd like that very much."

"Good. I have enough clothes in my suitcase for a day or two, especially as I can wash them at your place." She continues chatting as we drive down the lane to the house and I'm smiling when we reach the main gates. But the smile slips when I see Serena's walking to her car.

"What's happened now?" I say, that familiar feeling of uncertainty gripping my insides like a vice.

"Whatever it is, we'll deal with it," Isobel, the voice of sanity replies.

What happened to Piper Archer?………K.J.Rabane

She opens the car door and it's immediately apparent that Serena is worried.

"I'm so glad to see you," she is addressing Isobel. Her eyes won't meet mine.

In an audible whisper, she tells her what she found when she arrived at the house and rather than it disturbing me further I find I'm breathing a sigh of relief.

"Berry? What is it?" she asks, sensing I'm not as fearful as she'd anticipated.

"Nothing, except a gigantic feeling of liberation that my sanity is not hanging by a thread. You've seen it for yourself. Someone is trying to make me believe Piper's returned."

Isobel, who hasn't said a word, remarks, "But you said you'd seen her, spoken to her."

"I think I might have been suffering from some sort of psychotic episodes and I've stopped taking the anti-depressants. Some people have side effects from them, such as I've described; they are few and far between but they do happen. Piper wouldn't play mind games; she's far to uncomplicated for such a course of action."

Serena walks to the window. "The shower had been used, the mirror was still steamed up, wet towels on the floor. But there was no car in the drive."

This isn't like Serena. There is no stream of inconsequential nonsense. She's afraid, and her fear has made her succinct. "I think it's time you called the police, start another search for her, we need help."

Isobel puts her hand on my arm as I listen to Serena.

"And say what? Someone's used my shower, left a meal prepared, taken nothing?"

Isobel frowns. "None of this makes any sense but people do all sorts of unexpected things when they are upset, feel aggrieved, need to pay someone back for something they've done. Can you think of any reason Piper might feel the need to make you pay?"

I shake my head. "We were happy. That's why I found it so difficult to understand; when it happened and she left me I was devastated. It didn't make any sense. As for her meeting this man – Rowland Green – the police never found him – I don't believe he ever existed. There must have been another reason his name was in the diary on her computer. Maybe it was the name of a clothes designer, something completely innocent."

Serena sniffs.

"What is it, Serena? Don't you agree that Piper was happy?" Isobel asks

She shifts uncomfortably, moving from one foot to the other then walking towards the window she looks out over the countryside.

"Serena?" I prompt.

"Was she happy with you? Yes of course she was happy living in luxury with a husband who asked nothing of her. But….." She hesitates and I can see she's thinking about how to say what's bothering her.

"You may as well tell us, there's absolutely no point in hiding anything now," I suggest.

"Did you never think for one moment that she might have been missing having children?"

I'm stunned. "I don't understand. We'd discussed all that before we got married. She told me it was one of the reasons she'd decided we could make it work. She didn't want to be put in the position of having to go through endless investigations in order to satisfy a partner's need for a family. She couldn't face it, the disappointment, the false hope."

"Could nothing be done?" Isobel asks me.

What happened to Piper Archer?.........K.J.Rabane

"I considered the best course of action, under the circumstances, was not to suggest any investigations. Neither of us wanted children. I thought she'd come to terms with it years ago, before we met."

Serena turns to face us. "She had, but something had unsettled her. I didn't think too much of it at the time. I thought it was the court case – some of the details I read in the newspapers were enough to unsettle anyone – having to listen to all the ins and outs of such wickedness must have been a nightmare, although she never said so."

"But you've changed your mind?" Isobel asks.

Serena looks down at her hands as if the answer lies there. "Don't take any notice of me. Just old memories – nothing for you to worry about – clutching at straws – I agree – she was happy – must have been."

What happened to Piper Archer?………K.J.Rabane

Isobel

Chapter 16

The events of yesterday had shaken us all. Beresford particularly. He lay awake for most of the night looking up at the ceiling. In the morning I found him in the kitchen, cooking breakfast.

"I've decided to forget about it all," he said. "I'll just wait until she decides to contact me again and then we'll see. It's obvious she, or someone she knows, is disturbed. It might turn out like Serena suggested, she'll come to her senses and gradually she'll explain."

I sighed. "You really believe it?"

"Not really, but I'm not going to spend the rest of my life worrying about it. There's absolutely nothing I can do to help, unless she asks for it." He handed me a plate of scrambled egg. "Eat up, then let's go for a drive. I need to clear my head and although it's turned colder the sun is out."

"Fine."

"Then I'm going to ring Austin and see about going back to work."

I was shocked at the change in him. "Great. I'm so pleased."

He kissed the top of my head and walked to the window. "I'm sure it's going to be a nice day," he said, putting the kettle on.

Life seemed to return to normal after that. Beresford and I had a very enjoyable day in the country; we had lunch in a pub near a river and walked through the woods holding hands. Neither of us mentioned Piper and I was starting to think her ghost, the one, which had lingered between us, had eventually found another resting place.

A week later, I told Beresford I had to go home to get more clothes, tidy up my house and generally see to things. He was back in work now and agreed saying I was welcome to stay at his place anytime and suggested weekends to be spent together at Elm Tree House might be a favourite idea. I didn't need to think about it. I liked him and was enjoying our time together, hoping it would lead to something more, so I happily agreed. It was what I'd been aiming for, after all.

The phone call came out of the blue. It was a woman, both of us were certain - he'd put the phone on speaker. The line was bad, it crackled and there was a sound of traffic in the background. It could have been Piper but to be honest it could have been anyone.

"I'll be back as soon as I've finished here," she said, just as if she were continuing a previous conversation.

This time Beresford had a witness and he handled it differently. "Good. Thank you for letting me know," he said.

We rang Serena who, after hesitating, told us about her visit to Richard Stevens. Beresford was surprised to hear she'd contacted a Private Investigator but under the circumstances I thought it made sense.

"Perhaps I should go with Serena when she next goes to see this Richard Stevens," he suggested.

"I think that's an excellent idea. At least it will give you a chance to assess whether he might be doing a good job or just in it for the money."

"My thoughts exactly."

So, after speaking to Serena again, he arranged to go with her to see the Private Investigator on Saturday morning. The office was in Hastings Buildings, on the High Street. I didn't go with them, believing it was a family matter but agreed to meet them afterwards in the Sweet Pea Café. At last I felt as though Beresford was taking charge of his life again and I was beginning to hope it might lead to me achieving my objective.

I was a bit concerned when I had a telephone call from the Private Investigator the day following Serena's visit. But under the circumstances I thought it wise to see him, although I didn't have much to tell to him. But I was too busy that week and arranged to see him in the middle of the following week.

He was nice enough. I'd been surprised that Serena had taken the trouble to pay for such an investigation, after all the police had looked into Piper's disappearance ages ago. Surely there was nothing more to discover. What on earth could she hope to achieve?

What happened to Piper Archer?.........K.J.Rabane

Chapter 17

There was a soft breeze drifting in from the open window bringing with it the sound of the town waking up from the excesses of the weekend. It had been a disturbing night punctuated by the ghosts of his past. Richie had tossed and turned, unable to get to sleep. Eventually he'd managed to snatch a couple of hours and had woken with a thick head. Knocking back a couple of painkillers with a pint of water had enabled him to face the day.

Standing at the window, he contemplated whether it might be better to shut out the pollen-filled air but decided against it, as there was no way he'd been able to afford the installation of an air-conditioning system. He was missing Sandy, his assistant. It was only two weeks, just one more week of her holiday to go. Harry was doing the honours and was filling in for her again. He was nearly as efficient as his aunt and Richie felt fortunate to have him during the summer break from uni, but it wasn't the same. He could hear him talking on the telephone in the outer office. He was making arrangements for someone to call in at the office later that morning.

Richie turned away from the window; things were a bit slow at the moment. Perhaps his new client would give him something interesting to work on, other than routine divorce cases and finding Miss Clements's cat.

"A Mrs Serena Platt to see you at eleven, Mr Stevens."

"Thank you, Harry. What is she like?"

"Sounded middle aged, talked in a continuous stream, ran on and on about someone called Piper who was missing and someone called Berry." Harry tucked a lock of bright red hair behind his ear. Richie noticed that it was much longer than last year's close crop. Fashion went in circles it seemed.

Mrs Platt sounded true to form; he wondered whether Piper was a moggy or a poodle.

At five to eleven he heard the outer door open and Harry ringing through to tell him his eleven o'clock client had arrived. He made it sound as if she were one of many. Richie smiled, ran his fingers through his hair, tried to look efficient, and waited for Harry to show her in.

She was unremarkable in appearance - a woman in her early forties with died brown hair and carrying a little too much weight on her hips. She smiled but there were worry lines creasing her forehead and she seemed nervous.

"Please sit down, Mrs Platt. Now what can I do for you?"

She began to tell him the story of her sister's disappearance and as she talked Richie remembered reading about Piper Archer and her husband in the local paper some time ago. He also knew Beresford Archer indirectly, as Sandy's sister-in-law had been one of his patients and had spoken highly of him and his competence as an obstetrician when he'd delivered their Adam.

Serena Platt was, as Harry had intimated, a talker. He waited whilst she described her family situation, the woman next door, and her friendship with someone called Izzie, until he decided he'd heard enough.

"And you believe your brother-in-law when he says his wife returned and has been telephoning him?" Richie asked, stemming the flow of her conversation.

What happened to Piper Archer?.........K.J.Rabane

"I don't mind telling you, Mr Stevens, I don't know what to think. I'm beginning to believe he's imagining it. But he's such an intelligent man, well thought of in his field – he wouldn't make up something like this now would he?"

"People have been known to act strangely when suffering from post traumatic stress."

"Well, yes, but Piper left a long time ago – why now? Besides he's just met Izzie, as I said, and he was beginning to get his life together, if you know what I mean. I don't understand it."

Richie made some notes on his laptop then asked, "Can you give me a run down on Piper's life with her husband before she left him – did anything unusual happen, had there been disagreements, you know the sort of thing?"

She thought for a moment, sighed, looked out of the window and for once seemed speechless. Then she bit her bottom lip. "I can't think of anything really. She seemed happy enough, there was never any talk of them having affairs, quarrels, nothing. She was a bit stressed a month or so before she left but it was nothing to do with Berry."

"Oh, and why was that?" Richie looked up from his laptop.

"She'd been called to do jury service at Lockford Crown court. Didn't want to do it – well, who does? The case went on a bit too, nearly four weeks it took. I think if it had been me, I'd have found it *very* interesting, a chance to do something different, get away from routine but Piper didn't fancy it and of course she couldn't talk about the case when it was going on. I don't think I'd have coped very well on that count. Even afterwards she didn't say much. I wanted to know all the gory details but she said there weren't any to tell. Which wasn't true of course because the case made headline news."

"Did she have to take time off from work?"

"No. She didn't work. Didn't need a job." She sniffed and sat up straighter. "Neither of us worked – our husbands being in such good positions, you see." A smug little smile tugged at the corner of her mouth.

Richie closed the lid of his laptop and stood up. "Right, Mrs Platt. I'll certainly look into this and get back to you. I have your contact details and as I say, I'll be in touch."

"It's a relief to know I've done something about it at least," she said, shaking his hand.

Afterwards, Richie watched from the window as his client walked down the High Street in the direction of Primark and wondered if there was more to this case than met the eye.

After glancing at his notes, he rang the contact number for Isobel Myers, which his client had produced, and made an appointment to see her at half five in the wine bar on the corner. Then, in the outer office, he watched Harry completing a Sudoku puzzle.

"I'm taking an early lunch, Harry. When you've finished that, take a look at the net and see if you can bookmark a couple of sites dealing with the report of a woman called Piper Archer who went missing just over two years ago. Her husband is Beresford Archer a consultant obstetrician and gynaecologist at Lockford General. I'll look at the results this afternoon. You can take a long lunch hour when I come back. On second thoughts take the afternoon off; it's quiet enough here and I can manage."

Harry grinned, "Thanks, Richie, great."

He looked rather too happy, Richie decided. "Date?"

Harry reddened. "Might have. It's this girl who works in the Sweet Pea café. She used to be in my school. She's waiting to start uni in September and I'm hoping to persuade her to give Birmingham Uni a try."

"How is Brum by the way? You'll be in your second year when you start back in the autumn?"

"Yeah. It's great, actually. The Mailbox on a Saturday night is the place to be the clubs aren't bad."

"Oh to be young again!" Richie said, whistling through his teeth as he left the office, knowing he wouldn't want to be that young again for all the tea in China.

Chapter 18

The Sweet Pea café was full of the usual throng of office workers buying lunch to eat in the park or the confines of their workplaces, and the rest who, like Richie, preferred to sit at a table and watch the world go by.

"Same as usual, Richie?" Diane handed him the menu. "The fish is good today, if you fancy a change. Fresh, not that frozen rubbish, I picked it up from Lockford market this morning."

"Sounds good to me, Diane."

The view of the High Street was one of the reasons Richie favoured the Sweet Pea café rather than the numerous eating places in town, together with its proximity to Hastings Buildings. Whilst he was waiting for his fish to arrive, he watched the ever-changing scene outside the window. People watching, or research, as he preferred to call it when Sandy was around, gave him an insight into human behaviour when his subjects were unaware they were being observed.

A young guy wearing tight blue jeans and an Oasis tee shirt stopped to comb his hair via his reflection in the plate glass windows of Arbuthnot and Trent before sauntering towards the betting shop where, to Richie's knowledge, a shapely blonde called Carol had just started working behind the counter.

His meal arrived at the same time as he saw Serena Platt walking towards the car park carrying a large brown paper carrier bearing the name PRIMARK. She looked preoccupied, her eyes constantly searching the pavement as if she were being followed. Without having the distracting influence of her stream of conversation, he could see she was nothing like she had seemed whilst sitting opposite him in his office. If asked to assess her

What happened to Piper Archer?.........K.J.Rabane

he would have said she was frightened, in fact she looked scared stiff.

This thought was uppermost in his mind when he climbed the stairs to his office later. The unexpected sound of conversation met him and he increased his pace as he recognised the voice he'd been missing for the past week.

"Sandy! What on earth? I thought you'd be in Paris until Friday.

His secretary/PA looked tanned and, he had to admit, extremely attractive in a healthy, outdoor way. Today she was wearing a yellow vest top and pale blue cropped pants, her fair hair tied up in a ponytail. Sandy's constantly changing image was always a source of enjoyment to Richie as he could never second-guess how she was going to appear from one week to the next.

"Couldn't stay away," Sandy said. "Besides Harry told me you have a new case."

Richie frowned at Harry.

"Honestly, Richie, she forced it out of me before I knew what I was saying."

"Sounds about right," Richie replied. "Anyway, it's good to see you, Miss Smith. Now step into my office, would you please?"

He knew there was more to it. The Miss Smith thing made her smile, a long-shared joke between them, but he could see the sadness in her eyes.

"Sit down, now what's this all about?"

"I don't know what you mean."

"Things with Claude not turn out to be quite what you thought they'd be?"

Sandy avoided his eyes. "His parents were great. Paris was fantastic. His sister was a sweetie."

"But?"

"Does there have to be a but?"

Richie sighed. "Look, tell me it's none of my business if you like but if nothing else we've become good friends over the years and you helped me enormously after Lucy and the twins died, when I didn't know which way was up. If I can return the favour, you only have to ask."

Sandy bit her lip. He thought for one terrible moment she was going to cry but she held back the tears and gave a rueful smile. "He's a shit."

"Claude, I presume?"

"He dragged me to Paris to meet his parents then decided to dump me in favour of Mariette, his long time girlfriend, of which I knew nothing. I'm not kidding, it was obvious he was using me to make her jealous. As soon as I realised the game he was playing I took the next flight home."

"Wise decision if I may say so. And it's his loss. He obviously didn't value a diamond when he held it in his hands."

Sandy spluttered and her face broke into a grin as he'd anticipated it would.

"Can I tell Harry to finish up today and I'll be in tomorrow."

Richie hesitated. "Er, no. Let him work out the week, as promised. I can just about afford to pay him and employ my PA for a day or four."

"PA eh?"

"Yeah, but don't let it go to your head. It's secretarial duties again next week, I'm afraid."

"Right then, so tell me all about this new client of ours."

Richie told her about Serena Platt's visit and his proposed meeting that evening with Isobel Myers.

What happened to Piper Archer?.........K.J.Rabane

"Do you want me to come – as your PA of course?" Sandy looked at him expectantly. He'd been about to say no and that he'd see her tomorrow but found he was smiling and saying, "Only if you're sure; it would be a great help."

At a quarter past five Richie and Sandy left Harry to lock up and walked to the wine bar. It was a warm evening and office workers were taking advantage of the good weather to sit outside the Sweet Pea café drinking coffee whilst the owner of the wine bar on the corner, anticipating an early influx of customers, had arranged tables and chairs in a similar manner outside on the pavement.

"I can't understand why anyone would want to inhale traffic fumes with their Merlot," Sandy muttered, following Richie inside and sitting at a table facing the door.

"I'll get us a bottle of red and three glasses," Richie said, walking to the bar.

At half five on the dot Isobel Myers arrived. Serena Platt had described her friend and there was no mistaking her as she looked around. She was tall, with soft curls framing an attractive face. His immediate impression was of a career girl, competent and focused.

"Miss Myers?" Richie stood up and pulled out a chair for her to sit down. "This is my PA, Miss Smith, I hope you don't mind if she joins us."

"No, er, that's fine."

"Would you like a glass of red or can I get you something else?"

She hesitated. "Perhaps a small one. I'm driving."

What happened to Piper Archer?.........K.J.Rabane

"Do you mind if I take some notes?" Sandy asked, fishing out a small IPad from the depths of an oversized handbag.

"I'm not sure I can tell you anything which would require note taking. It's not as if I know anything about Piper Archer but you're welcome to, if you must - if it will help, Miss Smith."

"Thanks, and it's Sandy, by the way."

Richie poured the wine into her glass until she indicated it was enough and then said, "Mrs Platt is very worried about her brother-in-law and as I said on the phone she's instructed me to look into her sister's whereabouts. I gather you've become friendly with Mr Archer?"

She nodded and raised the glass to her lips. A sudden summer shower fell in rivulets down the window and momentarily took her attention.

"And he's mentioned the fact that his wife has returned?" Richie asked.

"I'm sorry," she turned towards him, "not come back permanently exactly. At least the impression I got was he'd seen her but she'd only stayed in the house a short while. I haven't seen much of him since, actually. We were getting along so splendidly, I thought he was over it, he was going back to work, planning on us seeing more of each other, but I've been busy and well, you know how things drift when work schedules intervene. Serena, Mrs Platt, told me he was convinced he'd seen her – I only really know what she told me."

"So there's nothing you can add?"

"Well, not really. He doesn't quite seem himself though. I thought at one point he was progressing but not now."

"What makes you say that?" Sandy asked.

"Difficult to say really. He's usually so together, you know, well a man in his position has to be. But now, I would say he was floundering a bit. I think he's avoiding seeing me, he keeps making excuses." She put down her glass and sighed. "I think it's the writing on the wall for us."

"Ever since Piper's come back?" Sandy asked.

"Mmm, that's the thing though; has she come back? No one else has seen her. But I did hear someone on the telephone – it could have been anyone – he seemed to think it was his wife – it definitely was a woman."

"I see." Richie bit his lower lip. "How would you describe Mr Archer's personality? Before, I mean, when you first met him."

She thought for a moment then said, "Considerate, charming, in an old-school sort of way. You know the kind of thing." She turned to Sandy. "Opens the door for you, takes your arm to cross the road."

"Helps you into the car?" Sandy offered.

"Exactly."

Richie looked at his watch. "I see, well we mustn't detain you any further, Miss Myers. You've been a great help." He stood up and handed her his card. "Perhaps you'd give me ring if you can think of anything which might help us with our enquiries."

"Of course." She followed them to the door and into the street. "Although I think it unlikely I'll see much of Beresford again."

It was raining harder as Richie and Sandy walked back to the car, which was parked in the basement car park of Hastings Buildings.

"Shall I drop you off?" Richie asked.

"I brought my bike," Sandy replied.

"Rubbish, you're going to get soaked. Leave it locked up and pick it up tomorrow."

"Yeah, perhaps you're right. Anyway what did you think of Isobel?"

"Certainly attractive and young enough to be Beresford Archer's daughter."

"Well not quite but I take your point. About the age of his wife I should think. I wonder if that's significant?"

"It's early days yet. I suggest we visit Lockford General tomorrow." Richie opened the car and hesitated.

"It's OK." Sandy grinned. "I don't expect you to hold the door open for me."

"Well that's a relief."

"How can we just turn up at the hospital without an appointment? It will look a bit odd surely?"

"I have ways, my dear, Miss Smith. Trust me, just wait and see."

What happened to Piper Archer?.........K.J.Rabane

Chapter 19

The following day began with a promise of hot, humid temperatures. Richie showered, drank his first cup of strong black coffee of the day, and decided he'd eat breakfast at the Sweet Pea later.

When he arrived at the office, Sandy and Harry were staring at the laptop screen on the desk and making notes, Harry by means of his phone and Sandy using her tablet. Never ceasing to be grateful to that quirk of chance that had led Sandy to him, whilst knowing she was more than capable of carving out a more lucrative career elsewhere, he smiled to himself then said, "I'm off for my breakfast as I can see you two are busy. Anything interesting?"

"Could be," Sandy replied. "What time do you want to go to the hospital?"

"One thirty."

She shook her head. "That's not visiting time."

"Don't worry about a thing. It's sorted."

In the confines of the café, he ate breakfast whilst thinking about how he should proceed with the investigation. There was very little to go on, apart from supposition and conjecture. However, there was always a possibility that someone would start a train of thought steaming through his brain and firing his enthusiasm for the case.

He picked up his mobile and rang his contact.

"OK for later?"

"Fine, the coast is clear. He's off on the sick again."

"I'm bringing my PA."

"She young enough to be pregnant?"

Richie nearly choked on his bacon. "Pardon me?"

He heard a chuckle from the other end. "Don't worry, I'll say you're her father."

"Don't push your luck."

The morning stretched ahead of him and he was putting off the moment when he would return to his office and search through the mound of information he was sure Sandy and Harry had accumulated since he'd first asked Harry to search the archives for anything connected to Piper Archer.

Later, leaving the café, he looked longingly at the trees in the park, their leaves whispering gently together in the morning breeze. Running a finger around the inside of his shirt collar he wished he could have worn something a bit cooler. But he'd dressed for the part and it wouldn't be too long before he could drive Sandy to Lockford General. As he climbed the stairs to his office he hoped the fan in his room had been switched on in his absence and on his arrival was pleased to see that it was.

Sandy was working in the inner office sitting at Richie's desk, leaving Harry to answer the phone and search through the bookmarked items on his laptop.

"Harry's done a great job." She beamed up at him. "I'm sure he's found everything there was to find."

"I don't doubt it for a second." Richie walked to the open window and took a deep breath.

"You look very, smart, I should have said earlier." Sandy raised an eyebrow.

"Glad you approve."

"Now will you tell me what's going on?"

Richie looked at his watch. "I will, after I've had a look at the newspaper reports and when we're on our way."

"Spoilsport," Sandy murmured, turning the laptop to face him. "Have a look at this then."

What happened to Piper Archer?.........K.J.Rabane

At first Richie couldn't see the significance of the headline, *Murdered in cold blood by her boyfriend.* There was no mention of either Piper or Beresford Archer in the report in the Lockford Times. He frowned then shrugged and turned his palms upwards as if asking for an explanation.

"Read on," she said.

Kayleigh Brown was only sixteen when she first met Keanu Collins. She was an innocent young woman ensnared by a sadistic killer. After suffering years of domestic abuse, Collins finally strangled her and left her battered body to be found by neighbours, who were concerned about her whereabouts. Twenty-one-year-old Kayleigh died in terror, alone and uncared for, whilst Collins went to the pub before taking a train to London.

The trial of Keanu Collins began at Lockford Crown Court over three weeks ago and today the Jury brought in a guilty verdict. Sentencing, by The Honourable Mr Justice Lawrence Bright, will be heard on the 27th, the court was told.

"And the significance is?"

"Piper Archer was a member of the jury."

"Ah, I see."

Sandy consulted the notes on her IPad. "Keanu Collins went down for life."

"Too good for him, in my opinion," Richie exclaimed.

"Do you think this might have anything to do with Piper's disappearance?"

"It fits the time frame. Serena Platt told me her sister left a month or two later. Good work, Miss Smith."

"It was Harry, actually."

Richie walked into the outer office.

What happened to Piper Archer?.........K.J.Rabane

"You've just earned yourself the day off tomorrow, Harry, a paid holiday of course."

Harry's smile was as wide as his aunt's but not so appealing, Richie decided.

"Miss Smith, if you're ready, we'll make a start."

The journey took a little over fifteen minutes during which he brought Sandy up to speed with events.

"You remember DCI Freeman, from the Met?"

"Your friend, Norman? Yes, of course. He's helped us enormously with some of our more difficult cases."

Richie drove into the visitors parking area and turned off the engine. "By pure coincidence his nephew Austin happens to be Beresford Archer's registrar."

"No! That's unbelievable."

"It's a coincidence, yes, but in actual fact the reason Austin is in Lockford at all is indirectly because of me. When Norm's sister's boy was looking to complete his speciality in Obstetrics, Cheryl suggested he contact Lockford General. She's been trying to persuade Norm to retire and move down here for years. Cheryl was great when..." he didn't complete his sentence. The memory of his family being wiped out by a drunk driver, whilst he was working in the Met, still haunted him and crept up on him unawares.

"Right," Sandy said. "So mystery solved. Austin Banks is going to give us the low down on his boss?"

Richie nodded. "Got it in one."

Inside the hospital Richie and Sandy followed the directions on the wall in the reception area, which lead to the consulting room of Austin Banks, senior registrar in obstetrics and gynaecology.

What happened to Piper Archer?.........K.J.Rabane

Austin was sitting behind his desk making short work of a ham and cheese baguette. He stood up as they entered.

"Good to see you again, Richie." He indicated they should sit down. "I'm sorry I can't give you more than twenty minutes or so. It's hectic here, what with the Boss on another planet."

"No, not at all. I'm grateful for any time you can spare. This is Miss Smith by the way, my er, PA."

Austin reached over the desk to shake Sandy's hand, after wiping his on a paper tissue. "How can I help?"

"I want to know all you can tell me about Beresford Archer's state of mind both before his wife left him and now that he believes she's returned."

Austin looked aghast. "He thinks she's come back?"

"You didn't know?" Sandy asked.

"No, not at all. I understood he had some kind of recurring tummy bug. And as to his state of mind, he sounded OK on the phone, said he'd be back next week."

"And before?" Richie prompted.

"Before? Well I would say he was his usual self, competent, focused, pleasant to work with, happy at home, in fact he was much envied by some of the staff as he seemed to live a charmed life."

"But all that changed when his wife left?"

Austin looked down at his hands. "He certainly went through the mill. Who wouldn't under the circumstances?"

"So there's nothing out of the ordinary in his behaviour, you would say."

"Precisely." Austin looked at his watch.

"I won't keep you much longer. Do you know where he worked before coming to Lockford General?"

"I do as a matter of fact. I believe it was at the Princess Royal hospital in the centre of Cardiff, although he didn't talk much about it."

Richie stood up and held out his hand. "Thanks for giving us so much of your valuable time, Austin. Give my regards to Norm when you next speak to him. Tell him I'll be in touch."

"Will do. Goodbye, Miss Smith."

Richie noticed the lingering glance Austin gave Sandy and smiled as they left the room and walked down the corridor towards the exit.

"What are you smiling about?" Sandy asked.

"You don't want to know."

"Where do we go from here?"

"If Harry can work a few extra days next week, I suggest we take a trip to Cardiff. When someone appears to be whiter than white, I often wonder if there's some dirty linen hiding beneath the clean sheets."

Chapter 20

It was something Serena Platt mentioned; Richie hadn't taken much notice at the time but at four o'clock in the morning, when the humidity was way above normal, it bothered him. He threw off the bed-sheet which felt damp, got up and had a cool shower. Feeling refreshed and able to think more clearly, he decided he would ring DCI Norman Freeman at the Met, later, when he knew Norm was likely to be having his second cup of tea of the morning.

Austin Banks's uncle had worked with Richie, what seemed a lifetime ago. Norm and his wife Cheryl were Richie's closest friends, the ones who had been there for him when the rest of his colleagues avoided his gaze. It was Norm who had backed him when he'd attacked Phillip Hatton, Norm who'd understood when Richie decided not to stay and fight his suspension but to seek another life on the south coast. There were so many reasons to be thankful for his friendship, not the least of which was his continued help with some of Richie's more difficult cases.

He'd opened all the windows in his flat the night before and could hear the sounds of the town waking up. His apartment was on the edge of Lockford, overlooking the river Locke, and if he leaned out of the window he could smell the vegetation on the riverbanks washed by the rise and flow of its waters.

Richie took a deep breath and closed his eyes. Once upon a time his mornings began with Lucy urging the twins to get out of bed, the smell of breakfast cooking and her lovely face greeting him as he entered the kitchen. It was getting more and more difficult to remember every detail of his wife's face, his children's voices, their teenage rants, their morning smell.

Forcing the images to remain, he stood a while longer, then sighed, opened his eyes, and returned to the present where each day they became his past.

His thoughts returned to the Archer case. Being called for Jury service in itself wasn't significant, vast numbers of people up and down the country were invited to fulfil their public duty every day. And although some cases were extremely unpleasant, after serving on a case, they returned to their lives without any undue ill effects. Piper Archer's disappearance coming within two months of her sitting on a Jury however, just might be related. He knew he was clutching at straws but without any other leads to go on it was worth investigating.

His client said she didn't know any details other than it was a murder case, something about a boyfriend killing a young girl who was pregnant by him. She seemed most put out that her sister hadn't shared the details with her at the time, even though she'd tried her best to get her to talk. She'd said she thought it would be good for her – it wasn't good for anyone to keep it bottled up inside – you never knew where it would lead.

With the newspaper report, Sandy had shown him, uppermost in his mind he opened his laptop and searched the court reports for the day Piper Archer attended Lockford Crown court for Jury service. The report of the Collins case was reminiscent of many he'd seen before whilst working in London, the same sad story, drugs, mental cruelty and control. Kayleigh Brown had paid with her life.

The trial took longer than expected as the Jury were out for nearly four days. Richie ran his fingers through his hair. Not unheard of, but slightly unusual as it was an open and shut case. But it was worth looking into. He made some notes on a pad in the kitchen, tore off a sheet and slipped it into his pocket.

By now the streets had woken up. The sound of cars revving up in the underground car park accompanied the far off cries of a baby, schoolchildren arguing as they climbed into a four by four with their harassed mother, curses flying in the morning air and car doors slamming.

Driving towards Hastings Buildings Richie wondered how much Norm would be able to help him. He recognised the restrictions imposed upon his friend and knew the limitations, which existed regarding disclosure of jurors' details. But maybe, just maybe, DCI Norman Freeman would bend the rules in his favour to some small degree. Anything he could come up with would be of help, as he knew he was struggling with this case. It was against his nature to go down without a fight but he had the niggling feeling that if he wasn't careful this battle would be one fight he would lose.

What happened to Piper Archer?.........K.J.Rabane

Beresford

Chapter 21

Sometimes I think I've dreamt it all and I'll wake up to find Piper in the kitchen preparing breakfast and none if this has happened. It's like living in the middle of a nightmare.

I thought I was getting over it but now I'm afraid to go to work in case she comes home and I miss her, afraid to deal with patients' problems when my own are all encompassing, and as for trying to operate - it doesn't bear thinking about. The hospital board will want an explanation soon; I can't keep avoiding it. Austin will require assistance; it's not right to expect him to manage my list much longer. And I'm not being fair to Izzie – she must wonder why I'm so changeable.

In the bathroom mirror the image that looks back at me is of a haunted man. It's what I am. Haunted by my wife, who flits in and out of my life like a spectre. It's my fault, all of it. I should have been more attentive. I should have realised what was going on. There must have been plenty of indicators, which I was too wrapped up in work to see.

The phone is ringing. It's half past nine. It's got to be Serena. She's worried about me but it's getting on my nerves, the constant asking 'are you OK, Berry love?' But if I don't answer the phone she'll come around, she'll be sure I've done something stupid. Too late now, the damage has been done.

I pick up the phone. "Hello?"

It's not Serena. It has to be Piper. No one speaks but I know she's there.

What happened to Piper Archer?.........K.J.Rabane

My hands begin to shake. I'm afraid to speak but in a whisper I stutter, "Pppiper?"

I hear a definite sigh. It's not my imagination. Then the connection is cut and I'm left looking at the phone, willing it to ring again. It's no use me trying ring-back – the digital display says the number is unknown. She won't come now - I know she won't, not today anyway. She'll come when I least expect her – when I can't arrange for anyone to be here to see her."

I put down the phone wondering if I've just heard the sigh of a ghost.

A car draws up outside and I start to shake. The doorbell rings. I can't move.

"Berry?"

It's Serena.

"Berry, open the door. I've got groceries. The frozen stuff is defrosting."

With no alternative left to me, I draw my dressing gown closer around me and go downstairs and open the door to my sister-in-law.

"Not dressed? It's nearly half eleven."

"Yes, er I was about…"

"Well, let me get these in your freezer, stock up your fridge and make us both a nice cup of tea, whilst you go and have a shower and put something on."

She's well meaning. She doesn't want me to starve. I know she wonders why Piper hasn't contacted her. I hear her singing softly in the kitchen as I climb the stairs. For a moment her voice reminds me of her sister's and I cover my ears with my hands and head for the shower.

Afterwards, we sit in the conservatory. The sun is high in the sky. I see she's opened all the windows but it's still hot.

What happened to Piper Archer?.........K.J.Rabane

"Not feeling well enough to go back to work then?" Serena asks.

I should tell her about the phone call but it sounds mad, even to me. So instead I mutter, "Er, no, not yet."

"Have you seen someone? What about getting a friend to take a look at you? Someone in the profession, someone who knows about Piper."

I make up a lie about having seen a psychiatrist friend of mine who told me I was just a bit overtired and to rest for a while. She nods. She's satisfied, at least for now.

"I spoke to Izzie on the phone last night. She was asking about you. Why don't you give her a ring, Berry? Take her out for a meal. It would do you good to get out."

How can I? What if we were to bump into Piper? How can I be seen socialising with Isobel when my wife is likely to come back into my life at any moment?

"I'll think about it," I reply, which seems to satisfy her for the moment.

She's talking. I can hear the words but feel no necessity to engage with her conversation. As long as I've known Serena, I've found the ability to disconnect from the drivel; it's the only way I can deal with the inconsequential stream of events with which she insists on littering each sentence.

"I said to Mike, only the other day, when next door's cat had done its business on our lawn again, Mike, I said, you've got to do something, say something. He was coming down the stairs, with a cup of tea in his hand. I always take a cup up to him, first thing in the morning. But did he talk to her, no, not on your life."

On and on it goes, like a never-ending stream, gurgling and spluttering it's way to its destination. I wonder how long it will take her to get to the point.

What happened to Piper Archer?.........K.J.Rabane

"I've been to see that private detective – remember I said I was going to ring him? I know you said you'd seen Piper but I can't think why she hasn't contacted me. I need to find out, you see. I won't be satisfied if I don't at least try."

I almost miss it, she's reached the pivot and I've switched off so completely I almost miss it.

"A private detective – investigator he calls himself?" She drinks her coffee as I assimilate this latest news. "Richard Stevens - got a place in Hastings Buildings - looks pretty genuine to me. Milly in the dry cleaners used him once to find out about Billy and his bit of stuff."

And she's off again. I try to divert the flow.

"What did he say?"

"Who?"

"This Richard Stevens."

"Said, he'd look into it and let me know."

"And has he?"

"Well, no. Not yet, said he didn't hold out much hope, as the police had investigated her disappearance thoroughly at the time. But he said, he'd give it a good go."

She shifts in her seat. She's embarrassed. I thought she wanted me to go with her but she obviously saw him alone. I wonder what she's told him about me? She doesn't believe Piper has come back. She thinks I'm having a breakdown, that I've imagined it. There are times when I'm inclined to agree with her. Until the next time, when I come home to find evidence of her having been in the kitchen, preparing my meal or ringing but not having the courage to speak to me. It's why I don't want to leave the house. I want to be here when she puts her key in the door. Next time I'll make sure she doesn't

What happened to Piper Archer?………K.J.Rabane

disappear. Next time there will be no mistake and they'll all believe me.

What happened to Piper Archer?.........K.J.Rabane

Serena

Chapter 22

He's not right. Not by a long chalk. But what can I do? Mike says I've been daft to pay out money to a private detective. I suppose he's right. He could be rubbish. But the thing is - if there is any possibility he can find my sister - I have to take it. At the very least he might find out why Berry keeps insisting she's come back.

I waited until Mike went off to work then I rang Mr Stevens. His secretary answered. He was the young lad with red hair. I thought he'd said he was filling in for his aunt. Obviously he was staying on a bit longer because I saw his aunt the last time I called at their office, pretty little thing, I did wonder if there was anything going on between her and her boss. Bit of an age difference but it happens in offices, people working closely together, sharing problems and who knows what else. The secretary, the young lad, he seemed quite efficient. He said Mr Stevens was working on the case at the moment. He was up in London, he said, visiting a professional contact, and if I was at all concerned about progress to ring at any time.

Whether he's good is anyone's guess, although I've heard good reports, and his office *is* near Primark. It's why I rang Richard Stevens in the first place. This business with Berry is making me wonder whether Piper is afraid to contact me directly. Well, we had our differences after all, and before she went away we had some issues. Perhaps she's afraid I'll tell him about her past, now that she's left. Of course I wouldn't. I'm not the vindictive type. If I was I could have told Berry before they were married. That would have put the cat amongst the pigeons and no mistake.

Later that afternoon I had a call from Izzie asking about Berry. I told her to go round; it was no good waiting for him to make up his mind. She sounded doubtful. I know she likes him, really likes him, I mean. I suppose he needs someone strong like Izzie to take him in hand, sort him out, make him forget this nonsense about Piper and get on with his life. But I can't bear the thought of it – not really – not when Piper's still missing. He'll forget about her and where will that leave me?

Just when I'd decided to ring my friend Shirley, who lives around the corner, to see if she fancied going for a Chinese because Mike had rung to say he was working late and would eat in the canteen, the doorbell rang.

"Izzie, fancy seeing you. I thought you were off to see Berry? Come in. God it's so hot. You'd never think it was six o'clock it's as warm as midday. Anyway, have you eaten. We could ring for a take-away, if you like."

She looked a bit worn, a bit worried.

"Have you seen Beresford lately? In the last day or two I mean."

"Yesterday."

"I'm worried about him."

"Shall I ring for a Chinese?"

She sighed, walked past me into the kitchen and out into the back garden, where I'd been sitting when she rang, and sat down on a garden chair. "Chinese is fine, I'll have whatever you're having. I'm not bothered, really."

Later, after we'd washed down the meal with a glass or two of Chardonnay, Izzie said, "I've been thinking. How did Piper and Beresford meet?

What happened to Piper Archer?.........K.J.Rabane

"Let me think. It was in Lockford General, that's right. The first time anyway. She'd been fundraising for the new sick-children's wing. She said he'd been very supportive and I knew by the way her eyes lit up when she talked about him that she fancied the pants off him."

Izzie spluttered and wiped her mouth.

"But they didn't meet up properly until six or seven months later. I think it was at a party and he recognised her from the fund-raising event. I remember what she was wearing as if it were yesterday. She did look lovely I have to admit, midnight blue she called it, a little backless number with a short skirt. Not too short mind you – not cheap looking – classy. Piper never looked cheap. Anyway, that was that and afterwards they couldn't get enough of each other."

"So they didn't meet in Gareg Wen?"

"Gareg Wen? That's a place I haven't heard of for a while." I tried not to show the effect it had on me. It was a shock, mind you. Over the years I've tried to forget the place ever existed. I think I pulled it off though; she didn't notice. "No. Why do you ask?"

"When I met Beresford there on holiday I got talking to someone in the pub called Lorna who said she recognised Beresford and remembered his wife visiting when she was a teenager."

"Well yes, of course, Piper and I often used to stay at our aunty Gwen's. She was our mother's sister. It was so tragic."

"Tragic?"

"She went on one of those coach holidays to Spain. It was awful. Piper and me - we were shattered. The coach was on a bridge, the driver lost control over a ravine...."

"Hey, I'm sorry, Serena. I didn't wish to drag up sad memories."

"Of course you didn't. We got over it; well you have to don't you? But mother was devastated and we were cut up about our aunt. Piper was very close to Gwen. Your friend probably remembered her from the time she went to stay with some friends after she'd done her exams-sixteen she was. She stayed for nearly two months. I went down to stay with her when I could. I was working of course and there was Mike. We'd only just started seeing each other.

"I see I expect that's when she got to know Lorna first. And afterwards, I understand she married Beresford and they used to go to Gareg Wen on holidays occasionally?"

I smiled. "Yeah, she always did have a soft spot for the place. She said it was good to get away from everything."

We chatted on, as the sun sank lower and a stiff evening breeze started to creep up the garden. Mike came home, had a glass of wine with us then Izzie said, "Thanks for a lovely evening, Serena, I'll be in touch."

Mike went up for his shower and I walked her to the gate and watched her car until it disappeared around the corner at the end of the road. I'd enjoyed our chat, well, most of it. But I didn't tell her everything, no, not the half of it – well I couldn't – it wouldn't be fair – if there's one thing I can do it's keep a secret.

Chapter 23

After Richie explained to Sandy that he'd spoken to DCI Freeman he made an appointment to see him the following day.

"So this is about the trial Piper Archer attended before she took off?" Sandy asked

"Right. It might be leading us nowhere but I'd like to have a word with the rest of the jurors or at least get a chance to assess their opinions of Piper Archer. This is going to be a difficult one for Norm though. It's against his better judgement for him to let me have a copy of the court list but he might be able to point me in the right direction."

Sandy nodded. "And you really don't want me to come? Harry's willing to pop in for a day or two."

Richie smiled. "I'll still want Harry to complete the week. But you, Miss Smith are required for greater things."

"You've noticed at last."

He was about to give a smart reply, to respond in kind, but instead said quietly, "I've always known it."

"Great, so what is it? "Sandy replied, unaware of his change of mood.

"Austin Banks. I telephoned him to make an appointment for you to see him but we agreed it would be better if you met up with him at *The Grapes* on the corner of Westmore Street at half-six tomorrow evening."

"And what do you have in mind?"

"I know Austin, he's intelligent, young and unattached and I saw how he responded to you – he likes what he sees."

"That's so sexist."

"Agreed. But it this case I think we'll use it to our advantage. Get him to unwind, ease the conversation around to his boss. Away from the hospital environment he might be more forthcoming."

"Won't he think it a bit obvious?"

"Of course, but I'm banking on him ignoring the fact and enjoying just being in your company."

Sandy bit her bottom lip. " You know that sort of thing is against my principles – I would like to register a strong protest."

"Protest noted, Miss Smith. Wear something appropriate though."

"Sexy?"

"Exactly."

The following day Richie drove to London without the apprehension he'd often felt previously when visiting the city. The events, which had preceded his departure from the Met and his flight to Lockford, still managed to catch him unaware at times but the feelings were less intense. He'd managed to dampen down his rage and sorrow in order to survive. Lucy would have been proud of him. She wouldn't have wanted him to grieve forever, to waste his life by living in the past.

He'd spoken to Angie and made arrangements to visit her after he'd seen Norm. He was looking forward to seeing her again. The twins were growing up. They'd be three now. She'd said Grant was in New York trying to close a deal, so asked him if he'd call at their apartment. Her jewellery business had begun to sell in the States and he felt a great pride in watching her spread her wings. From the first moment he'd come across her selling her original pieces from a stall in Covent Garden market, he'd been drawn to her. It was during the early days when he was fearful of walking around the city, which had been his home, and she'd reminded him of the daughter he'd lost. He'd been able to talk to Angie about his loss and the anger he'd felt towards the drunken driver who'd robbed him of his family. She understood his pain but didn't trot out the usual well-meaning platitudes. They'd been friends ever since.

DCI Norman Freeman was sitting in the lounge bar of the St Ermin's Hotel near the building, which housed New Scotland Yard. He was reading *The Daily Telegraph*.

"Richie," he stood up. "Good to see you again, my friend."

Richie shook his outstretched hand and sat opposite him, a low coffee table separating them. " How's Cheryl and the family?"

"Great. She sends her love and asks when you're coming up to stay. The rest are jogging along nicely until the next drama."

"Perhaps when this latest case is over I might be able to take some time off to visit my two favourite people."

"What's all the secrecy anyway? Something illegal you want me to do?" His smile took the sting out of his words and Richie relaxed.

"I need a court list for a trial that took place in Lockford Crown Court over two years ago."

His friend frowned. "You know that's impossible."

"Yeah, but it was worth a try. Although, I thought maybe there might be another way around it. There usually is; you and I both know that from bitter experience."

"Bending the facts to fit. We've seen it and fought against it often enough."

What happened to Piper Archer?.........K.J.Rabane

"You said it."

Richie explained the reason for his visit and waited for Norm's reply.

Eventually, the detective stroked his chin and said, "You haven't heard this from me but there was a court official called Derek Baynton who was working in Lockford at the time of the trial. Roughly about three months after Collins was sent down for the murder of his girlfriend Baynton was in financial trouble. I remember it because Dick Dawson was working undercover on a case involving gambling and illicit drugs and Baynton had come to London to play at the Casino where Dawson was working."

"How much trouble was he in?"

"Big enough. Baynton had a habit, which hadn't been apparent before, as he'd managed to keep it well hidden. He was a gambler who got into some trouble with unpaid debts. But he managed, with the help of some friends, to repay his debts and by some miracle escaped coming to the attention of the court. How he didn't lose is job over it is still a mystery."

"Perhaps he was lucky?

"You and I both know that's rubbish."

"Yeah. Swept under the carpet then?"

"More like it. He still lives and works in Lockford, I believe."

"So he's vulnerable where money is concerned?"

"Got it in one, Richie."

"He won't remember who was on that list though surely?"

"Unlikely. But he could find out. The details would be on file on computer somewhere in the archives ."

"Great. I can't thank you enough, Norm."

What happened to Piper Archer?.........K.J.Rabane

"He might not be willing to help though. I would think he'd be a bit cautious to say the least. It all depends how much of a hold his gambling habit still has over him. Once an addict always an addict as we've discovered on more than one occasion."

"Right, it's a start anyway. Now tell me how is Cheryl managing to cope with an empty nest now your youngest is in Uni?"

Later that afternoon, Richie took a cab to the smart new development in Covent Garden where Angie and Grant's apartment was situated. When she opened the door to him he noticed she'd cut her hair into a curly bob, which stopped at her chin. It suited her.

"Whatcha Sport," Angie said, kissing his cheek.

"Whatcha yourself," he replied, giving her an affectionate hug. "Where are the little ankle biters then?"

"Gone to Hyde Park with the nanny."

"You've got a nanny?"

"It's the tradition in Grant's family, apparently. Gives us time to have a proper chat though. You'll see them later, plenty of time for them to get to know their adopted uncle Richie."

The apartment was expensively and tastefully furnished, attributes, which, in his opinion, do not necessarily always go together. In spite of her change of circumstance when she married Grant, Angie hadn't changed. Richie found her to be the same, delightfully uncomplicated, girl he had met years before, when she'd arrived from Australia with ambition, talent and little money.

Although the air conditioning produced a comfortable temperature on such a hot afternoon, Angie suggested they take their drinks onto the balcony. The sights and sounds of cosmopolitan London drifted up towards the penthouse, muted by their elevated position, as they sat shaded by a striped awning and chatted about old times and Angie's career prospects in the States. Finally she said, "OK, now tell me what's really bothering you."

Richie smiled. "That obvious?"

"Only to me."

He told her about his latest case and how he intended to proceed. "Any ideas on why a woman who seemed to have it all should leave her husband in the first place and, if her husband is to be believed, reappear two years later."

Below them the sound, of a baritone singing to a crowd of tourists, drifted upwards on the breeze.

"Did she have it all?" Angie mused. "I don't think a woman who is truly happy ever leaves that kind of marriage. There has to be something missing."

Richie sucked in his bottom lip. " Sandy and you are reading from the same page."

"She's still with you then?"

"Yeah. And I'm permanently crossing my fingers. She's too well qualified, she could go at any minute."

"It's like I said though, people who are really happy don't." Angie smiled.

Richie heard a door slam followed by children's voices. Angie's three-year-old twin boys raced towards them, their curly hair mirroring their mother's. Richie's face stretched into a wide grin. "Now let me see where have I put the presents I bought for my favourite little boys," he said, as hugs and sticky faces swamped him.

Later, when the children were fast asleep and night had fallen, Richie kissed Angie's cheek and left her standing on the balcony waiting to wave a last goodbye. In the street he hailed a black cab and returned to his hotel.

Before sleep overtook him, he pondered over Angie's assumption that no one who was truly happy would leave such a marriage. Many times in his life he had wondered whether that was true. It was certainly the case that no one knew what went on behind closed doors, which metaphorically speaking could include the mind. How many secrets did we hide, even from ourselves?

What happened to Piper Archer?………K.J.Rabane

Beresford

Chapter 24

I've not moved from the house in five days. But she hasn't come back. There have been no further phone calls. I can't sleep. I look like shit. The situation is impossible. I have to pull myself together. This can't go on. I must forget I ever knew her.

It's Friday. The sun is hot on my arm as I open the window. I'll have a cool shower, change into some clean clothes, go to the supermarket, take charge of my life and start again. I've done it before, when life has slapped me in the face; I know I can do this.

The traffic is busy on the road leading to the large supermarket on the edge of town. Piper hated shopping here, 'it's too big,' she would say, 'why would I want to walk down rows and rows of cheeses to get to the one I want?' I know I won't see her here.

There are children everywhere, screaming, crying, running between the aisles, parents shouting at or ignoring, their offspring. I feel sweat running in rivulets down the back of my neck. My forehead is wet. Hurrying along each aisle like a marathon runner, I fill my trolley with little heed to my purchases. Panic sweeps over me, as I fear I'll see her around every corner.

"Eighty-four pounds sixty three pence, dear," the checkout assistant says, her voice and demeanour robotic.

I place my card in the reader, punch in the pin with fingers that won't stop shaking, and hurry towards my car. I can't breathe properly until I drive out of the car park heading for home and my panic attack recedes.

The house looks the same, no strange car in the drive but my heart races. I know she's there - waiting.

In the kitchen a casserole is cooking and the appetising smell nauseates me. There's no note from Serena, who is the only one who has a key, apart from Piper. She's upstairs. I can hear her footfalls on the wooden floor. I race up the stairs and throw open our bedroom door.

She's naked. Her hair is wet and she's drying her body with a towel. "It's so hot, I decided to take a cool shower, darling. You're home early." She glances at the clock on the bedside table. "Are you OK? You don't look well."

I don't know what to say. How to answer such a simple question? It shouldn't be difficult but the words stick to my tongue like Velcro.

"Why don't you take a shower? It will help, I'm sure. A change of clothes," she hesitates. "Why are you wearing cotton trousers and a yellow shirt to work, Beresford?"

"I've not been to work."

"Why not?"

Again the words feel sticky in my mouth but I manage to reply. "Taking a short break – tummy bug."

"Well then. All then more reason to cool down in the shower. I'll bring you up an Alka-Seltzer to settle you tummy. It's the heat. Change your clothes in work, did you? Austin's by the look of them." When she reaches the door she says, "I won't be long, be back in a tick."

It's what she always says – 'be back in a tick' – it's one of her sayings.

What happened to Piper Archer?.........K.J.Rabane

I shower. Letting the water wash away my fear seems a reasonable thing to do. Something normal. I know she won't be there and that I'll go downstairs and find her gone. I know it's an hallucination, a fantasy.

I've dressed in a pair of shorts and fresh T-shirt. Serena's daily, Vera Dawes, has been looking after my washing and cleaning since Piper left. She comes in once a week on a Monday. I don't hurry. There's no need. When I eventually drag a comb through my wet hair I go downstairs.

"There you are. Feeling better? I popped the casserole into the freezer. It's far too hot to eat a cooked meal, especially if your tummy's playing up. Cold salmon and salad do you?" Serena is sitting in the conservatory under the ceiling fan, reading a book.

"Thanks. You shouldn't worry about me, you know. I can manage." Of course I don't tell her about my fantasies.

"You really don't look at all well. Perhaps you should see Doctor Baxter."

Nodding I say, "I will, if it keeps up."

"Good. I've laid the table outside. It's cool under the canopy. Go on out and I'll bring it to you. Then I must go home or Mike will think I've left him." She doesn't see the irony and I don't comment.

Sitting at the table in the shade I close my eyes and pray I'm not going insane. I've no appetite for food or conversation. But Baxter is a last resort. I have to try and beat this myself. The thought embeds itself, becomes a distinct possibility, a way out of my predicament, a way back down the road to sanity - no one can help me but myself. I watch the approach of night as I wait for Serena to return with my meal.

What happened to Piper Archer?.........K.J.Rabane

After I hear the sound of her car driving away I go inside to the silence of an empty house.

What happened to Piper Archer?.........K.J.Rabane

Chapter 25

"Well?" Sandy was alone in the office, Harry having taken a chance on a last minute trip to visit a friend in the south of France. She was wearing a short blue and white cotton frock, her blonde hair tied back in a low knot from which tendrils escaped. Richie felt a fluttering somewhere in his chest and swallowed.

"Yes thanks."

"Do I have to spell it out?" she asked with a grin.

"Make me a brew and come into my office, Miss Smith."

Whilst Sandy was boiling the kettle the telephone rang. Richie picked it up. It was Serena Platt.

"Mr Stevens? I'm really worried about Berry. He looks terrible." She launched straight into it, the point of her phone call almost being missed by the descriptive element of how Beresford Archer had come home after shopping. She nearly described what he'd bought in the supermarket then ended with him waiting on the patio for the salmon salad, looking as if he'd seen a ghost. Apparently he didn't say as much but she was convinced he thought she'd been back to the house again.

"I've been thinking, Mrs Platt. On these occasions does no one else see his wife? What about the neighbours for instance?"

"Neighbours? There are none. I think I gave you their address, didn't I? It's Elm Tree House. You drive out of town towards Manor Way, take a sharp left at the Cuttings then down the road leading to the Common. The house is on your right, down a country lane. It's massive. Beautifully done mind you. No expense spared. There were stables, when they bought it but Beresford had them made into a spa area – hot tub – you know the sort of thing."

Richie ran his fingers through his hair, he wasn't sure if he did, never having been in a position to afford such luxury.

"I see. Right, well I've been visiting a friend in London and have some information, which might be of help. Is there anything you can tell me about the people who served on the jury with your sister? Perhaps after the trial she might have spoken about some of them?"

"No, I don't think she did. She wasn't given to small talk, our Piper. Reticent, even with me." She sighed and it spoke volumes.

Not like her sister then, Richie thought.

"I see. OK, thanks for the call, Mrs Platt and if there's anything that comes to mind, please don't hesitate to contact us."

"How long d'you think this will take?" She was obviously worried about his bill. He wanted to say as long as it takes but replied, "I'll follow this line of enquiry and by the end of the week I'll have an answer to your question. But be assured I won't let this drag on longer than is necessary."

She seemed satisfied by his reply and he replaced the phone and followed Sandy into the inner office.

After he'd told her about his meeting with DCI Freeman, Sandy said, "This Derek Baynton, have you decided how to go about arranging a meeting?"

Richie looked up from his desk and frowned. "That depends on you."

"Me?"

"Yeah. Knowing your chameleon-like ability I wondered if you'd be up for a role as a gambler? Especially as I've already seen your skill at poker."

What happened to Piper Archer?.........K.J.Rabane

Sandy laughed. "You're serious?"

"Baynton has two weaknesses Gambling and a pretty face. Norm said he's to be found at the Lockford Heath Casino most Friday and Saturday nights."

"Do I have expenses?"

"Of course. I don't expect you to gamble away your wages."

"What if I win?"

"OK, look on it as the bonus I can't afford to pay you."

"In that case, when do I start?"

"I think we'll try this Friday."

"Are you coming with me?"

Richie stroked his chin. "Not exactly. I'll be there but it is essential that you arrive alone and don't acknowledge me. I'm just there to keep an eye on things and if he doesn't show then I'll see you home."

"And if he does?"

"I'll leave that up to you. I'll be watching your back but I suggest you don't go to his place afterwards."

"Don't worry. I'm a big girl now. I can deal with creeps like Baynton."

"I'm glad to hear it. So it's business as usual till then."

During his lunch hour Richie drove out of town following the directions to Elm Tree House given to him by his client. As he approached the house, he saw she hadn't exaggerated its grandeur. Beresford Archer's work as a consultant surgeon, although well paid, surely couldn't run to such a place. The money had to have come from somewhere else. Speculation was useless; he considered it could be anywhere these days, lottery, inheritance, stock market success. He wondered what

What happened to Piper Archer?.........K.J.Rabane

had driven Piper Archer to leave her marriage because outward appearances suggested she had a loving, wealthy husband and an enviable lifestyle. And if Beresford Archer was to be believed what had made her return and behave as if the past two years had never occurred? Was she playing some sort of sick psychological game? None of it made any sense. Was this case the one to break the camel's back? No ready answer sprung to mind so he'd have to wait to see whether Sandy would make the difference and point him in the right direction.

Chapter 26

It was raining hard when Richie left the taxi and entered the Lockford Heath Casino, a summer storm accompanied by thunder and lightning the severity of which he hadn't experienced since being caught in a tropical storm on a family holiday in Florida when his children were small. The doorman nodded in his direction and as he handed his raincoat to the cloakroom attendant he was dismayed to see Micky Parsons from the Courier bearing down on him from the direction of the Gents.

"As I live and breathe, Richie Stevens – not the place I'd have expected to see you on a Friday night."

"Mick. I could say the same thing."

Parsons fell into step alongside him as they made their way to the bar. "Yeah, well, you know how things are."

"Ferreting out a story then?"

"My lips are sealed. Got anything for me?" Mick looked hopeful.

"Not a thing."

"Don't believe you've suddenly taken up gambling – not for a minute."

Richie knew he'd have to feed him something, as from past experience he recognised he wouldn't give in without a struggle. "As a matter of fact I've heard on the grapevine that one of the croupiers is sifting off more than she should from the customers and my client would like my opinion."

"Sounds like a story to me."

"Possibly, but I don't want you planting your size ten shoes in my patch and messing things up before I decide for myself."

What happened to Piper Archer?.........K.J.Rabane

Parsons tapped the side of his nose. "A nod is as good as a wink, my old son. I'll be in touch."

Watching Micky walking off towards the tables, Richie breathed a sigh of relief and finished his drink. Half an hour later he saw her. She was wearing a red halter neck dress, which flattered her figure to the point at which Richie wondered why he'd never noticed such attributes in his assistant before. Her hair hung loose to her shoulders and shone in the light from the overhead spots, her legs, elongated by sky-scrapped heels, were tanned and toned to perfection. Sandy caught his eye for a fraction of a second then looked away.

Ordering another drink, he found a seat at a table on an elevated section from which he had a panoramic view of the punters. He watched Sandy playing Black Jack and held his breath. She was no fool, where the tables were concerned, having spent part of her gap year as a croupier in Las Vegas. In addition to which getting a first in Psychology gave her an insight into the minds of the punters. She was on a winning streak but gave no outward sign of it. After a while she headed for the Roulette table where Derek Baynton was seated.

Richie saw her watching the action for a bit before waiting for a vacated seat at Baynton's side. Then, after appearing to hesitate, she sat down. If Micky Parsons hadn't been at the bar Richie would have taken a seat at the same table but now he had no option other than to watch from a distance, hope Micky hadn't recognised Sandy, and wait for her report.

Even from this distance he could see that their quarry was losing badly. At one point Sandy leaned across to him and he saw the man smile and place his remaining chips on red. The croupier spun the wheel and red came up. Richie sat back in his chair certain that Sandy could more than handle the situation. However, there was no way he was going to leave her alone, not a snowball's chance in hell.

Two hours later, Richie was sipping coffee whilst Sandy and Derek Baynton were seated at a nearby table. Not near enough for him to hear their conversation but close enough to see they'd made a connection, the look on Baynton's face said it all. Thankfully Micky Parsons seemed to have called it a night and was nowhere in the vicinity.

After a while he saw Sandy take her mobile from her bag and watched as Baynton leaned across her obviously trying to dissuade her from calling a cab. Richie's inclination was to intervene but he sat tight and waited.

He saw Sandy smiling and shaking her head. She stood up and, followed by Baynton, made for the exit. Richie hurried towards the door. In the street, he saw her getting into a taxi with Baynton and watched helplessly as they drove away. It was too late for him to do anything to help her now and could only pray she could handle anything Baynton had in mind.

What happened to Piper Archer?.........K.J.Rabane

Isobel

Chapter 27

I left Serena's sure she was keeping something from me. I get these feelings occasionally and usually I'm right. My mother was convinced I had psychic powers but then mother was an uneducated person with a penchant for visiting fortune-tellers. Thankfully I'm more prosaic. However, instinct wasn't going to unravel Serena's secrets neither would it get to the bottom of what was going on with Beresford.

Deciding that, if I wanted to continue with my resolve to have him come hell or high water, I'd have to make some of my own investigations where Piper Archer was concerned. So where did I go from here? Serena's detective seemed, as much in the dark as anyone, if what she'd told me was correct so the place to start had to be in Elm Tree House. But would he let me in? I couldn't get him to speak to me on the phone longer than a couple of seconds and as for arranging for us to go out for a meal, it was one step too far. I was afraid he was on a downward spiral into depression and having had experience of the condition, with a close friend, I thought I knew how to handle it.

The delicatessen near Hastings Buildings was busy with the after-work rush. I waited in line to be served whilst deciding which would be the most appetising meal to take-away. Surely he wouldn't be able to resist if I made it impossible for him to do so.

Driving out of town, the appetising aroma of our evening meal filling the car, I pondered over how I would continue with my plan. As I turned into the lane leading to the house, a car drove towards me and I stopped to let it pass. I had a brief view of someone in the driving seat but the tinted glass of the side windows made identification difficult.

When I arrived at the house the front door was ajar.

"Beresford?" I called out.

I heard the sound of someone rushing along the upstairs landing, followed by Beresford hurrying downstairs. His face fell and he clutched his chest when he saw me.

"Isobel? I thought…"

He slumped and sat on the lower stair.

"You look terrible." I put the food carrier on the hall table and went to him. "You're not well, are you? Come into the living room and I'll pour you a brandy."

He didn't argue, just did as I'd asked, sat in a chair and stared out of the window as if in a trance. Once the brandy began to slip down his throat, he spluttered and turned to face me. "She was here. I was upstairs. I heard her moving about in the kitchen but when I called out there was no answer." He put his head in his hands and shuddered. "I must be going mad."

"I don't think so - not at all. Something's happening here. Have you thought that someone might be playing a cruel game by impersonating your wife? Someone who dislikes you, someone you've upset, perhaps?"

"It's Piper. I know it *has* to be her." He was getting angry. "But why is it only me seeing her?"

"I saw someone driving along the lane from this direction when I arrived."

He removed his hands from his head and looked up at me. "You saw her?" He was so anxious for a favourable reply I almost lied.

What happened to Piper Archer?.........K.J.Rabane

"I saw someone but to be honest it could have been anyone. The car approached and as the lane is so narrow I pulled into the side and waited for it to pass"

"What make was it?"

"I don't know. It was black or navy blue and quite high up from the ground. At least the bonnet was higher than mine."

"That's not saying much, yours is an Audi sport." I realised it was the nearest he was going to get to humour. "So it could have been her you saw?" he asked anxiously.

"It's possible," I replied, and saw the muscles in his shoulders relax.

"If only I could be sure." He was picking at his thumbnail.

"Let me heat this up and we can eat outside. I'm famished," I said. "And besides you look as if you could do with fattening up."

"It's very kind of you, Isobel but I've no appetite. I think I'll just lie down for a while. Please, eat your meal and let yourself out when you've finished."

So this was how it was going to be I thought packing up the meal and taking it home with me. There was simply no more I could do for the moment. However, I was determined that Piper Archer was not going to deter me from my goal. She'd had her chance and thrown it away. If she had some sick ulterior motive for behaving in this way, I'd find out, if it took all my resources to do so. I did realise it could all be in his mind and that something had tipped him over the edge to the point at which he believed he was seeing his missing wife around every corner. And if this were the case, I'd help him to recover. One way or another I'd make sure it happened between us if it was the last thing I did.

What happened to Piper Archer?.........K.J.Rabane

Serena

Chapter 28

We used to go on holiday in August, once Ellie broke up from school. Now it didn't matter when we went. Ellie was in Spain and Mike suggested we visit her and then drive up to the south of France. I liked the idea of seeing our daughter but was anxious about staying away with this business with Piper hanging over us. Then Mike came home from work and said a mate of his had dropped out of a golfing holiday in Alicante and wondered if he could go instead, if I wasn't too bothered either way. He looked at me with those brown puppy-dog eyes of his and I didn't have the heart to refuse. To be honest it suited me to stay at home, as I've said.

I must admit though, after I drove Mike to the station, I felt lost. So I parked the car in the High Street and walked towards Hastings Buildings.

The temperature was climbing as I opened the office door and felt the cooling breeze from a ceiling fan.

"Mrs Platt." Richard Stevens was standing at one of those water bottle dispenser things that give you the option of water with or without ice. He's quite attractive, not in the same league as my Mike, mind you, but the sun had caught his hair and made it look quite blonde. He was alone in the office.

"I wondered if you had any news for me?" I asked

"Come and sit down. Can I get you a drink? Tea-coffee?"

"I'll have what you're having. It's so hot and it's not ten o'clock yet. On your own today, are you?"

What happened to Piper Archer?.........K.J.Rabane

The phone rang and he went to answer it before he could reply.

"No hurry. Yeah, I can't wait. It could be good. As I said, take your time. No don't bother, Harry. I'm fine. See you later then."

He put down the phone and looking at me, said, "I am but my secretary will be in later. Now what can I do for you? An update, I presume?"

"Well, yes, that and to let you know that I'm now convinced it's all in Berry's head. There's no way my sister wouldn't come and see me if she was in the area."

He frowned and handed me a polystyrene cup of iced water. "What I don't understand is why you would think so, Mrs Platt, after all, you presumably haven't heard from her in a year or two, why would she suddenly get in touch now?"

The water made me feel better; the heat had quite got to me. "I get what you're saying, of course I do. And it might seem a bit odd. But you see, the way I looked at it was this. Piper wanted to disappear. OK, so she might have run off with some bloke or other. But I thought the reason she hadn't phoned me was because she didn't want Berry to know where she was. She would know I couldn't keep it from him, not with him being so upset at her going. Also, I thought she might have had that amnesia thing, people do, don't they, so that might be another reason she hadn't phoned. But when Berry started saying she'd come back, well that's when I knew she'd have let me know how she was."

"I see."

"It makes sense, doesn't it?"

"Well, some sort of sense, yes. I can see your reasoning. But if you're now convinced your brother-in-law is imagining seeing his wife, presumably you want me to finish up my investigations."

I was in two minds, to tell the truth, I really wasn't as positive as I'd sounded that Berry was imagining it all, so I replied, "Well not exactly. I've decided to let you continue for the next two weeks. My Mike is away and there's no point in you stopping now – perhaps when he comes back you'll have some answers for me. If not then I think we'll have to forget it."

"Very well. I have a couple of avenues to explore as a matter of fact and two weeks should give me a chance to do my best before calling it a day."

"Can't say fairer than that then." I stood up and he walked me to the door.

"Be assured, Mrs Platt. I will do my very best to find out what happened to your sister." He smiled and held out his hand. As I shook it I shivered, deciding he was definitely attractive in a comfortable sort of way. It was just as well there was no one for me but my Mike, I thought, leaving the building and walking towards Primark.

What happened to Piper Archer?.........K.J.Rabane

Chapter 29

From the office window Richie watched his client walking down the street, wondering if two weeks was enough to wrap up the case. A while later, sitting behind his desk drinking his third cup of tea of the morning, he heard the door to the outer office open, followed by Sandy's distinctive footsteps.

"I told you not to hurry," he called to her.

She stood in the doorway, hair scraped back from her face, wearing a navy and white cotton dress and navy pumps as different from the image he'd seen in the Casino as it was possible to be.

"You didn't have to come in at all today. I'm finishing up here after lunch anyway. There's nothing going on and we can leave the answer phone on for appointments. Not that there's likely to be any. Most people are on holiday."

"I know, but I knew you'd want to hear it all first hand and I'm meeting a friend for lunch later anyway."

"Not Derek Baynton by any chance?" Richie found he was silently praying she'd come up with the right answer.

"You've got to be joking! It's a friend from school, Louisa, if you must know."

He silently sighed with relief. "OK then, let's have it."

Sandy sat down opposite him and crossed her long legs. "He's a sleazy nutcase and one which I found easy to crack."

"Go on."

"I started with flattery, which he fell for like a drunk looking for his next drink. Then I brought the conversation around to work and he said he was a court official, made it sound as if the whole legal system depended on him."

"Not given to modesty then?"

"Quite. But I listened intently, still massaging his ego."

Richie avoided the obvious pitfall of interjecting that he hoped that was all she was massaging. "And?" he asked.

"And it worked. Eventually, I asked about some of the more lurid cases he'd worked on, bringing the conversation around to the Collins case. When we were sitting at the bar he told me he'd worked on the case and mentioned some of the sickening details, all of which could be found in newspaper reports at the time." Sandy fanned her face with a cardboard file on Richie's desk. "And the more I oood and ahhhhd and said what an interesting man he was, the more he talked."

Richie leaned back in his chair and closed his eyes.

"Am I boring you?" Sandy asked.

"On the contrary. I'm trying to picture you pandered to that jerk and failing miserably. Please continue, Miss Smith."

"I said I'd always wanted to be called to jury service and wondered what it would be like."

"And he told you, of course."

"In great detail. But when I asked what were the people like who were sitting on the jury in the Collins case, he shrugged and said he didn't remember."

"And you don't believe him?"

"No doubt he doesn't remember most of them but I think Piper Archer might have rung a bell, not that I fell into the trap of mentioning her name. He'd remember her all right, if only from the publicity at the time – I expect he dined out on the fact without going into enough detail to get him the sack. But it will take more than one night to get it out of him."

"Did you get the impression he was short of cash?"

"Not last night. He was winning at Roulette. But I noticed frayed cuffs on his shirt and there was an air of desperation hanging about him like a bad smell."

"Have you made a date to see him again?"

"He tried but I was enigmatic enough to make him wait. He has my number though. I thought if he wants my company bad enough and if the money runs out, I might be in a better bargaining position."

"Sounds good to me but time *is* running out for us. Serena Platt has retained our services for another two weeks and that's it."

Sandy shrugged. "I'll just have to up the anti then. I'll have that list for you by Monday morning at the latest."

The day passed slowly, as days when nothing much happens often do. He was alone when he locked up the office. Sandy had left hours ago. He'd intended to finish up himself after lunch but decided to do some routine spadework before calling it a day. He'd also rung Austin Banks. Sandy had other fish to fry and it wasn't fair to expect her to work on both Baynton and Banks, enticing though her charms might be. She'd met him once but he'd been a bit tight lipped about his boss. So it was up to him to ease her load.

There was a cool wind blowing down the High Street as he left the office. Richie was grateful for the drop in temperature, as the heat had been oppressive over the last few days. There was a time when he'd have looked forward to a weekend of good weather to take the family to the beach. But he could hardly remember what it felt like to be part of a family; all he had left were snapshots in his mind of a life that was beginning to feel as if it belonged to someone else.

The wine bar was busy and it was a while before he saw Austin sitting at a table overlooking the High Street.

"Thanks for meeting me, Austin," Richie said, as he sat down. "I know weekends are precious for busy doctors and I won't keep you longer than is necessary."

"It's no problem. I'm meeting Jen, a nurse at Lockford General later so I'm killing time until she gets ready, as it happens. You said on the phone it had something to do with Beresford Archer?"

Richie nodded, "I'll get us a drink first then I'll explain.

A short while later, with a glass of red in front of him, Richie said, "You mentioned when I last saw you that you thought Archer had done his training in Cardiff, at the Princess Royal. When would that have been exactly?"

Austin stroked his chin, thought for a moment then replied, "He was an SHO at the Princess Royal. He told me once that the Cardiff night life was second to none."

"So he was a young man; mid twenties would you say?"

"That's an accurate approximation. He didn't go into details but I had the feeling something happened to stop him from continuing in Cardiff. I thought it odd, as he seemed to like the place so much and wondered why he moved from the area."

"Surely it's not unusual to move for advancement in your profession?" Richie picked up his glass.

"Quite. But apparently the registrar on the team was dismissed and I would have thought Beresford would have been a natural replacement."

"Did he say why?"

Austin raised his eyebrows. "Not in a heartbeat, very uncommunicative, if he wants to be. No. It was Miles Lawrence told me, and he'd heard it on the grapevine, apparently."

"I see. Might be something to look into. Thanks Austin. Now tell me when are you thinking of settling down and not playing the field?"

Austin sighed. "You've been talking to my uncle Norman I presume."

When he'd finished his drink, Richie shook Austin's hand, thanked him again for his time and said he would give his good wishes to Norm when he next spoke to him.

It had started to rain by the time he left the wine bar and walked back to the basement car park in Hastings Buildings. It was a welcome change from the heat of the past few days. Whether his conversation with Austin would be of any use was another matter but his natural optimism was leading him to believe that he might have stumbled upon some vital link in the chain of coincidences. Turning up his shirt collar, he whistled softly, as he considered his next move.

What happened to Piper Archer?.........K.J.Rabane

Serena

Chapter 30

The money wasn't a problem. Well not at the moment but I wasn't going to let on to Richard Stevens. Let him think I couldn't afford to retain him for more than a week or two – keep him on his toes. But I was determined to get to the bottom of this and if it took all my savings to do so, well I'd have to live with it. It wasn't as if we were destitute after all. We'd always been careful and when Mike's promotion came through and Ellie was more or less off our hands we were comfortable enough. Not in the same league as my sister and her husband, granted, but look what had happened there. Money can't buy happiness as Mike is always saying. And I have to agree with him. Berry's not happy, anyone can see that and Piper? I wish I knew what was going on with her. There are nights I can't sleep for worrying.

Some days I'm sure Berry's gone around the bend then I wonder whether she's actually come back and *she* is sick. In the head, I mean. It's not unheard of. Only the other day I was reading the Daily Mail and there was a story about a man who went missing and his son found him living on an island in Greece. It was only by chance he found him at all. The son was on holiday and he saw his father fishing from a rock in a small beach well away from the tourist area. The father didn't know who he was and couldn't remember how he'd got there.

It's got to be something like that otherwise I know she would have phoned me. She's had her secrets in the past though. I suppose most of us have. But I found out

What happened to Piper Archer?.........K.J.Rabane

about that one and I'll do the same with this, if it's the last thing I do.

I like Richard Stevens and his PA. They seem as if they know what they're doing. I trust them. Trust is a funny thing I always think. They say when trust is gone from a marriage nothing's left. That's what happened with Izzie. It was a marriage destined to fail from the off, she told me. He was in his early fifties when she married him and her just out of university. He was a man about town, if ever there was one, so she said. Liked young women, if you know what I mean, very young women, girls really, and there was the violence. She was naïve, she told me. It took her years to come to her senses. She's not like it now though, one bitten twice shy, as the saying goes. No one will put one over on Izzie. I did think her and Berry would get together but I'm not so sure now and in a way that's a huge relief. Berry's a mess at the moment. I hope he'll pull himself together soon and start looking for Piper seriously.

I was in the conservatory the day before yesterday and the phone rang. It was Izzie. "What is Beresford's favourite meal?" she asked.

When I told her she said, "Right. He's got to shape up and I'm going see he does." She sounded determined and I was in two minds whether she would succeed – only time would tell.

Yesterday, I called her and she said I was right, he's in a state and she got nowhere with the meal thing. It's not a good sign, the old saying, the way to a man's heart is through his stomach, is true. But she didn't even cook it herself so what did she expect. Mike's never kept a quarrel going when faced with a steak and kidney pie.

Wishing there was more I could do to help Berry isn't enough, I know. There must be something I can do.

What happened to Piper Archer?.........K.J.Rabane

After all, he's the next best thing to a brother I have. I wonder if Piper leaving had anything to do with that awful Collins bloke who killed his girlfriend? Being on the jury really upset her at the time. She never confided in me but I don't think she was ever the same afterwards. Well, who wouldn't be upset having to sit through it all day after day for over three weeks?

I must admit I thought she'd soon get over it though. It was bound to fade after the sentence was passed and life returned to normal. Although, I didn't see much of her during the weeks before she left. Being busy with Ellie studying for her exams and Mike having just got promotion I didn't have much time to dwell on Piper's problems.

Anyway she'd never really ever confided in me. Not like I did with her. I'd tell her everything and she'd just sit there, listen and nod her head, like she was somewhere else. Even when she was in real trouble I had to drag it out of her. But did I let her down? Not on your life, I was there for her every step of the way. Which makes it surprising she didn't tell me, if there was something wrong in her marriage, something that was upsetting her or just if Berry was getting on her nerves.

Envy is too strong a word for it. I've never been envious of Piper, even though she's always been the pretty one, not even when she married into all that money. If I'm honest there were times when I slightly begrudged her good fortune, especially when Mike was working all the hours God gave and I was stuck at home with a young baby. I distinctly remember having a terrible winter with Ellie having one chest infection after another, Mike coming and going and never having time to talk to me and Piper and Berry spending a three-month break in Australia. Well it wouldn't be natural

What happened to Piper Archer?.........K.J.Rabane

not to want to change places in such circumstances, would it? But I'd always comforted myself by thinking, I had Ellie and I'd always have one over on my sister in that department.

Chapter 31

A welcoming cool breeze drifted up from the river to where Richie sat on the balcony of his flat reading the Sunday papers. In the distance, church bells rang out over the town, as swallows darted and dived in the trees bordering the silver ribbon of the river Locke below him.

The buzzer in the hall heralded the arrival of an unknown visitor. Stretching his legs, Richie walked towards the small screen near the front door. He smiled. He had a feeling she'd come.

"Miss Smith what a welcome surprise on this Sunday morning. Can't you sleep? Have you forgotten it's the weekend?"

"Just let me in, will you; you know you're dying to hear what went on last night."

In a matter of minutes Sandy was sitting on the balcony admiring the view.

"Cool drink?" Richie asked.

"I'll have what you're having," she sighed, making herself comfortable on the lounger and leaving Richie to sit on the chair and pour the iced tea into her cup.

"Right then, you've had the drink, you've liked the view. Put me out of my misery."

Sandy grinned. "I knew it," she said, "you can't wait."

She began to relate how she'd met Derek Baynton at the *Ivy Tree* for dinner at eight then afterwards he'd suggested they finish off the evening at the Casino.

"Last night, he couldn't do anything right." She sat forward.

"He lost?"

"Heavily. Which was as much as I'd suspected he would. He was getting more and more agitated as the night wore on until I managed to steer him towards the bar. I waited until the right opportunity arose then said," 'Derek, I've a proposition for you.'

"Not that kind of proposition," she told Richie, quickly. But he thought otherwise and smiled; an expression, which made my flesh creep, then he took my hand.

Richie frowned.

So I explained, 'Last time we met I asked you about the Collins case. I have a particular interest in it as I'm writing a dissertation on it for college. I desperately need some inside information. Ideally I'd like to contact some of the jurors, to get a feel of what they were thinking at the time but it's impossible to find out who they were.'

The penny suddenly dropped and he sat back in his chair and bit his lip. He looked around the empty bar area and, realising we were unlikely to be heard, leaned forward again and in a low tone said, 'What if I could get you a list of all twelve of them?'

'I'd be eternally grateful,' I simpered. At which point he stroked my hand suggestively. I felt like throwing up on the spot, I don't mind telling you."

"That would have put the cat amongst the pigeons," Richie commented wryly.

"Yes, well, instead I told him I'd be willing to pay for the information."

I could see him assessing how much, but he said, 'I see. And that's all is it?'

'I like you Derek,' I lied. 'But I don't want to get involved, I'm too busy at the moment. Who can say, when I've finished my exams, perhaps we could catch up again.'

'So, how much are we talking about here?' His eyes narrowed into slits.

What happened to Piper Archer?.........K.J.Rabane

Sandy, watching a cat chasing a bird on the riverbank, turned to Richie and continued, "I told him the amount we'd agreed, less two hundred, and he hesitated. I could see him assessing whether there was more to be had."

'Couldn't do it for that,' the greedy little creep replied.

"So I added the extra two hundred, whilst saying I was really stretching things and it was all I could offer being a student etc."

"And he agreed?" The newspaper fell from Richie's lap and he bent down to pick it up.

"He agreed. We're meeting tomorrow at lunchtime to finalise the deal."

"I knew he couldn't help himself if money was involved." Richie said, " I'm willing to bet he would sell his own grandmother, if the price were right. When you came along you were the answer to a gambler's prayer. Unsuccessful gamblers are usually on the lookout for ways to make money, not always legitimately, I might add."

Sandy yawned.

"What time did you get to bed then?"

"Half three, I think."

"Any trouble?"

"None I couldn't handle. He pushed his luck a couple of times but soon got fed up when I put him straight."

Richie winced.

"I shouldn't have let you get involved. I should have been the one to get the info out of Baynton." He looked down at his hands.

"I'm not a kid, you know. It's work and I'm willing to bet you'd have come up against a brick wall. He's no fool; he'd have seen through you in a heartbeat. Women are a different matter with the likes of Derek Baynton – it's a macho thing – he likes to impress."

"So tomorrow you should have a list of names and we can move forward?"

Sandy nodded.

"Nice work, Miss Smith."

"Thank-you, Boss. Now if you'll excuse me, my bed is waiting and I need to catch up on my beauty sleep."

Far below him, Sandy raised her hand before opening her car door and driving towards the flat she shared with her cousin Hugh, which overlooked Lockford Common. Hugh was in his final year of a performing arts degree course at Lockford college of Music and Drama and had been staying with Sandy, at her uncle's request, for the duration of his course. There had been times when this had caused problems but now that Sandy could see an end to her shared living status things seemed to have settled down between them. Richie knew she loved her little flat and living on her own, whilst being near enough to visit her father. Bernard had given up the family home in favour of a warden controlled flat near the Common.

However in some ways she would miss sharing with Hugh; she'd told Richie there were times when she'd used him as an excuse not to become too involved with some of her more intense boyfriends. He suspected that Hugh had come in handy when Derek Baynton had insisted on seeing Sandy back to her flat. Privately Richie hoped her cousin wouldn't be in too much of a hurry to leave.

However, it was with an uncomfortable feeling in the pit of his stomach that he picked up the newspapers and empty cups and sought the relatively cool interior of his living room.

What happened to Piper Archer?.........K.J.Rabane

Chapter 32

The following day, when the time drew nearer for Sandy to meet Baynton, Richie felt the necessity to leave the office and secure a place in the wine bar ahead of her. She had the money in an envelope in her handbag and he decided she needed a bodyguard in case anything went wrong. At least that's what he told himself. In actual fact he wanted to see how Derek Baynton would react to his PA. He believed he'd be able to tell by the man's body language alone if she were heading for trouble where he was concerned. He'd hardly slept and had second thoughts about letting her go through with the transaction. Keeping an eye on her was his way of making up for it.

The French windows of the bar were open to the street and Richie saw Baynton heading for the wine bar from the direction of the station. He stopped to comb his hair in his reflection in the Estate Agents' window, slicked back each side with his hands and then entered the wine bar, whilst looking around presumably to see if Sandy had arrived. Five minutes later Sandy passed Richie's seat, glared in his direction then walked towards Baynton.

By the time Richie had drunk a small glass of red wine and an orange and lemonade, Sandy had handed Baynton the envelope and received one in return. He saw her stand up, and walk into the street followed by Baynton. Through the window he saw Baynton lean forward to kiss her cheek but Sandy avoided it by holding out her hand. Watching Baynton's embarrassed handshake Richie smiled with relief. He needn't have been concerned; she knew what she was doing. Finishing his drink, Richie walked out into the sunshine and back to his office with a spring in his step.

"You didn't need to follow me!" She was angry and attacking him before he'd closed the door.

He hung his head. "Sorry," he said.

She sighed in exasperation and handed him a sheet of paper. "Here's the list of jurors."

Richie ran his eyes over the typed sheet. "It looks genuine, Piper Archer, heading the list of names and addresses, I see. Good work, in fact excellent work. I can't believe he produced this without any further conditions."

"We don't know that he hasn't."

"In what way?"

"Extortion springs to mind. Most people have a secret or two they'd prefer being kept secret."

"Possibly, but I don't think he'd have bothered to investigate these people in any detail, after all it's just made up of the ordinary man in the street."

Sandy considered his words for a moment. "Yes. But what if he didn't look any further than the first name on the list - Archer. In addition to which she's not short of money."

Richie frowned. "Maybe. I suppose it's worth thinking about. In the meantime, have a look at these addresses and plot them on the map in relation to each other then we'll get started."

Later that afternoon, Richie sat alongside Miss Laura Bentley on a seat in her garden. The scent of rose petals lingered in the warm air as he sipped his tea from a wafer thin cup.

What happened to Piper Archer?………K.J.Rabane

She was a woman in her early sixties, thin as a stick with short, straight, grey hair. "I don't know if I'll be able to help you, Mr Stevens. I didn't really bond with Mrs Archer during the three weeks we spent together, other than to discuss the details of the case in the jury room. I seem to remember she was a pleasant enough young woman, kept herself to herself. However, from my experience of serving on juries, I've served on three now, I've noticed that some people do seem to become close during the short time they are closeted together, especially if the case is a particularly unpleasant one."

"So you didn't notice Piper Archer forming such an attachment?"

"Not really. There was a woman she regularly sat by in the jury room. Her name was Joyce something or other. You know how it is, we are all creatures of habit, and we seemed to gravitate to the same seats day after day, almost as it they were our personal property and woe betide someone who violates our chosen space."

Richie nodded. She was an intelligent woman who would be an excellent witness. "It is good of you to try to help, Miss Bentley."

"Not at all. How did you say you found me?"

"Mrs Archer's sister remembered her saying you were with her during the trial. She remembered that you lived in this cottage, the one with the roses around the door. I just called on the off-chance that she was right." Richie lied.

"That's right, of course, I remember you saying as much on the telephone. I'm just sorry I can't be of any further help. And I do hope you find Mrs Archer. It must be very distressing for everyone involved."

Closing the garden gate, he raised his hand to her. This one had been easy, the explanation for his visit tripping glibly from his tongue. But he wasn't looking forward to making his way down the list in such a manner, even if Sandy was easing the situation by seeing six of them.

The next morning, Richie arrived at the office to find Sandy already hard at work.

"How did it go yesterday?" he asked, switching on the kettle.

"OK – you?"

"The same. Do you want to compare notes?"

"Not at the moment. I wondered if it might be better to see them all and then discuss our findings. What d'you think?"

"OK by me."

"My first appointment is at a quarter past twelve. When are you leaving the office?" Sandy asked, her diary open in front of her.

"Ten. I'll just have a quick brew and I'll be off. So there was no trouble yesterday, was there?"

"No. The stories we'd concocted seemed to hold up. No one challenged my right to ask questions about the trial or their fellow jurors. But I have the feeling they won't all be like that."

"Quite. But as I said, at the first sign of confrontation, quit."

"OK, Boss."

"Right then, "Richie glanced at his watch. "I'm off, see you later."

Joyce Leatherhead worked part-time in a shoe shop but met Richie in the Sweet Pea café prior to her afternoon shift. She was a woman in her early forties with raven black hair, which was cut in a spiky style. It would have suited someone younger but was at odds with her pale complexion and tortoiseshell framed glasses.

"I won't keep you long, Mrs Leatherhead. As I explained I'm working on behalf of Piper Archer's sister."

"Yeah, so I understand. How did you get hold of me though?"

Richie gave her his little boy lost look – the one Lucy used to say wouldn't work – but in his experience it always had. "I'm afraid, I found you via someone who is helping us with our enquiries, another member of the jury."

"Got to be Bill Roberts, he can't keep his mouth shut. Three weeks of listening to him going on and insisting he be put forward as foreman, I don't mind telling you, Mr Stevens, it was three weeks of pure hell. If it hadn't been for Piper making it more bearable, I have gone potty."

He let her think it was Roberts, there was no need to use Laura Bentley's name, which made things a bit easier.

"So you and Mrs Archer became close?"

"Not exactly close but we did sort of chat now and again. We had a bit of a laugh too, which was difficult under the circumstances, not many laughs to be had on the Collins case or with the rest of the jury."

"Did you meet up after the case finished?" Richie asked.

"We did, as a matter of fact. Only the once, mind you, and that was by accident. I bumped into her in John Lewis's. We went for a coffee."

"Did you ever meet her husband?"

"No. She didn't say much about him. Doctor, isn't he?"

What happened to Piper Archer?.........K.J.Rabane

"Yes."

"Too posh by half for me then. But we got along, Piper and me."

"Was she upset by the case?"

"No more than any of us. You read the newspaper reports, I expect. There was no doubt in any of our minds that he was guilty, not for a second. Of course Bill Roberts had to make a song and dance about it but eventually was persuaded by the rest of us. Not before we had four long days deliberating though. Pain in the neck he was."

"He thought Collins was innocent?"

"Not as strong as that. He thought the girlfriend might have asked for it. Made us all mad as hell when he said that, you can imagine."

"What about the other men on the jury? Anyone Piper got close to?"

She laughed and spluttered into her coffee. Dabbing at her mouth with a paper napkin, she replied, "Sorry, but if you'd seen then other men you'd understand."

"Why was that?"

"They were a rum lot to say the least. Tom Harris was nice enough but a bit of a geek, loved trials, used to go and sit in the public gallery in his spare time – knew all there was to know about procedures. I think he was a student." She thought for a moment. "Let me see now, it was a while back, I can't remember all their names but there was an elderly man, must have been all of sixty, bald, walked with a limp, Ray something. Nice sort but too old to be interesting."

Richie winced.

"Jim wasn't too bad, builder, in his thirties but he liked to talk about his family until we were sick of hearing about them. So that was the lot, the rest were women, a couple of old dears, a girl with a young family, two giggly twenty somethings with skirts up their back sides, oh and I nearly forgot Piper used to talk to Jean Montgomery."

"Young was she?"

"Jean? No, that was the funny part really; she must have been fifty-five if she was a day, loads of wrinkles, dark rings under her eyes, looked like an unmade bed some days. I couldn't see what Piper saw in her. But towards the end of the trial they often sat together chatting, on their own, until I arrived, and then Jean gravitated towards the old dears. Oh yeah, and there was Ronald somebody, funny surname, quiet type, bookish, if you know what I mean?"

Richie nodded. "Did you have any idea that Piper was unhappy in her marriage?"

She sipped her coffee thoughtfully. "No. Like I said, she didn't say much about her husband, just that he worked in Lockford General. I knew he was a doctor but she didn't go on about it."

"So it came as a surprise to you when she left?"

"That's an understatement, Mr Stevens. I was shocked rigid. She seemed so contented, especially at the start of the trial. Most of us were strung out by the end of the three weeks, understandably considering the evidence, and Piper was no exception. She was twitchy and not as composed as before – as I said, none of us were, myself included."

Richie leaned across the table and held out his hand. "Thank you so much for your help, Mrs Leatherhead."

Her hand was ice-cold in spite of the fact she'd been nursing her coffee cup. As he left the café, Richie wondered if he could read anything into the fact that Piper Archer's disposition began to change towards the end of the trial or whether it was, as Joyce Leatherhead had suggested, understandable under the circumstances. By the time Sandy and he had interviewed all the members of the jury he hoped to have an answer or at least a clearer picture of the woman who, it seemed, had suddenly come back into her husband's life. But the fact remained, if Beresford Archer was to be believed then where was his wife now and what game was she playing?

What happened to Piper Archer?.........K.J.Rabane

Chapter 33

Richie yawned and put his feet up on the desktop. The Indian summer was definitely over. He hated cold, dark, mornings and short days; in fact he hated anything to do with the thought of winter approaching. The central heating clunked, the water gurgled in the pipes and he shivered as a cold wind slid through the ill-fitting windowpanes. Sandy said he should invest in double-glazing, if only to keep the noise of Lockford's High Street from invading their space but Sandy hadn't taken a look a his bank balance lately. The Piper Archer case was the only one on his books at the moment and he needed to bring it to a swift conclusion if only for his bank account's sake.

Throughout last week he'd been concentrating on interviewing the members of the jury in the Collins case and hadn't come up with a thing he could use. The sound of footsteps running up the stairs heralded Sandy's arrival. Through his open door he could see her standing in the outer office raindrops dripping from her hair, as she shook her head.

"You remind me of Bruce."

"Thanks. It feels good to be compared to my old Labrador, especially as he's passed over."

Richie grinned. "Still miss him then?"

"Of course. And you had to admit he was a good cover for surveillance work." Sandy hung her raincoat on the hook.

"The best. Remind me - who are you going to see today? There can't be many left on the list.

"Only one – Ronald Wengren in the antiquarian book shop on Milton Road."

What happened to Piper Archer?………K.J.Rabane

"Right, that's our last line of enquiry sewn up then. I have to admit defeat as I have absolutely no idea what happened to Piper Archer or where she is now."

"Coffee?" Sandy asked.

"Thanks. You know I've got Serena Platt coming in tomorrow morning to see if there are any developments?"

Sandy nodded.

"She rang me to ask if I'd mind if her brother-in-law came as well. I wish I had more for them but it looks like I'll have to wrap it up."

"Perhaps Wengren knows something."

"Clutching at straws comes to mind but you never know, give it your best shot. I'm counting on you, Miss Smith."

There was something in the self-satisfied expression, which crossed Sandy's face that made him sit up. It was only fleeting but he'd seen it before and knew she was keeping something from him. Past experience with his talented colleague made him ignore it for the moment. Making no further comment, he opened the bottom drawer of his desk and removed the packet of biscuits he'd bought on his way to work.

"Fancy one?" he asked.

The earlier rain had continued through the lunch hour and showed no signs of abating whilst Richie waited for Sandy to return to the office. He'd been reading over the Piper Archer file hoping for some inspiration in preparation for his meeting the following day. It occurred to him to wonder why Beresford Archer had suddenly taken an interest in this investigation and whether there had been any developments at their end.

What happened to Piper Archer?.........K.J.Rabane

It was nearly four o'clock, and the office was so dark he'd switched on the lights just after lunch. When he heard Sandy opening the door to the outer office he stood up and went to meet her, eager to know the outcome of her meeting with Wengren.

"Well?"

"Yes thanks."

Richie bit back a retort and waited until she'd removed her raincoat and was sitting behind her desk.

"At first I thought he seemed rather attractive," she began, "dark hair and deep brown eyes. He showed me into a room behind the shop, whilst an elderly lady frowned and, obviously against her better judgement, allowed me to pass behind the counter, her domain, and into the back room."

"How old is Wengren?" Richie asked, having had the impression he was too old to hold any attraction for Sandy.

"Early thirties, could even be late twenties but it was when he started to speak I had the impression of someone much older. Perhaps it's because of his fondness for ancient books but I thought he had a sort of old world charm. Anyway, I started to ask him about the trial and what he thought of Piper Archer and the longer he talked the more I became convinced he was lying."

"What made you think so?"

"You know me, Boss, I can't explain it, just a feeling."

"And one which I have grown to respect," Richie walked towards the kettle. "Cuppa?"

"Please. He said he'd met Piper, just the once after the trial, when she'd popped into the shop as she was passing. He ran his finger around his collar and I suppose that was when I knew he wasn't telling the truth."

"Just because he ran a finger around the inside of his collar? I can see I'll have to be careful not to do the same." He was teasing her and being used to his humour she didn't respond just smiled and raised her eyebrows.

"As we talked I became certain he was hiding something."

Now Richie knew she was up to something, holding something back, like dangling a bone in front of a dog and waiting for him to pounce.

"OK. I give up. What is it?" Richie said, handing her a mug of coffee.

She'd raised the mug to her lips but her carefully constructed wall collapsed. "OK!" she said, putting the mug down on the desk. "I give in. It's his name – it's been niggling away at me from the moment he let me into the shop. She picked up a piece of paper from her desk. "Here, take a look."

Richie was well used to seeing Sandy completing *The Telegraph* crossword, anagrams written on scraps of papers, words crossed through, others highlighted. He glanced at the arrangement of letters and sighed. "It's obvious but why didn't I see it before?" he said. "I must be getting old."

"Well, I shouldn't worry. It took me long enough."

"Ronald Wengren – Rowland Green," Richie said, it's been staring us in the face all the time.

What happened to Piper Archer?.........K.J.Rabane

Beresford

Chapter 34

Austin has done a splendid job of keeping the ship ticking over. His team are working flat out and I can see he is relieved at having an extra pair of hands on board, in addition to which he can now relax and leave the helm to the captain.

Sailing metaphors, it seem, spring to mind on recalling the past few days. I can see a stretch of calm water ahead. I've not been imagining Piper coming into the house, Serena has seen the evidence and Isobel is where she has always been, supporting me throughout.

When Saturday morning arrives, I shower and dress casually taking care to put on a coat, as the weather has changed dramatically, summer having given way to winter in a matter of weeks. Our appointment with Richard Stevens is at eleven and I wonder whether he's a charlatan only interested in taking Serena's money, of which I am determined to reimburse her, regardless of any protestations to the contrary, or whether he is genuinely trying to discover what happened to Piper.

Serena is nervous.

"I'm so glad you're coming with me, Berry. I was beginning to think I've been a bit foolish but I didn't know what else to do. I can't understand why Piper hasn't rung; I'd begun to think she might be dead. Well, you know how the mind races. I said to Mike, I said….."

I switch off, as always, when Serena starts to move into nonsense mode, she'll be saying how it was only a day or two ago, now let me think was Mike wearing his golfing trousers? I do remember it because I'd just made

What happened to Piper Archer?………K.J.Rabane

a cup of tea……..It was all rubbish but it was Serena and she had a good heart, so I tuned out and concentrated on looking for a parking space on the High Street.

What happened to Piper Archer?.........K.J.Rabane

Isobel

Chapter 35

I wasn't sure what to think about Beresford visiting Serena's Private Investigator. Part of me thought it was a good idea but another part was afraid he'd find Piper, that they'd fall into each other's arms, and I'd be right out of the picture. I'd invested too much of my time and energy trying to make this relationship work to have it all go down the pan now, just when I thought I was getting somewhere.

He said he'd give me a ring later this evening. It was Saturday and I'd hoped he'd suggest an evening out, especially as he was now back in work, but all he was offering was a phone call, 'to keep me in the loop,' he'd said.

The thought of going through another winter without any firm commitment from him was getting to me. Yet I wasn't about to call time on this relationship if I could help it. I was determined to hang on to what I'd established ever since the day I'd 'accidentally' bumped into his car.

I was shopping in Kents department store in the High Street when I saw Petra Gibbs. I'd worked in the same office as her when I was doing some work for an Insurance firm, a while back. I remember her particularly because most of the men in the office were mesmerised by her large bust, blonde hair and brown eyes. I seemed to remember her conversations were limited to fashion, hair, and television sitcoms. I tried to avoid her.

"Hello. It's Izzie, isn't it?"

What happened to Piper Archer?.........K.J.Rabane

"Hi, Petra. Still working at Marshalls?" I've always been able to hide my feelings. I sounded almost pleased to see her, I thought.

"Yeah, but I'm looking for somefink else. It's a dead end job."

"Really? Anything in mind?"

"As a matter of fact, I have. A year or so ago I was called to do jury service and I met a cool girl called Aisha, who worked in her father's shop selling clothes, high fashion they are. Well, we became good mates and last week she said her dad was looking for someone to do his books and if I wanted I could come for an interview. I've always been interested in fashion. I've got an eye my Carl says."

Wondering briefly who the unfortunate Carl might be, I said, "Just up your street then."

"Yeah. Thinking about Aisha, d'you remember a year or two back there was a big fuss about a woman going missing called Piper somefink? Well, me and Aisha was doing jury service and she was on the jury with us."

Genuinely interested in the conversation for the first time, I said, "You in a hurry, or d'you fancy a coffee and a catch up?"

"Great, always up for a coffee and a chat, me. Where you working now?"

In the coffee shop, facing each other, Petra chatted on about people we knew in Marshalls then during a break in the conversation, I said, "You were telling me about your time as a juror earlier. That's something I've always wanted to do but never been called."

"Yeah, well take my advice, it's not all its cracked up to be – sitting around listening to some terrible stuff, over and over again. If it hadn't been for Aisha, I'd have been well bored."

What happened to Piper Archer?.........K.J.Rabane

"Did you say Piper Archer was on the same case?"
"She was. Know her did you?"
"No. But I know her sister, Serena."
"Right. Well she was OK. She didn't bother with me and Aisha much though; pleasant, always smiling, quite pretty really. Couldn't believe it when her photo was all over the papers. They say she went off with some man and left her husband without telling him. Poor man thought she was dead, I heard."

I wondered where she'd got that from but knew rumours spread like Chinese whispers and Petra would have been only too eager to mention a connection with someone who was 'in the papers'.

"Did she make friends with anyone on the jury – like you and Aisha did?"

"Let me see now. I think me and Aisha thought she was a bit cosy with one of the blokes – nice looking, dark curly hair, always reading, but then thinking about it she wasn't any more friendly with him than the rest of us. They just used to eat their lunch together sometimes."

"I see. What was his name?"

She looked at me then, a bit too intently and I thought if I was too eager she might smell a rat.

"Not that it makes any difference only Serena, being my friend, still hasn't heard from her sister and I wondered if this bloke might know something."

She thought for a moment. "No, can't remember. But I think he owned a book shop in town – not sure where though."

I nodded and decided it might be time to change the subject. "Looking for anything particular today?"

"Yeah. Me and Aisha are going to *Bruno's* tonight."

What happened to Piper Archer?.........K.J.Rabane

I looked at my watch. "I must let you get on then, Petra. Lovely to see you again."

Outside, I looked down the High Street; Waterstones and Bargain Books, both of which I often visited. The manager of the former was in his fifties and I knew the man who owned Bargain Books and he was bald. My car was parked in a road behind the department store and as soon as I was seated, I removed my phone from my handbag and searched though the Internet to find the location of independent bookshops in the area.

Blackman's Christian Literature shop was on Bank Street, which was short drive away but Antiquarian Books was nearer, being on Milton Road. Deciding to walk, I left my car, turned up the collar of my coat against the wind, and set off in the direction Milton Road.

The Antiquarian bookshop, looked from the outside, as I'd imagined Dickens's Old Curiosity Shop would be, through the bow-fronted window I could see shelves of leather-bound books and furnishings to suit the era. The overall effect was charming. I opened the door and stepped inside.

A woman in her sixties, with iron-grey hair, looked over the top of her half-moon glasses and smiled at me. "Good morning. Let me know if you need any help."

"Thank-you. I was looking for the owner actually."

"I'm afraid Mr Wengren is unavailable. I'm the manager, can I be of assistance?"

"Not sure. You see I need to speak to him about a personal matter. Perhaps you could tell me when he's likely to back."

"I'm sorry, that's not possible. You see, Mr Wengren has taken leave of absence and I'm not sure when he'll be back."

"Right, I see. Well I'll try again sometime. Thanks anyway."

I made an attempt at showing an interest in an arrangement of books on a table near the window then turned to say goodbye. But the woman was closing a door behind the counter, leaving me alone.

Either extremely trusting, a pressing call of nature, or maybe my visit had prompted some other urgent action on her part. Leaving the shop, I decided I'd never know one way or the other and wondered whether it really mattered anyway.

What happened to Piper Archer?.........K.J.Rabane

Chapter 36

Richie glanced at his watch as he heard Sandy talking to someone in the outer office. At least they were on time, he thought standing up and opening his door.

"Mrs Platt, Mr Archer, do come in," he said, "Thank you, Miss Smith.

He held out his hand and felt Archer's grip – firm, the skin cold. He'd imagined a shorter, rounder man with thinning hair but had been quite wrong. Archer was at least six-foot tall with thick, almost silver, hair, slim, and looked ten years younger than his age. He could see why a woman like Piper would have been attracted to him, apart from his wealth and prestigious job.

Serena Platt said, "Berry wants to know how things are going, as I said on the phone, we both know she's been in the house; I've seen the evidence with my own eyes."

"Yes, I understand. But you do realise it might be misleading."

"How? The shower was used; it was obvious she'd been there. Can't think why anyone else would use the shower or why?"

"It is possible that someone who wants you to believe Mrs Archer has returned could leave a false trail."

She sniffed and looked away. "They'd have to have had a key – nothing was broken, no forced entry. I had to unlock the front door myself when I arrived and only Berry, Izzie and I have a key."

Beresford Archer hadn't spoken. Richie addressed him, "What is your opinion on this, Mr Archer?"

He didn't answer immediately just looked down at his hands but when he did Richie was surprised, as the voice didn't fit the rest of him. On first sight, he looked like the sort of man who'd have a gentle, soft voice, used to imparting good or bad news in an appropriate manner. However, there was nothing soft or gentle in his tone. The voice was deep, loud and rich in timbre; he sounded like an actor used to projecting his voice, the words were clipped and to the point. "It's true I had the distinct impression that my wife had been in the house, Her perfume lingered and there was evidence in the shower tray – strands of black hair in the sink trap etc."

"Not conclusive I'm afraid."

"So you think it wasn't my wife?

"I can't say one way or the other at this moment. It might have been but then it might not. I don't want you to think of this as definitive proof that your wife entered the house. There are too many variables to consider."

Beresford Archer narrowed his eyes. "I understand."

"However, Miss Smith and I have made progress with our investigations. We now know the identity of Rowland Green."

Serena sat forward. "You do? Well what are we waiting for – he must know where she is."

"Hold on, let's listen to what Mr Stevens has to tell us first, shall we, Serena?" Archer placed a steadying hand on her arm.

"There was a man, who was on the jury the same time as your wife, Mr Archer. His name is Ronald Wengren. Miss Smith noticed the similarity in the lettering of both names and with a little ingenuity managed to form the name Ronald Green."

"So it looks like it's true, she was planning to leave me for this Wengren fellow?"

"We can't be sure. Miss Smith and I are going to try and track him down and then I can give you a more conclusive answer to your question, Mr Archer."

What happened to Piper Archer?………K.J.Rabane

"I see, well perhaps you will contact either Mrs Platt or myself after you've talked to him."

"So you want me to continue, Mrs Platt? I'll understand if you find this process to expensive."

"Of course." She sniffed again. "Whatever it takes."

Richie watched Sandy showing them out of the office and sighed. Would a visit to Wengren wrap this case up? He could only hope so, because, if not, he was staring failure in the face.

What happened to Piper Archer?.........K.J.Rabane

Beresford

Chapter 37

I'm pleasantly surprised at Serena's ability to find a competent Private Investigator. Richard Stevens seems to inspire confidence and his assistant is obviously both intelligent and attractive. I get the impression she's working in Hastings Buildings whilst she decides to move on to something more fulfilling, otherwise why would she waste her talents in such a small-time outfit.

However, although Stevens is more than capable of handling his workload, reading between the lines, I don't think he anticipates solving this case in the near future. I doubt if anyone will. Piper has disappeared as effectively as Lord Lucan did in the nineteen seventies and he has remained so ever since.

The thought doesn't depress me as once it did. Isobel and I are spending more time together and work has helped to put me back on track mentally. I decide to leave it in the hands of Richard Stevens to discover the identity of who has been entering Elm Tree House and at last have come to terms with the idea that it might not be her. I ring the locksmith and arrange to have new locks fitted.

"Hello? Anyone home?"

It's Isobel. She's calling through the letterbox. I open the door to find her standing on the step her key in her hand.

"I've had the locks changed. I thought it was about time," I say taking her key. "I'll have a new one cut for you."

She smiles and I wonder why I haven't noticed the dimple in her cheek before. "Come in, it's a lot warmer inside than shivering on the step." I kiss her cheek and inhale her perfume.

In the kitchen I pour her camomile tea into a cup and myself a strong black coffee. "How did it go?" she asks.

I hesitate.

"With the Private Investigator?"

"Oh yes, sorry. I forgot to ring you. Well, he was better than I expected actually. Seems competent enough to me, didn't give out any platitudes about being able to wrap this case up with a flick of a finger or anticipate hanging it out longer than is necessary. He said he has a few avenues to explore, after which he'll arrange another appointment with Serena and myself."

"Right. You look happier today."

I reach across the table and take her hand. "I am, Isobel. At last I feel able to put the past behind me. Whatever the outcome of Richard Stevens's investigations, I will meet it head on."

"Great. I'm so glad. You sound really positive about the future," she says.

"Our future, I hope."

Her smile broadens as she lifts her teacup and clinks it against my mug. "To our future then," she says.

As I drink to her toast, part of me is still clinging to the past. I know my words sound more positive than I'm feeling about sharing my future with another woman but the warmth of Isobel's smile is so enticing, that the thought is but a fleeting one.

What happened to Piper Archer?.........K.J.Rabane

The following day Serena arrives. We are still in bed. I go downstairs and open the door, still wearing my dressing gown.

"Oh, sorry, Berry. I just brought you some home made pasties for your lunch but my key wouldn't work. Sorry to disturb you. I see Isobel is here." She turns her head and nods at Isobel's car.

"Come in. Yes, Isobel and I had a late night. It's good of you to think of my lunch but you don't need to go on spoiling me. I'm better now – and I can cook, you know." I smile to soften the words.

"I know but I'd made too many for Mike and me and well, you know what I'm like. Can't stop worrying about the people I care about." Her manner suddenly changes and I see a tear in the corner of her eyes. She's thinking about her sister.

"Let me put the kettle on and we can have a chat, leave Isobel to catch up on her beauty sleep eh? Oh and I'll have a new key cut for you for when I go away etc., just like before."

"You've changed the locks then?"

"At last, yes. I've given up expecting her to come back."

She looks down at her hands. "You're probably right."

I reach over and pat her hand. "It will work out. She'll be in touch with you at some point, I'm sure of it. Perhaps when she's more settled in her new life."

Serena sighs and tries to smile. "I hope so, Berry. I do hope so. It's like losing a limb, to lose a sister and not to know what's happened to her. I was telling Mrs Roberts from the paper shop only the other day, when Mike had done a double shift and he was exhausted, I said, …"

What happened to Piper Archer?.........K.J.Rabane

So I sit at the table and hear the inconsequential flow of Serena's conversation and wonder why Piper hadn't bothered to contact her. It's so out of character. It's part of a mystery, which I hope Richard Stevens will be able to solve. But whether he does or not, I know my life can't stagnate. I must move on.

Chapter 38

It was one of those rare autumnal days when winter is begging to begin and the weather has decided not to let summer go just yet. Richie stood at the window and waited until he saw Sandy riding her bike down the High Street. Her hair was tied in a ponytail and from his elevated position she looked like a schoolgirl rushing to school. The sight of her brought a smile to his lips and tugged at his heart as the memory of the daughter he had lost swamped him in a rush of mixed emotions.

A short while later he heard footsteps running up the stairs followed by Sandy's appearance. Her cheeks were pink from her exertions and as their eyes met she said, "What?"

Richie coughed. "Nothing. Have a nice ride?" He turned away and continued to look out of the window.

"OK, what is it?" Sandy asked.

"Nothing. Let's get down to business, Miss Smith." He knew he sounded harsher than he felt but he couldn't begin to explain to her without sounding maudlin.

"Right. Would you mind if I had a coffee first?"

"No time. We are off to visit Mr Wengren this morning. I've no appointments and the answerphone is on. Hurry up, Miss Smith, remember it's the early bird who catches the worm."

She didn't comment, just picked up her handbag from the desk and sighed.

Sitting in Richie's car, a while later, Sandy said, "Do you really think he's involved in all this?"

"I think it's a strong possibility. Either way we need to talk to the man, if only to decided whether he's been telling the truth or not. You said the battle-axe you spoke to on the phone was less than helpful?"

What happened to Piper Archer?.........K.J.Rabane

"She reminded me of a protective mother hen guarding its chicks."

"Really, I wonder what gave you that impression?"

Richie had learned to trust Sandy's intuition, which was usually spot on. During the short drive to the bookshop they discussed how they were going to proceed.

The inside of the shop smelled of leather, old paper and Lily of the Valley, the latter wafting towards them from the woman Sandy had referred to as a mother hen.

"We'd like to speak to Mr Wengren, please," Richie said. "Richard Stevens, Private Investigator, you spoke to my PA on the phone yesterday."

The woman looked at Sandy with a sour expression. "I think I told you, young lady, that Mr Wengren is not available."

Ignoring her comment Richie asked, "It's very important that we speak to Mr Wengren. Do you have a contact number?"

"I'll pass on a message."

"Not good enough," Richie said, firmly. "I don't think you realise that if I am unable to conclude my investigations in a satisfactory manner then I'll have to hand over my files to Lockford Police, who will no doubt be very interested to know of Mr Wengren's unavailability."

He waited whilst the woman frowned, sighed, opened a diary sitting on the counter and made a show of examining its contents.

"Ah, well, looks like you're in luck, Mr Wengren will be calling in later, after lunch. Will you come back then?" She attempted a smile, which only emphasised her pinched expression.

"We will. You can be certain of it."

Richie and Sandy left the shop aware of the woman watching them intently over the rim of her glasses.

"Coffee?" Richie asked, heading for a café tucked away in a side street.

Sandy nodded, "At last," she muttered.

When they were seated, Richie said, "I agree, something's not right. She's protecting him from something."

"So they are in it together? Whatever it might be?"

"Succinctly put, Miss Smith. Whatever it is, I think they are most definitely – in it together."

Chapter 39

"Do you believe him? Sandy asked later, as they drove back to Hastings Buildings.

Richie parked the car before answering, "I think I sort of do, although everything points to the contrary. He's lied before, remember, when you first spoke to him?"

"And what about his protector Nancy Smedley? I'm sure she's up to something. Have you seen the way she looks at him?" Sandy followed Richie up the stairs and once inside the office sat at her desk.

"I agree. She'll be a harder nut to crack though." Richie watched her as she opened her laptop and accessed the Archer file.

"Would you say we've had a breakthrough?" She looked up at him.

"Most definitely but it's just the beginning. Ring Mrs Platt and say I'd like to have a word with her please, Miss Smith. Then I suggest you make us both a cuppa."

Serena Platt was alone this time. She sat opposite Richie, patted her newly-styled hair into place and said, "Berry's working, so I told him I'd let him know what you had to say, Mr Stevens. He's very busy at the moment, operating and stuff. He's such a clever man, so well-thought-of. Piper was such a lucky girl to have married him. I told her often enough."

Richie coughed. "To get to the point, Mrs Platt. I've recently been given some new information regarding your sister. Apparently she was last seen sleeping in the front seat of a car, which was parked in a motorway service station car park. When the owner of the car returned, he found she'd disappeared."

What happened to Piper Archer?.........K.J.Rabane

She sat forward in her seat and Richie could smell hairspray wafting across the desk towards him. "When? I don't understand. Who was she with?" She bit her lip then said, with conviction, "Rowland Green, the man she was meeting before she left. So she was having an affair."

As she'd supplied an answer to her question, Richie didn't reply. He preferred to keep Ronald Wengren's anonymity just that for a while at least.

"So she's left another one then. I suppose that's the end of it. I don't mind telling you, Mr Stevens, I'm disappointed in my sister. Why she hasn't let me know she's safe is beyond belief. And what Berry's going to say when he knows she's been with that man all this time and hasn't had the decency to contact anyone, well, it doesn't bear thinking about."

She picked up her handbag. "Send me your bill, Mr Stevens. I'm sorry you've been troubled."

Richie raised his hand. "Wait a minute, Mrs Platt. You don't understand. I haven't finished with this case. I still haven't found your sister. This is just a breakthrough in my investigation."

She shook her head. "As far as I'm concerned, Piper can stew in her own juice. When I think of all the sleepless nights I've had worrying about her, believing she'd been harmed, or worse that she was dead. Well I don't mind telling you, I'm done with it."

She stood up. "As I said, send me your bill please and the sooner the better. Thank you. I'm sorry I've been wasting your time."

Richie stood up. "You're welcome, Mrs Platt."

In the outer office Sandy looked up as Richie walked their client to the door. "Prepare an invoice for Mrs Platt, Miss Smith," he said, over his shoulder.

What happened to Piper Archer?.........K.J.Rabane

The click-clack of heels on the stairs receded to a distant tapping when Sandy said, "I don't understand. She doesn't want us to go on with the case?"

"That's the long and short of it. We'll get paid and hope another client is waiting just around the corner."

"So, you're going to leave it and we'll never know what happened to Piper Archer?"

Richie walked over to the kettle, filled it and switched it on. "What do you think, Miss Smith?" He grinned.

What happened to Piper Archer?.........K.J.Rabane

Ronald

Chapter 40

When the letter came to attend Lockford County Court for jury service, I contemplated postponing my summons – I had a shop to run and Maddie was too young to look after the place for any length of time. However, fate took a hand in the shape of Nancy Smedley, mother's best friend.

She'd been popping into the shop with gifts in the shape of cakes, biscuits and casseroles, ever since mother passed away and the day I received the summons she 'just happened' to be passing with a box of buns; she'd baked too many 'apparently'. When I told her about my predicament, she smiled, patted my hand and said, "There's no problem Ronald. I'm always willing to help, you know, you can safely leave me in charge of this place." She'd worked as a librarian until she retired and knew all there was to know about books, she informed me. So I replied to the court confirming my ability to attend on the 20th of the month.

I was a little apprehensive about becoming a member of the jury, wondering what sort of depravity we'd be likely to hear and whether I was the right man to sit in judgement upon another. I'd always been of the opinion that one should live and let live in this life. It was impossible to know how any of us would react given a certain set of circumstances.

When the day arrived, I made sure I was early and sat outside the court on a bench near the jurors' entrance waiting to see what my fellow jurors would look like. Of course, never having been in this position before I hadn't realised that there would be so many people or that there would be so many cases to be dealt with. Eventually, I entered the building and was faced with two security officers and an airport-style archway, which bleeped in the presence of metal.

"Just walk through here, sir. Your bag if you please." The larger of the two security men had a jolly face and a gold tooth, which shone when he smiled.

My canvas bag, which contained my lunch and a paperback, was searched and I walked through the archway, thankfully not accompanied by a peel of bleeps. In front of me was a sign, which said *Jurors this way*. I walked down a corridor, passed two giggling girls and an elderly lady walking with a stick, towards a locked door at the side of which was a keypad and a buzzer. A tall woman with curly grey hair standing in front of me pressed the buzzer. "This looks like the right place," she said. "So many rooms, so many people." I wasn't sure who she was talking to so didn't answer. A short while later a clerk admitted us into a cloakroom area with lockers, beyond which was a large room, seemingly filled with a cross section of society. As I said, I was surprised to see so many people.

"I hear there are at least six, quite unpleasant cases to be catered for today," a tall woman said, presumably to me, although she didn't look in my direction.

"Really?"

"Yes, so the court usher told me. I spoke to him when I arrived." She walked towards an empty seat near the window and I searched for another unoccupied seat, wishing I hadn't sat outside for so long. Finding one alongside a large man with a red face, reading the Lockford Times, I sat down.

What happened to Piper Archer?.........K.J.Rabane

"Done this sort of thing before, have you?" The man asked, lifting his eyes from his newspaper.

I shook my head, "You?"

"Yeah, my third time. You'll soon settle in once you're called. Then you'll stick with your crowd."

"I beg your pardon?" I had no idea what he was talking about.

"You have to wait here until they call your name – then you go into court and wait to see if the accused objects to you – they don't often do that in my experience. Then, you get told what the case is all about and they choose the twelve – from the fifteen or so who go into court. If you're one of the twelve that's it – those are the people you'll see for the rest of your time – if not you come back here and the same process begins again until you are finally chosen."

"I see, thanks," I replied, thinking it all sounded very complicated. Looking around the room, I wondered with whom I'd be sharing the next couple of weeks and whether, amongst the sea of faces, there was anyone of interest.

My name was called for the first case and I followed the other fourteen potential jurors and the court usher, along the corridor to court number two. When the proceedings reached the stage where we were asked to form a jury we were told the case we would be hearing would be likely to take up to three weeks or more. Although there was a certain amount of grumbling to be heard, only one asked to be pardoned and we were discharged and told to come to court by ten o'clock the following morning.

At first I didn't notice her, not even on the second day. She was one of the twelve and the trial was going to be a complicated and harrowing one so I didn't have time to properly assess my fellow jurors. But on the third day she and I sort of clicked, if you know what I mean – she was someone who thought like me and I think she recognised it. In fact from then on, during the lunch hours, she began to search me out. We would talk as if we'd known each other for years. It helped that she was beautiful, but it wasn't the only reason I was attracted to her. Beauty fades, changes, is often only skin deep but this was something else, an instinctive understanding, which was only partly due to the situation in which we found ourselves.

It was during the second week that she told me about her past and dissolved into tears, it broke my heart to see her so upset. I tried to comfort her without being overly intrusive in case I frightened her and it seemed to work. Afterwards, I felt as though a bond had been established between us.

The trial was at a particularly gruesome stage and being unable to talk to anyone about it, other than our fellow jurors, was a strain. Piper told me she found it particularly difficult not to discuss some of the details with her husband at the end of the day. I sympathised, even though I was not married. I suppose I could have talked things over with a close friend, or possibly Nancy in the shop, who was like a second mother to me but we were warned over and over again not to discuss the case with anyone outside the jury room.

When the trial finished I didn't think I'd see her again but told her to pop into the shop when she was passing and we could have a chat over a cup of coffee. I thought it unlike she'd do anything of the kind but I was wrong. How was I to know she'd want my help and how could I have known how it would affect my safe and comfortable life?

What happened to Piper Archer?.........K.J.Rabane

Piper

Chapter 41

To understand it all you'd have to start at the beginning. I fell in love with Simon Roach in the summer of the year before he went up to university. He was eighteen and I'd just had my sixteenth birthday. We began by travelling on the same bus home from school and would meet in secret in the evenings. We had to keep it a secret because he was dating Melissa Hardwick from year eleven at the time and my parents would think I was too young to have such a serious relationship, besides Dad was ill and I didn't want to cause them more stress.

First love is always serious, especially as I later discovered it was one-sided. He was tall, dark and most of the girls thought he was handsome. I used to lie awake at night reliving our moments together, sometimes in the back row of the cinema or in the park, after the gates had closed.

"I've chucked Melissa, " he told me one day when the rain drummed on the roof of the park shelter and the words were like music to my ears.

Looking back I suppose it was inevitable, it was an accident waiting to happen. I was young, Dad died, I was vulnerable and he was careless. Falling in love with him had made me reckless. I yearned to feel him hold me, kiss me, comfort me and want me.

When I told him I was pregnant he didn't want to know. He told me it was my problem, to do something about it and besides he was spending the rest of the

What happened to Piper Archer?.........K.J.Rabane

summer in Spain at his parents' time-share with Melissa and the rest of the gang.

Heart-broken I hid my secret for nearly a month, then was in tears when I told Serena. " Leave it to me, don't worry. I'll sort it out for you. But remember don't say a thing to mother – not after Dad – she couldn't cope, Serena said.

As it turned out, her boyfriend Mike had an uncle who lived in South Wales in a place called Gareg Wen and he worked in the IT department of a hospital in Cardiff.

Serena arranged that we should tell Mum we were going to stay in Gareg Wen for the rest of the summer with Mike's uncle and his family. In the meantime Mike's uncle Emrys would make an appointment for me to see an obstetrician friend of his at the hospital. It's hard for me to think about it even now without crying, especially as I know the truth and how it could all have been avoided.

So Serena and I stayed at Emrys's house. He lived on his own and was glad of the company. He was working during the day, which gave us plenty of time to ourselves. We often visited the Anchor, which was quaint and under other circumstances I would have loved to stay there. Lorna, the barmaid, was a scream and we soon became friends. Of course she had no idea why I was in Gareg Wen; she thought Serena and I were holidaymakers spending the summer with a relative.

I was so scared when we went for that first hospital appointment. Serena comforted me and somehow I got through it; the embarrassing questions, my reasons why I couldn't continue with the pregnancy, had I considered the wider picture, etc.,. I blubbed my way through the answers and couldn't wait to get out into the sunshine.

What happened to Piper Archer?………K.J.Rabane

Mike's uncle had pulled a few strings and the termination was due to take place the following week. I didn't really understand much about the reasons why it was going to be an operation under a general anaesthetic, rather than a more routine procedure, even though they explained it. I suppose I didn't want to think about it – it would make it all too real.

If it hadn't been for Serena, Mike and his uncle I don't know what I would have done. Serena held my hand as I waited for the pre-med to take effect. I remember feeling great then, floating and giggling, the faces of the porters taking me to the operating theatre, the nurses in their surgical masks and the surgeon gowned and masked, all drifted past me as the anaesthetist tapped the back of my hand and asked me to count to ten.

When I awoke, they told me there had been a problem and that Doctor would explain later. I felt raw inside, Serena looked as if she'd been crying but she smiled and held Mike's hand as they sat at the side of my bed. Then Mike went to the shop to buy a morning paper. Serena was with me when the Consultant arrived. I was in a side ward, so we were alone, no one to overhear our conversation.

"Miss Sandford, I'm afraid I have some bad news for you. Although your pregnancy was successfully terminated, there were a few problems." The Consultant was a short, thickset man with thinning hair. He hesitated and looked down at the floor. I remember the sound his shoes made on the laminated floor. "I'm afraid you will be unlikely to conceive a child in the future due to complications resulting from your termination." He had a kind face. He patted my hand. I was numb. All I could think about was I wasn't pregnant any more and could get now on with my life. I was too young to absorb the implications of his words. Too young to know how I would feel in the future.

When the door closed behind him, Serena said, "Piper, are you OK? You don't have to be brave. It's all right to cry."

"No, it's fine. At least it's over."

The words haunt me now. I had no idea that it would never be over and in the future it would shape my life as no incident past or present would ever do.

What happened to Piper Archer?.........K.J.Rabane

Chapter 42

Serena told our mother we'd be staying on in South Wales until school started in September. I think it was a relief, as after father died mother was not in good health. Serena was amazing as were Mike and his uncle. They really looked after me. I was a bit mixed up about it all and if I'd been at home there would have been questions, which I didn't want to answer. As it happened no one in Gareg Wen suspected a thing. I wasn't exactly showing before, so there was no reason why they should.

At the end of her two week holiday from work Serena called in sick, the local doctor gave her a sick note as she'd managed to convince him she'd hurt her back water-skiing and couldn't possibly go home in her condition. The man was old and I think he signed her off work to get rid of her. Serena is like a steam train when she starts talking. Mike went back home after the termination and we were left to our own devices. Gradually I began to recover and to forget about my ordeal. Lorna helped. I became close to her during the summer holidays and we spent long hours walking along the cliff paths and sunbathing on the beach.

At the beginning of September, I said a tearful farewell to my new friend and followed Serena on to the train taking us back to Lockford.

Two years later, I had a choice to make. My A level results were OK but I wasn't going to set the world alight academically, so I came to the decision not to go on to further education, in spite of mother wanting me to do so.

What happened to Piper Archer?.........K.J.Rabane

"You're lucky, you do know that don't you?" Serena, who was replying to an invitation to a friend's wedding, looked up.

"Lucky?"

"To be able to work in Haughtons. Especially as you haven't been to college." There was an implied criticism in her tone. I wondered if she was really thinking, 'especially after what happened.'

Lily Haughton had been in my year school. She said if I wanted it then the job was mine. I'd have to start at the bottom, office junior. I thought it would mean making the tea and emptying the bins but I didn't mind.

Eric Haughton, Lily's father, owned Haughton's, Insurance brokerage and Financial Services. Lily was going to college. Her father wanted her to take his place one day and Lily seemed keen to do so.

I'd been working in Haughton's for six months when Serena and Mike got married. And a year later she fell pregnant with Ellie. I can't deny feeling a slight pang of envy, my own predicament coming to the fore for the first time since it happened. But it soon passed and I became an indulgent aunt at the first sight of my niece resting in her mother's arms.

My life now consisted of work and Serena's family. I helped with Ellie as often as I could. It made me feel as though I was worthwhile. This makes me sound as if my life was devoid of male company, which wasn't the case. I had a succession of boyfriends. I was attractive. None of them however made me feel as abandoned as Simon Roach had done. Perhaps it was a feeling that could only be attached to first love and maybe I would never find 'the right one'.

With this thought uppermost in my mind, a few years later, I attended Lily's graduation party, which was held in the Manor Bridge Hotel on the outskirts of town. I'd bought a new dress in Selfridges in London, when Serena and I had been on a shopping trip several weeks before and the opportunity to wear it hadn't arisen until then.

I piled my hair up on top in an attempt to look more sophisticated, in view of the people I was likely to meet at such an event, and gave the figure-hugging red dress its first outing.

I'd been talking to Lawrence Daly who worked in the accounts section when Lily tapped me on the shoulder, "Piper, I'd like you meet Beresford. He's just started working in Lockford General and could do with some entertaining company."

I remember replying something like, I hoped I wouldn't fail on that count and he chuckled. I liked him straight away. He was older, which under the circumstances suited me.

We talked endlessly. He was so interesting, he told me about places he'd visited, books he'd read, people, he'd met and as the night blossomed around us so did our relationship. We left the party in the early hours and walked the short distance to the Common where we sat and watched the first faint fingers of dawn approaching.

"I'd like to see you again," he said, kissing my fingertips one by one. It was an old fashioned gesture but somehow it seemed right. Everything was right.

We arranged to meet up for dinner the following Saturday and as the week progressed I found I couldn't wait to see him again. He picked me up at eight and we drove to *The Riverside.* I'd never been there before having heard it was terribly expensive. As it turned out it was an enchanting evening. After soaring temperatures throughout the day, a cool breeze sprang up as we sat sipping cocktails on a veranda overlooking the river.

"That was a lovely meal. Thank you," I said.

"I'm glad you enjoyed it. And I hope it will be the first of many." He leaned towards me and kissed my cheek.

Intoxicated by the night, the alcohol and being with him I relaxed, and realised it was the first time I'd felt really content since Simon Roach had broken my heart all those years ago and indirectly ruined any chance I had of becoming a mother.

"It's good of you to drive, especially as you've been restricted to soft drinks and I've drunk far too many cocktails," I said.

"Nonsense. I'm intoxicated enough just being in your company." He laughed. "God, that sounds so corny. But it's the truth."

We parked on the Heath overlooking the town, neither of us wishing the night to end. Beresford wanted to know all about me and for the most part I told him the truth, leaving out that bit of my life which I'd purposely pushed to the back of my mind. Everyone has secrets and now I know that fact also applies to Beresford.

"How old are you?" I would never have come out with it quite like that under normal circumstances. I blamed it on the cocktails.

He chuckled. "That's my girl, straight as an arrow. I'm thirty-eight."

Being twenty-three I thought it seemed ancient. But it was only a number, he didn't seem old at all and I told him so. As we talked and morning approached, he told me about his life before he met me. After he graduated from medical school he married one of his fellow medical students. But the marriage didn't work and they'd called it a day within two years and gone their separate ways.

"You didn't meet anyone else?" I asked.

"No one who mattered. Not until now."

"You've no children?"

"No. I'm not sure I ever wanted any. Perhaps that's not quite true, when I was younger I thought it would have been nice to have a family. But not now."

I was so elated; we were two sides of the same coin. And, most importantly, I would never have to explain.

Chapter 43

Six months after we first met at Lily's party, we drove to *The Riverside.* It was the second week of December. The River Locke was in full flood after the recent rains and the frozen riverbanks shone in the moonlight as our taxi drove away and we walked the short distance to the entrance.

"Looks like snow to me," Beresford said, taking my arm.

I think I knew that was going to be the night. He'd been leading up to it for weeks. Christmas was approaching, he'd recently been appointed as a Senior Registrar on the team at Lockford General and he'd been looking at a magnificent property called Elm Tree house on the outskirts of town, with the intention of moving from his flat in Manor Road.

Although the property was outrageously priced I think I'd always know Beresford was independently wealthy. His father had been a partner in Archer and Thorne, a law firm in London and when is parents died in a tragic accident whilst on holiday in South Africa, he'd become their sole heir.

"A bottle of Bollinger, please."

So I was right, I thought.

When the champagne arrived, Beresford took my hand in his. "My darling girl, will you do me the honour of becoming my wife?" he said taking my hand and searching my eyes for an answer.

His proposal was like something out of a nineteen thirties film but it was perfect. The ambiance inside the restaurant where there were very few diners, even though Christmas was approaching, was ideal; it wasn't the sort of place office parties favoured being far too expensive.

What happened to Piper Archer?.........K.J.Rabane

The lighting was soft and romantic and to add to the magic, flakes of snow drifted down like a shower of confetti pattering softly against the windowpanes.

"Yes please," I answered, as to my delight he produced the ring of my dreams and placed it on my finger. The large oval diamond flashed in the candlelight when he leaned forward and kissed my lips. It was, as I said – perfect.

We married on New Year's Eve in a register office in London. Serena was outraged – why weren't we getting married in Lockford – why didn't I want a church wedding – what was the rush, she stopped short of asking was I pregnant. Our witnesses were two strangers we met in the street; they were young and full of fun.

The New Year started with our honeymoon. We travelled around the Western coast of the United States, visiting California, the Mohave Dessert, San Diego, Las Vegas and ending our tour in San Francisco. We made love under the stars on warm oceanic nights and I couldn't have been happier. Beresford was a loving and attentive husband and we suited each other. When it was time for him to return to work we settled into married life in his flat whilst making arrangements to complete the move to Elm Tree House.

Waking up on the morning after our first night in our new home, I felt the luckiest person in the whole world. I had an intelligent, caring and loving husband who asked nothing from me but to return his love and who provided me with a luxurious lifestyle, the likes of which I could only have dreamed.

There was no need for me to work so I decided volunteer for shifts at the charity shop in Lockford High

Street and to start delivering books to people too infirm to travel to the library.

Life settled into a steady rhythm and it wasn't until I'd been married for just over four years when I felt the first painful pangs for motherhood tugging at my sleeve. I tried to forget the obvious joy my friends displayed when telling me of their pregnancies and ignored the ache around my heart whenever I saw a new-born baby in a pram.

I didn't mention any of this to Beresford of course. He knew I was unable to conceive, although I hadn't told him of my earlier pregnancy. It was one secret I preferred to keep. He didn't even suggest I might like to have my infertility investigated as he assumed neither of us was keen to start a family.

I was certain that, as the years passed, I would conquer this longing, so chose to ignore it and throw myself into my charity work with renewed vigour. And I suppose it would have worked had it not been for the brown envelope on the mat in the hall one Monday morning.

Chapter 44

"You'll be fine." Beresford put down the morning paper and patted my hand. "It will be a drunk driving case or someone stealing a car, you'll see.

"I've often wondered what it would be like to do jury service but now the call has come I'm not sure I want to know," I replied.

"If you're really upset about it you could always defer, make some valid excuse, but my love, you are going to have to face it some time or other as they won't accept another postponement."

"In that case, I have to bite the bullet as the saying goes. I'll look on it as an adventure, another stitch in the rich tapestry of life."

My husband raised an eyebrow and picked up a slice of toast. "Very poetic and admirable, sweetheart, and you never know, you might even enjoy the experience."

On the morning I was due to attend Lockford Crown Court, I dressed in lightweight cotton black trousers and a cool white blouse then drove towards the centre of town. The building was impressive from the outside, solid and reassuring. I'd seen it many times before but never looked at it in detail. Now, as I approached the jury entrance, I saw the stone pillars with their trefoils and curlicues and it was with the slight feeling of apprehension I parked the car, showed my jury summons to the security officer and stepped inside the ancient building.

In front of me stood a red-carpeted corridor and a sign saying *Jurors this way* with an arrow pointing ahead. At the end of the corridor I saw a woman in her late thirties, who was looking lost.

What happened to Piper Archer?………K.J.Rabane

"Oh good, you look as if you're going my way. I've been down this corridor twice and can't find the jurors' room," she smiled. "I'm Joyce, by the way, Joyce Leatherhead."

"Piper Archer. I think it might be down this way. Shall we take a look?"

We walked towards a closed, half-glazed, door at the side of which was a keypad and buzzer. I pressed the buzzer and waited, gave our names to the disembodied voice and heard the door click open. Inside, we followed a court official into a larger room filled, it seemed to me, with a crowd of people.

"Blimey, I never thought there'd be so many of us," Joyce said, echoing my thoughts.

"There's a couple of empty seats near the window," the young woman wearing a name badge said. "Make yourselves comfortable." She handed us a folder each. "Fill out the forms and let me have them back when you're finished."

We were then shown an explanatory film about what we would experience during our term of duty. Thanking us for doing our public duty the court official finished by saying, "Listen for your names to be called over the intercom system then follow the usher to the relevant court.

As it turned out, my new friend Joyce and I were called to attend court number two. Whilst waiting in an anteroom before entering the court, a girl with dark brown hair tied in a ponytail and wearing a very short skirt and skyscraper heels turned to me and said, "I've been talking to the court official, he couldn't take his eyes of my legs. I asked what sort of case we were likely to be on and he said they were all bad ones – six of them, each as bad as the other he said, then asked me for my phone number."

I heard a sharp intake of breath from Joyce. Glancing around the anteroom, I tried to assess which of us would make the final selection and which of the fifteen would return to the main area to possibly sit on another case. The court official, who'd asked for the girl's number, was decidedly creepy, I thought. Just our bad luck that he was attached to us.

"Right then, ladies and gents, line up please we are going in."

The court was much as I'd expected it to be, as it was representative of most of the crime drama productions portrayed on TV. But the judge was a woman, with a kind face who looked benevolent. However, once she spoke the image was dispelled; her voice was sharp, her manner abrupt. She waited as the clerk of the court read out our names one by one giving us each a chance to make an appeal to the judge for being excused as it appeared the case would take longer than the normal two weeks of our mandatory summons.

A large man with a red face whispered something to the creepy official whose name was Derek Baynton.

"If it please your honour, Mr Hughes has to attend to an aging relative and would find it difficult to prolong his attendance."

The Judge frowned, all trace of her benevolence having disappeared like ice melting in the sun. "Couldn't you make other arrangements for your relative to be cared for?"

The red faced man became animated, the colour of his cheeks deepening. "I tried, your honour, but mother can be very awkward; she doesn't like strangers; she's a very private person."

What happened to Piper Archer?.........K.J.Rabane

The judge sighed, "Very well, you're dismissed. Next!"

This process continued without any further interruptions until the twelve members of the jury were sworn in. I sat alongside Joyce and an older man with a smiling face. Then the judge instructed us upon the case we would be hearing and I heard a slight gasp from Joyce as the accused stood, ran his eyes along each of us in turn and nodded.

"Very well then, ladies and gentlemen." The smile was back; she was the genial judge once more. "I thank you for your time and look forward to seeing you all in the morning. Once more I must impress upon each of you that the details of this case are not to be discussed outside the confines of the jury room, that includes members of your family and other jurors."

In the cloakroom, Joyce said, in a whisper, " I didn't like the look of him at all, did you? Those eyes! I can well imagine him being a murderer – the eyes are the windows of the soul – as my old mother used to say."

Obviously I didn't want to comment, hadn't she been listening to the judge's words?

"So, Joyce. I'll see you in the morning. Bye now, I must dash."

Before she could follow, I rushed through the foyer and out of the double doors, then took a deep breath of untainted air and walked towards my car. I can't deny feeling apprehensive about what we'd be hearing during the coming weeks. Joyce was right about one thing Keanu Collins certainly looked the part. I wondered how hearing the gruesome details of his girlfriend's murder would affect me, especially as I couldn't confide in Beresford. Only time would tell.

What happened to Piper Archer?………K.J.Rabane

Chapter 45

The first few days of the trial were filled with routine procedures, witness statements and police reports. During the lunch hour, on the first day, I sat with the others in the canteen but like Joyce they thought it OK to discuss the case. So in order not to be put in such an awkward position, I decided that in future I would sit in my car, eat a packed lunch and listen to some music to take my mind off the case. I had noticed that not everyone ate in the canteen, after that first day; some ate their sandwiches on the grassy bank surrounding the court, whilst others made for a nearby café.

On the third day, the weather was unbearably hot and sitting in the car during the lunch break was not an option. There was a tree on the bank, which offered a degree of shade, and it wasn't until I was sitting down that I noticed I wasn't the only one who'd sought to put a distance between themselves and the rest of the jury members.

"Hi, it's Piper, isn't it?" He glanced up from his book. "Gets a bit much, all that chatter about the case, doesn't it?"

"It's embarrassing."

"My thoughts entirely. The judge couldn't have been plainer but that Leatherhead woman hasn't taken any of it on board," he smiled, to soften his words. "Rant over. I'll leave you to eat your lunch in peace."

"It's OK. I don't mind, really. I enjoy a good natter, just not about the case."

He put his book down. "So, I understand you are married to a doctor?"

Usually I skirt over the subject of Beresford's profession. He's so well qualified – at the head of his profession – I feel some people are intimidated by it or make superficial judgements based on his career. "That's right. He's a surgeon at Lockford General."

Ronald just nodded and changed the subject asking me what books I liked to read. As I ate my lunch we chatted and I was almost sorry when the hour passed and we were back in the jury room. He was pleasant, easy company and a welcome change from Joyce and her incessant nattering.

We'd been sitting in the jury room for about ten minutes when the usher arrived to show us into court. He made my flesh creep. The way he looked at Aisha and Petra, undressing them with his eyes. I'm no prude, but there are some men, like him, who have no respect for women, some men who will pick you up and drop you from a great height when it suits them. It was more than obvious Derek Baynton was one of them.

Justice Rose Devonshire thanked us for arriving on time and gave a short summation of the evidence, which would be heard that afternoon. She warned that some of the photographs, in the folders on our seats, we would find distressing, so too the evidence which would be heard from the forensic experts.

She hadn't been exaggerating; I left the court that afternoon feeling sick to my stomach that anyone, calling themselves a human being, could inflict such pain on another. Collins had been systematically abusing his girlfriend for years, culminating in her painful and totally unnecessary death.

"You OK? You look like I feel," Ronald was getting into his car, which was parked alongside mine. I was searching for my keys, which had dropped to the bottom of my handbag.

"I've felt better. More of the same tomorrow I gather."

"Doesn't help when you can't talk to your husband about it, I'm sure."

"That's right."

"Doctors usually have the ability to make one feel better," he said, with a half-hearted smile.

"Yes. I'll see you tomorrow then, Ronald." I grasped my keys and opened the car door, giving him a little wave as he drove past me.

The following day I was the first to arrive in the jury room. I've always been punctual, and since I married Beresford, even more so. He's so organised; I hate to be the one to keep him waiting. It's an admirable quality I think but there are times when I wish I were more like my sister and not so organised and routine driven.

"Hello. I'm glad I'm not on my own. I really need to tell someone our good news." Laura Bentley ran her fingers through her short grey hair and sat down beside me. She was tall and stick-thin. She'd told me she regularly ran five or six miles a day, even though she was in her early sixties, and jury service had interrupted her early morning running routine.

"Jackie is pregnant! John and I are ecstatic. We'd almost given up any hope of becoming grandparents. She told us yesterday that she's sixteen weeks gone. The little minx hadn't told us before because she wanted to be certain about keeping it."

The knot in my stomach tightened. "Congratulations. I expect your daughter and her husband are thrilled." I think I managed to smile.

"Thank you dear, but Jackie isn't married. She's gay but she and her partner Josie are made up. Apparently

Josie's brother provided the necessary – I don't want to think about how they went about it – anyway as I said, we are all over the moon."

One by one the rest of the jury arrived and Laura spread her good news like a forest fire in a heat-wave. Inside me the knot was gradually unwinding but I knew it would always be there – waiting to strangle me.

Tom Harkins, twenty-one years of enthusiasm, rushed through the door and slid his backpack to the floor. "Sorry I'm late everyone, missed the bus." He smelled of chewing gum, body spray and hair gel. "I think today is going to be the day we hear all the gory details, guys."

Petra Gibbs and Aisha Patel, who were his contemporaries in age but nothing else, had formed a giggly bond on day one and seemed to talk about nothing other than clothes and hairstyles. They stopped talking and looked across at Tom. "Really! Do you think they'll put Collins on the stand today?"

"Yeah bound to."

"He's lush looking," Petra said.

Ray Pickford, the oldest member of the group, looked over the top and his glasses and shook his head. He'd been talking to Beryl Barker-Lloyd about her career as a concert pianist.

Beryl stretched her long neck and patted the bun, which was perched like a bird's nest on top of her head. "Perhaps by the end of the day you'll see how lush he really is. Never be fooled by a pretty face, girl - it's only ever skin deep."

Petra raised her eyebrows at Aisha and they giggled.

The door opened and the usher announced. "Everyone line up then, here we go again."

What happened to Piper Archer?.........K.J.Rabane

By the time midday arrived I doubted if any of us had an appetite for food. Petra looked pale and I could see Beryl's words had hit home. Leaving the others I sought the relative seclusion of the grassy bank and the shade of the oak tree, sat down, drank from my bottle of water and nibbled on a cereal bar, all I could face after hearing the evidence.

"How are you bearing up?" Ronald asked, striding towards me.

"The same as any of us, I should imagine."

"No appetite?"

I nodded.

"Right, I'll leave you to read in peace." He went to walk around the tree to the other side.

"No. It's all right. You're welcome to sit here. I could do with a distraction from my thoughts."

"Well if you're sure. I don't want to intrude." He put his book down on the grass and opened his lunch box. "I shouldn't complain, it's not as if many single men of my age have the benefit of having their lunch prepared for them. But I'm getting a bit sick of tuna-fish sandwiches," he grinned.

"You're not married then?"

"Nearly tried it once but we split before the big day."

"And your mum loves having you to fuss over?"

"Oh no. Sorry I should have explained. My mother died just before Dad and my sister moved away. They live in Canada now with my sister's husband, who is Canadian. I have a flat in town but Nancy, my godmother and mother's best friend, treats me like her son. She works with me at the bookshop occasionally and every day since I've been here she's taken it into her head to provide me with my lunch. I feel a bit like a child on his way to school. I can't be treated like a child at thirty-one without it having some sort of detrimental effect, I suppose, but I don't like to offend her."

"I'd lie back and enjoy it, if I were you."

"You would?"

I thought about it. "No, not really," I replied, and with a smile, accepted the tuna-fish sandwich he offered me.

Chapter 46

"You look pale, darling. Case getting you down?" Beresford asked over breakfast the next morning.

"Ah ha," I replied.

"Don't worry, I know the score. I won't ask for any details. But I'm here if you need a shoulder to cry on, as always."

"Thank-you. I appreciate it. I just hope it doesn't go on too long. There is talk that it will definitely last into a third week, possibly longer. Some of my fellow jurors are champing at the bit as they work full time – others are enjoying the break from the nine-to-five routine."

"Must be hard for some people. Imagine those high profile cases that go on for months. I don't know how a small business could survive if it had employees who were called for such a case."

"Have you got a busy day?" I asked.

"Not too bad, ward rounds this morning and ante natal clinic this afternoon. Austin's on holiday so I'll have the dubious pleasure of Mr Jonathan Rawley, ex public-school, medical exams passed by the skin of his teeth and the old boy network, this afternoon."

"What's he like?"

"Eager. Just a bit too eager for Lockford General."

"Well then, go easy on him, darling. Remember you were young once."

His face clouded over and he bit his lip. I'd seen him do this before and took it to be when he was concerned about something. "Have a good day," he said, kissing my cheek as he headed for the garage."

"You too, " I replied but he'd gone.

What happened to Piper Archer?.........K.J.Rabane

Jean Montgomery was in front of me going through the security gate and we walked towards the jury room together. Jean was in her early fifties, with curly brown hair peppered with grey. Her face was prematurely wrinkled, I presumed as a result of her fondness for sitting in the sun. She gave the impression of being a rather nervous, mouse-like person.

"I hope it's not going to be another day like yesterday," she said, falling into step alongside me. "I hardly slept a wink last night."

"I'm afraid we're in for more of the same. There's quite a bit of evidence we've yet to hear, or so I understand."

She blew her nose into her handkerchief then stuffed the tissue up the sleeve of her cardigan. "I never thought for one moment it would be like this. I was hoping we'd have a drunk driving case or a robbery – not this. The only time I've ever been in court was when I got divorced but it was nothing like this."

I sympathised and, as we reached the jury room, we were soon joined by Jim Baines, a local builder who was in deep conversation with Joyce, no doubt going over the case in great detail.

"Don't know about you two," Joyce said, "but I haven't been able to stop thinking about Collins, I said to Gary, I said, if you only knew what sort of day I've had."

"You didn't tell him, I hope," Bill Roberts, overhearing the conversation, interrupted her.

"Well, nothing that would matter."

Then the creepy usher arrived to take us into court and the day began again.

What happened to Piper Archer?.........K.J.Rabane

Nearing the end of the second week of the trial, we'd listened to about as much evidence as any of us could stand and I found it intriguing as to the effect it had on us as individuals. The men were as affected by the brutality of the accused as much as the women. We'd endlessly discussed the evidence in detail at every opportunity afforded to us, whilst we were in the jury room, during breaks when points of law were discussed without the jury, and sometimes when it was raining and we stayed inside eating our packed lunches, most of us having decided it was cheaper and more appetising than eating in the canteen.

At the end of the week we were told the case was expected to run for a further week at least, and we were again instructed not to divulge the details to anyone. Leaving the court that afternoon I saw Jean in the car park looking particularly distressed as she put her mobile back into her handbag.

"Are you OK, Jean?" I asked.

Her face looked even more wrinkled as she answered, "I'm in a bit of a fix, actually. My lift can't make it and the busses to my end of town only run every hour and I've just missed one."

"Can I give you a lift?"

"Oh, I wouldn't want to take you out of your way. The thing is I've promised to look after my next-door-neighbour's little girl, until her husband gets back from work and I don't want to let her down."

"No problem. Where so you live, Jean."

"The Cuttings. St Julian's Close."

The Cuttings Estate had once had a bad reputation. Beresford told me it was a paradise for drug pushers. But after the council had invested in a clean up programme, the houses had a make over, the pushers moved out of town, and the area had become trouble free.

"No problem."

During the drive Jean told me that when she was young, like many of her contemporaries, she had married because she'd become pregnant by her boyfriend. They'd had little money to spare but had managed to rent a property in the Cuttings, which she'd later purchased from the council.

"I didn't know you had children Jean."

She cleared her throat. "I don't. I lost it."

"I'm so sorry. I didn't mean to pry."

"You weren't to know. I couldn't have any more, there was a mess up."

I wasn't sure whether she wanted to tell me or not. My instinct was that this was a story she needed to get off her chest but I hoped she'd keep the story to herself for obvious reasons as it was a bit too near home for my liking.

"It's down here," she said as I turned into the estate.

The house was painted white, a semi-detached with a small neat garden, which was filled with flowers.

"What a lovely garden," I said.

"I try. Thanks again, Piper. You must let me pay for the petrol." She opened her handbag.

"I wouldn't hear of it. It's on my way home anyway. Look Jean, why don't I pick you up on Monday morning? It makes sense and I'd enjoy the company."

This was a lie but I felt sorry for her situation and more than anyone was able to empathise.

She brightened immediately. "Would you? That's so kind. I can tell my cousin Billy not to bother then?"

"Of course. It's no problem, honestly. Pick you up at a quarter past nine?"

What happened to Piper Archer?.........K.J.Rabane

"I'll be ready." She stood at the gate and waved until I'd driven out of sight.

What happened to Piper Archer?.........K.J.Rabane

Chapter 47

During the lunch break on Monday Jean suggested she buy me a coffee in a nearby café, as she wanted to thank me for the lift. I told her there was no need but she insisted. I sensed she was eager to talk and hoped it wasn't about the case as it would be in a public place and it had been a particularly harrowing morning.

We sat at a table outside in the sunshine and were alone, the rest of the customers having sought the relatively cool interior. She seemed even more jittery than usual and the feeling persisted that she wanted to get something off her chest.

She began by telling me about her relationship with her ex-husband, how it began and how it ended. It was a tragic tale a love, loss and heartache. I felt my throat close as I listened to how she lost her baby, the medical negligence case that followed and the gradual breakup of her marriage based on the fact that she could no longer have children. Tears flowed down her cheeks as the pent up dam of emotion broke down with such force I feared she would never stop crying.

Handing her all the tissues I had in my handbag, I said, "I'm so sorry, Jean. If there's anything I can do to help……?"

She shook her head, "Thanks, but no one can."

Eventually, she calmed down and added, "It's been ages since I've talked to anyone about it. It's such a relief. I don't know why I've burdened you with it all thpugh. I just sort of felt you'd understand."

"I do, Jean, believe me I do. I'm very pleased you felt able to trust me enough. Now, I'm going inside to fetch us a large slice of that chocolate cake and we're going to eat it without the slightest bit of guilt."

What happened to Piper Archer?.........K.J.Rabane

She blew her nose, smiled, and nodded and I felt as if the burden, which had lifted from her shoulders, had found another resting place.

The afternoon session was every bit as distressing as the morning's had been. Both Jean and I were quiet on the drive home and after diner I told Beresford I was going to have a long soak in the bath then have an early night.

I knew I was uncommunicative at breakfast but my husband didn't seem to notice. He was reading the morning paper and only commented when something outrageous came to his notice. All that was required of me was to agree and he was content.

Jean rang just as I was looking for my car keys. "Billy has a job on in town and he's called to say he'll pick me up this morning. So you don't have to bother, love."

A wave of relief swept over me and I wondered if Billy's sudden appearance had been engineered. Perhaps Jean also felt uncomfortable about baring her soul to me the previous day. I felt concerned that she might regret having been so frank with me. Under the circumstances the turmoil of the trial was enough to cope with without the trauma of Jean's revelation.

But if I thought yesterday had been bad, nothing could have prepared me for the sister of the victim and her statement, together with gruesome pictures of the systematic attacks Collins had made on Kayleigh prior to her demise.

I arrived early again, too early to go into the jury room and sit on my own thinking, so I parked my car and walked to the café nearby.

What happened to Piper Archer?.........K.J.Rabane

"Hi, you couldn't sleep either?" Ronald was sitting by himself in the deserted café.

"Would you mind if I joined you or would you rather be alone?"

"Please, take a seat and I'll get us a drink, what will it be?" he replied, standing up.

"Coffee – black please."

When Ronald returned with the drinks, he said, "How are you feeling after yesterday? A bit much wasn't it?"

To my astonishment I burst into tears.

"Hey, I'm sorry. I shouldn't have said anything. Here." He thrust a clean white handkerchief across the table but I just couldn't stop crying. The emotion, which I'd managed to suppress successfully for years burst through in an embarrassing rush of tears and snot. It wasn't a pretty sight.

However, Ronald waited patiently until I'd finished, seemingly unconcerned by the spectacle. Then, spent of all emotion, I apologised. He stretched forward, took my hand and patted it. "Anything I can do?" he asked.

I lifted my cup, drank the dark glutinous coffee and thought for a moment. This stranger just might help. "Do you know I think perhaps you can, but not here, I need to talk to you, to explain, properly. I think that's half my trouble, it's why it all came out now. Jean told me something yesterday which brought it all back and I can't talk to my family about it."

"It sounds as if what you need is a shoulder to cry on and I'm more than willing to provide one, no strings attached."

I sighed with relief. "When?"

"If you aren't in a hurry, this afternoon. When we finish up here we could go somewhere private to talk."

"The Common?"

What happened to Piper Archer?.........K.J.Rabane

"Excellent. I'll meet you there as soon as we leave here. How do you feel now?"

"Better." And for the first time since it happened I was beginning to think I was telling the truth.

What happened to Piper Archer?………K.J.Rabane

Chapter 48

Joyce Leatherhead stuck to me like a fly to flypaper all day. She chatted on and on about Collins and his actions whilst likening them to her ex, who had suddenly become a monster in her eyes. Anyone could see she was focusing all her pent up feelings of frustration towards her divorced husband onto the accused. I had no doubt Collins was a guilty as anyone could be, but I hoped I was being more objective in arriving at that conclusion.

Later, Ronald was waiting for me parked on a part of the Common, which was fairly secluded being surrounded by trees in full leaf. As soon as I drew up, he left his vehicle and walked towards me.

"It's so hot. Do you want to walk, or sit on the grass?"

"Walk I think. If we start off to our right there's a fair bit of open space looking down on Lockford. We won't be overheard and it's unlikely we'll be seen together."

He smiled. "This is very intriguing. I feel like a secret agent already."

"It's just, well, my husband – I wouldn't want him to get the wrong idea."

"Don't worry, I understand completely."

I knew he would. We were two sides of the same coin in temperament – it made it all so much easier. Once I'd started talking, I couldn't stop. I told him everything, explained how awful I'd felt every time someone in the family had a new baby to show off. How I'd deliberately chosen a man who didn't want children and how I hadn't even been able to tell *him* the full story.

He listened without interruption and when I'd finished said, "So this business with Jean has made you think you might have been put in the same position? Medical negligence?"

"I'm not sure. That's the problem. But it did start me thinking."

"Can't you talk it over with your husband? Didn't you say he was an obstetrician? Wouldn't he be in a perfect position to advise you?"

"That's part of the problem. I think Beresford would find it a conflict of interests to become involved."

"Surely not! You're his wife; there's no contest."

"It's not quite as straightforward as that. I'd have to explain why I'd lied in the first place."

"Lied?"

"Yes. Before we married I told Beresford I couldn't have children. But I said it was because I'd had a problem with an ovarian cyst, which had caused complications. He didn't know I was pregnant. I managed to skirt over the details of who was responsible for my pregnancy and he could see it was an uncomfortable topic for me, which he sensitively avoided afterwards. You see, Beresford didn't want children, so I suppose he was relieved that I was in such a position. It suited us both."

He thought for a moment. "Obviously not."

"Sorry?"

"We'll it's obvious to me that it's been eating away at you ever since it happened. Certainly after you married your husband. Having to accept it is one thing but as for it suiting you, that's quite another subject, in my opinion."

He was frowning and suddenly stopped walking. "Do you want to get to the bottom of this? Is that what this is all about?"

"I'm not sure. I think it just helps to get it off my chest, to talk to someone who won't judge."

"Well, that's fine. I'm always available, Piper. But if at some point you want to take it further......"

"You'd help?"

"I'm your man. Anytime, just let me know."

For the first time since we'd started talking I felt as though a gigantic weight had been removed from my chest. "Thanks so much, Ronald. I doubt if I'll need to bother you but it feels great to have your support and to be able to talk freely to someone who isn't involved."

The following day we heard the judge's summing up and were instructed that she required a unanimous verdict. Derek Baynton, the court usher took us back to the jury room then said, "I'll be sitting outside the door should your require anything and I'll be waiting until you've reached your verdict. The foreman of the jury will then let me know and we'll go back into court."

It was the most professional attitude I'd seen from him throughout the whole trial. He was usually leering at the young girls or winking in my direction.

Finally, it took us four days to reach a unanimous verdict but it would have been much sooner if it had not been for the pedantic nature of Bill Roberts, the self-appointed foreman of the jury, who insisted on looking for trouble where none existed.

It was an uncomfortable feeling to be sitting in judgement on another human being, however monstrous his actions. His family, obviously upset by their son's horrific behaviour, sat and listened whilst the foreman announced the guilty verdict; his mother's distress was plain to see. I couldn't wait to get out of the court, to leave my fellow jurors behind and hopefully to never see

What happened to Piper Archer?.........K.J.Rabane

any of them again, however close we had become through necessity in the past three and a half weeks. But, fate had other ideas, and my path would cross with one of them in the future with devastating consequences.

Chapter 49

A couple of weeks later, I was shopping in town when I bumped into Joyce Leatherhead. I'd hoped to avoid her but she greeted me like a long lost relative and insisted we have coffee together. I thought about saying I had no time to spare, that I was meeting Beresford but she looked so eager, I didn't have the heart to refuse.

Sitting in the Sweet Pea café overlooking the High Street, we drank coffee and chatted.

"I told my sister how the twelve of us really bonded. Being forced to listen to all that for over three weeks and spending so much time together, it was bound to happen. I'm really glad we bumped into each other."

"Me too," I said, not wanting to hurt her feelings.

"Have you met any of the others?"

"Er, no."

"Oh, you should join us on a Friday night at the Lockford Arms. Tom, Ray, Aisha, Petra and Laura, we'll have a laugh. They'd be glad to see you. What about this Friday?"

I was put on the spot. "Sorry, love to, but Beresford is taking me to the cinema." It was a lame excuse.

"Oh, really, what you going to see?"

My mind went blank. "Not sure, he said he was going to surprise me."

She looked at me over the rim of her coffee cup. I think she saw through me.

"Right, well, if you change your mind, you know where we'll be. It will be good to see all the old gang again. We've decided to make it a fixture, Friday nights are Karaoke nights at the *Lockford Arms*."

"Thanks. I'll bear it in mind."

"What d'you think! He's only going to appeal."

What happened to Piper Archer?.........K.J.Rabane

"Collins?"

"My sister's married to a solicitor out Fenbury way. He said he'd heard it on the grapevine that Collins was shouting the odds, saying it was a miscarriage of justice and he was going to appeal as he was innocent."

"They all are," I said, absentmindedly.

"What was that?"

"Nothing. I shouldn't think he'd get anywhere with his appeal."

"That's just what I said. Well, we know what he did, don't we."

"In graphic detail," I replied.

"Seen anything of Ronald, since?"

"Who?"

"Ronald Wenger, the bookshop chappie. You and he seemed to get on." She was looking at me as if there was some secret I was keeping from her – some juicy piece of scandal perhaps. "Couldn't get hold of him to ask him about Friday. I went to his bookshop but a sour faced old biddy gave me the brush off."

"We did share lunch occasionally and have a chat about books, but no, I haven't seen him since."

She chatted on until I thought I could safely leave without appearing rude. "It's been so nice to see you again, Joyce, give my regards to the others when you meet them. I must rush now."

"Don't forget – Friday nights in the *Arms*," she said, as I backed out of the door.

Whether it was her mention of Ronald that prompted me to walk in the direction of the Antiquarian bookshop in Millbrook Avenue, or not, I wasn't quite sure, but I soon found myself standing outside the window looking in.

What happened to Piper Archer?.........K.J.Rabane

"Hello? I thought it was you. See anything you might like?" Ronald held the door open for me. I took a deep breath inhaling the scent of aged bindings and paper. It made me think of old libraries, studies in stately homes; it made me feel relaxed.

"This is lovely. You've decorated the interior to complement the books."

"I've tried to create the period but I'm not sure I've succeeded."

"It's perfect."

"I'm so glad you think so. It's nice to see you again, Piper. How've you been? I've been worried, especially as you were so upset when we last talked."

"I..." Not sure how to answer truthfully, I left the question hanging in mid air.

"Why don't we go into the back room and I'll make us a cup of tea? Nancy will take care of the shop."

A lady in her sixties, with grey hair curling untidily to her shoulders, appeared from the depths of a large freestanding book case, nodded in my direction and began arranging books on a table display.

The room at the back of the shop was comfortable, two tapestry-upholstered easy chairs stood to each side of an ancient fireplace, which had been restored, the patterned tiles polished and gleaming. Scented candles were arranged in the fire grate and on a small table near a window was a bowl of pot-pourri. Again I complemented him but he shook his head. "All Nancy's work, nothing to do with me. She's the one I told you about, a friend of my mother's."

"The lady of the tuna fish sandwiches?" I asked

He grinned. "The same."

We chatted about the trial and some of the jurors but I felt he was waiting for the answer to his original question. Eventually, I said, "I can't get it out of my head. Medical negligence was so far from my mind after my termination. I was young, desperate for it all to go away, to forget it ever happened. It was only when I talked to Laura during the trial that I realised what happened to me all those years ago should be investigated, because I'll have to live for the rest of my life with the knowledge that I'll never have a child of my own. At the time, it was only hinted at, after the operation. They said there'd been some complication and I might find it difficult to conceive in the future. Only Serena and I were there, we were protecting my mother, she wasn't well and would have been devastated to think I was pregnant. So we just accepted it all without question."

Tears pricked at my eyelids and I swallowed hard. I'd cried buckets on his shoulders during the trial – no more – I had to be strong.

"Do you want to do something about it?" He'd asked the question before and now I began to think about it.

To give myself some time whilst coming to a decision, I replied, "I beg your pardon?"

"I said, do you want to investigate the possibility of a claim for negligence?"

"I, er, I don't understand."

He leaned towards me. "Remember I told you I studied law at university before dropping out? Well, I understand in cases where medical negligence is suspected the Limitation Act comes into force, only after the patient has become aware that the injury caused by the alleged clinical negligence was serious enough to justify legal proceedings. In addition to which you must know the identity of the potential parties to the action before the limitation period of three years starts running."

"I'm not sure if I know what your saying."

"Sorry, in plain language – you might still have a case against the person who carried out the operation which left you infertile. That's if we can be certain the consultant in charge of your case was the person who actually performed the operation and if not we need to discover who that person was."

"You're serious aren't you?"

"You seemed so upset I thought it might be worth looking into in case you wanted to go ahead with it. As I said I'll help all I can."

I put my cup down on the table, stood up and walked to the window. Did I want this? Was this something, which had been niggling away at me for years? Could I face finding out the answer?

"Thank you, Ronald. I rather think I do," I said, at last. "But where do we go from here?"

"First, don't you think you ought to tell your husband?"

"No, not at present. You see, he'd be sure to try to stop me. He would think it's best to let sleeping dogs lie. He's in the profession – it could be highly embarrassing for him. I'd prefer it, if we kept it just between us, for a while at least."

"OK. So you want me to see what I can find out. Right, then you'll have to give me some details. Do you have any paperwork?"

I thought for a moment then remembered the box I'd placed firmly at the back of my bedroom closet when I'd first moved into Elm Tree House. I nodded.

"Good, then I'll meet you here, same time next week, with the relevant papers?"

"Yes. Thank you."

Leaving the shop, I felt as though a cloud had lifted from my shoulders, one of which I was previously unaware I'd been carrying quite so heavily. My burden being made lighter was only the start of it. How could I have known the train of events Ronald would set into motion would shake the foundations of my comfortable existence with Beresford and make the life I knew come tumbling down about my ears.

Chapter 50

After I'd spoken Ronald, I went home. Beresford was still in work. In one of the spare bedrooms I opened a closet door. Reaching behind a large hatbox containing hats I'd worn for weddings, fascinators, and baseball caps, my hand touched an old shoebox. I lifted it out.

Removing the lid, I saw a selection of black and white photos of our family, my parents when they were young, their wedding, Serena and my baby photos. Tightly wedged underneath them was an envelope. I don't know why I hadn't throw it out years ago but something had stopped me, a thread to the past, I suppose.

It was a letter headed The Princess Royal Hospital of Wales, Grafton Hill, Cardiff – Obstetric Department. The letter was confirming a routine clinic appointment six weeks after my termination of pregnancy. The signature at the bottom of the letter above the typewritten words, Angus Sheridan, Consultant Obstetrician and Gynaecologist, was an indecipherable scrawl.

I remembered Serena telling my mother we were going shopping in Cardiff as they'd opened a new department store and she wanted to buy some things for her forthcoming wedding. She said she needed me to help her and we'd probably stay the night as it was too far for her to drive in one day. Mother had accepted the excuse without question. I know now she had other things on her mind, her own health issues for one thing.

I have a vague memory of sitting in a consulting room, with the sun slicing through grey venetian blinds, a large man with long tapering fingers looking down at the floor, the word infertility floating in the air, like a

What happened to Piper Archer?.........K.J.Rabane

dust mite trapped in a sunbeam, and spending the night in a hotel room in the centre of town.

Removing the letter from the shoebox, I folded it up and thrust it into the pocket of my jeans. It was all I had, whether it would be enough for Ronald I wasn't sure but in the study I opened my laptop, accessed the diary page, and made a note of my forthcoming meeting with Ronald. But before I typed in the name Ronald Wenger, I stopped. There was just an outside chance that it might be necessary to keep his identity concealed. This investigation into my past was way too important for me to risk compromising it before it had a chance to begin.

Doodling his name on a piece of scrap paper I arranged the letters as if completing an anagram clue in the Telegraph crossword. Rowland Green was the name I chose for my deception.

Beresford was particularly busy that week. He arrived home each evening complaining about staff cutbacks and restricted funding. I sympathised, made his meals, and listened as usual. But my thoughts were focused on my forthcoming meeting with Ronald and my hope for the future. I needed some answers, someone needed to be accountable for what happened to me at such a young age and the more I thought about it the more convinced I became that I was the victim of medical negligence and had been fed a version of the truth by the consultant Angus Sheridan, who was no doubt protecting his back.

"You seem preoccupied tonight," Beresford said, on the evening before my meeting with Ronald.

"Sorry, I was thinking of writing my shopping list for tomorrow, what did you say?"

"Nothing really, just I might be home a bit late, end of the week, you know how busy things have been lately. I promise I'll book a table at Hamptons for Saturday night to make up for it." He kissed my cheek. "I'm off for a shower and an early night. Leave the dishwasher, I'll stack it in the morning."

I smiled, "You'll do no such thing. Why don't you run a bath and relax, I'll bring you up a glass of wine and light a few scented candles."

"Excellent, I knew I'd married you for something." He kissed me again and left the room humming an aria from Tosca.

Although it was hot, there was a fine drizzle falling as I parked the car and walked the short distance to Ronald's bookshop. Nancy was serving a customer, a man wearing a shabby jacket and blue jeans; under his arm he carried a stack of books and nodded to me as I stood behind him, waiting. When she'd finished serving him, Nancy said, "Ronald said for you to go into the back room." She frowned and I wondered whether she disapproved of me meeting him, perhaps she was looking out for his wellbeing, as a friend of his mother, or perhaps she had other ideas.

"Come in," Ronald was sitting in the same chair I'd seen him sit in before. He stood up. "I wondered if you might be having second thoughts."

I shook my head. "On the contrary. I can't wait for you to begin. I've been on pins since we last talked."

"Good. I've learned from a friend of mine from my college days, who has a law firm in Lockford, that you could possibly have a case against the surgeon who performed your operation, but it is extremely difficult to prove medical negligence as the profession usually closes ranks in such situations. However, in your case it might be more straightforward. You were a young, healthy, girl, who had a routine termination procedure.

There is no reason why you should have expected it to be compromised by future infertility problems."

"I've brought the letter from the consultant."

"Excellent. It's a start. You realise I can't promise anything though. But I'll do my best. I have a cousin living in South Wales and I plan to spend some time with her whilst I carry out my investigations."

"This is very good of you, Ronald. You must let me have your bill."

"Nonsense. It's my pleasure. I hadn't realised until now how much I'd missed the investigative part of legal work. You'll be doing me a favour."

He was such a kind man. I had no doubt I could leave it in his capable hands. There was no reason why this should not turn out to be the result I required – at least – that's what I thought at the time.

Chapter 51

The following Friday afternoon I called at the bookshop as arranged but as I got out of my car, Ronald was waiting for me.

"What is it?" I asked.

"I think we should take a ride. Nancy is suspicious."

"Suspicious? I don't understand." However, I did as he suggested and waited until he sat in the passenger seat and we'd driven out of town to the Common before I received a reply.

"I'm afraid things are complicated, Piper. I don't want to cause you any embarrassment. Nancy has always taken my welfare, as one of her main priorities, after mother died. She's very kind but it does get a bit overpowering at times. Risking her thinking of you as anything other than a friend is naturally something I'd rather avoid, under the circumstances."

"I see. That's very considerate of you. I wouldn't want Beresford to start putting two and two together and making five either."

"Precisely."

"Do you have any news for me?"

"I do. It's just a start but I don't think Angus Sheridan carried out your operation himself. He was off sick at the time and his senior registrar, a man called Shelby Whittaker took over his operation lists."

"So we know who caused my condition?"

He hesitated and looked out of the windscreen at the trees bending in the strong winds. Summer was fading fast and rain clouds hung threateningly on the horizon.

"Not exactly. We can't be sure at this stage. What I understand from my source is that there was a flood in the department, which caused havoc to the bed situation.

What happened to Piper Archer?.........K.J.Rabane

Some of the patients were transferred to another local hospital in order to relieve the pressure on wards in the Grafton Hill Hospital. The members of staff in both departments were working under extremely difficult conditions and from what I was told Shelby Whittaker was not the most reliable surgeon they'd had to work with."

"Can you confirm that he carried out my op,.?" I was afraid he'd say there was no way of knowing."

He bit his lip. "Not at the moment. But I'm working on it and hope to have an answer before we meet again next week. Try to think positively. I won't let you down."

I reached over and patted his arm. "I know you won't, Ronald," I said.

"Then I suggest we meet here instead of at the shop. Two-thirty next Friday suit?"

"Fine. Now where would you like me to drop you off?"

"I told Nancy I was going to the library in town to do some research. The High Street will be fine."

I stopped the car near Hasting Buildings and, after Ronald had started to walk away, caught sight of a thick set balding figure approaching him. Bill Roberts was wearing his golfing clothes, flashy, logo ridden, and as loud as his personality. His insistence on becoming foreman of the jury was just another symptom of his overbearing nature. I didn't envy Ronald's chances of getting to the library any time soon.

Over dinner that evening Beresford talked about his day and I took the opportunity to ask a few questions, which I hoped wouldn't sound too unusual.

What happened to Piper Archer?………K.J.Rabane

"How on earth do you manage when there are staff shortages, surely it must put pressure on surgeons to hurry operations?"

He looked up from his plate. "Hurry, is possibly the wrong word, darling. We are always aware we are dealing with living patients and not mortuary slab cadavers." He sliced through his steak and raised the fork to his lips.

"Of course, but surely there must be some corners which are cut?"

"Well, put it this way. The team may be lacking a few members, which puts pressure on the remaining staff but we only agree to operate if we are able to perform to the best of our ability – non-essential operations are postponed until a more convenient time so we can concentrate on the emergencies."

I wanted to ask more but knew to do so would arise his suspicion as to my reasons for such in-depth questioning. So I talked about the weather, shopping and the state of parking in the centre of town and let my heart rate slow to something approaching normal.

What happened to Piper Archer?.........K.J.Rabane

Chapter 52

When the following Friday arrived I was waiting on the Common for Ronald as arranged, but he didn't come. Frustrated and worried that something had happened to stop him, I decided to go back into town and see if he was at the bookshop. It was so unlike him to have forgotten.

A young girl with curly fair hair was serving an elderly gentleman at the till and I waited to see if Nancy or Ronald would appear but there was no sign of either of them.

When the young girl had finished serving I said, "Excuse me, could I see Mr Wenger, please?"

"I'm sorry. Mr Wenger isn't in today. Can I help?"

"No thank you. Is his assistant available, her name is Nancy, I don't know her surname?"

"Mrs S is off on the sick, don't know when she'll be back."

"I see. Could you tell Mr Wenger that I'm sorry he missed our appointment earlier and perhaps we could meet next Friday at the same time."

"Name?" she asked opening a note pad.

"Just pass on the message, please. He'll know who it's from," I replied, feeling very secretive.

The following Friday he was there, waiting. The trees on the Common bent in the wind and scattered leaves onto the roof of his car as I watched him slowly closing the door and walking towards me. His face was serious. There was no smile, no wave of his hand as he'd done previously. I began to feel alarmed.

"What is it?" I asked.

What happened to Piper Archer?.........K.J.Rabane

"I'm sorry I missed last week. I'm afraid I couldn't face you."

My heart started to race. "Ronald? What on earth is the matter?"

He was silent for a moment watching a leaf twisting and turning in the breeze until it fell to the ground. Then, taking a deep breath, he replied, "I've discovered the identity of the surgeon who performed your operation."

"Excellent. That's good, surely?"

"Not exactly."

My hand flew to my throat. "I can tell by your face, it's someone I know."

"You do."

"Who?" It still didn't dawn on me – how could it?

"Your husband – Beresford Archer – he was a young senior house officer and his registrar was supposed to carry out the procedure but apparently he was in the habit of disappearing without warning from time to time. Apparently he'd scrubbed up, Archer was assisting, then with a shake of his head he insisted Archer take his place and he left the operating theatre with his patient prepped, ready and waiting. There was very little your husband could do and afterwards there was the usual cover up, naturally. But my source is a reliable one, and I have no reason to doubt its authenticity."

My hand began to shake; my mind was in turmoil. He leaned towards me and gently took my hand in his. "I didn't want to tell you, that's why I couldn't face you last week."

Unable to think clearly, I thanked him for the information and said I'd think about what to do next.

"If I can help, anytime, you know you only have to ask."

"Thanks. I'll be in touch. Right now, I need to think."

What happened to Piper Archer?.........K.J.Rabane

"You'd prefer to be alone?"

I nodded, tears not far away, and then waited whilst he walked to his car and drove away. I took a deep breath to stop my hands from shaking. My husband, the man I loved, had been responsible for my inability to have children. The sentence hung in the air like an unpalatable truth. How I was going to behave when I saw him was anyone's guess. I had absolutely no idea. I'd make his meal, sit at his table, let him kiss me and sleep at his side. I couldn't contemplate the thought of his lovemaking; it was one step too far.

As it turned out, Beresford rang to say he'd be late and to eat dinner without him, he'd grab something in the hospital canteen. I couldn't face eating so I sat in the kitchen nursing a mug of coffee and stared out of the window at the garden and the surrounding fields, as the sun sank lower in the sky and shadows lengthened.

The more I thought over my earlier conversation with Ronald the more confused I became. Why hadn't Beresford recognised my name when he first met me? Piper Sandford surely would have stuck in his mind, not to mention the outcome of his disastrous surgery. I had never met anyone else called Piper, wouldn't it have rung a bell when we were introduced?

Thinking back to the time I was sixteen and the trauma of discovering I was pregnant was difficult enough. My mother never knew and Serena had been amazing. I picked up the phone.

"Hi, it's me."

"Pip, everything OK, is it? You don't usually ring this late." Serena was eating.

"I won't interrupt your meal, I'll ring again tomorrow, it's not important."

"Nonsense. I'm on my own, Mike's had to go into work, some emergency or other and Ellie's out with her friends. Now what is it?"

"I've been looking at old photos," I was thinking on my feet, "you know I try not to think about it – the op and everything."

"Come on spit it out. It's all in the past, nothing can change it, I said to my friend Rita, only the other day, the past is a road we can't travel – none of us can and she said.."

I had to stop her or I'd start crying for sure and that would have her coming around and tearing a strip off Beresford and starting something I wouldn't know how to stop. "I just wanted to know how Mum never found out. Surely the hospital would have written to her afterwards and asked to see me, if only for a follow up appointment. I know I wanted to forget it all, at the time, to escape, and believe it never happened. How did you manage to keep it a secret? I've never asked, never thought about it until now."

I heard the sigh and could imagine her biting her lip and hunching her shoulders. "I used your middle name when I registered you for treatment – you were booked under June Sandford and I was your sister, your only living relative – all correspondence came to me at the flat – don't you remember?"

I did, I remembered it all now, it was still in my brain but I'd refused to think about it for so long, I needed a prompt. If I'd have been thinking clearly I'd have remembered it was all in the letter I'd hidden in my shoebox – the one I'd given to Ronald.

"Yes, of course, that explains it."

"Are you sure, you're OK, Pip? Do you want me to come around?"

I forced a laugh. "I'm fine, just a bit nostalgic, looking at old photos of Mum and Dad. You get back to your meal. I'll ring on Sunday as usual."

But I wouldn't ring on Sunday. By Sunday my world would have collapsed and I'd be starting a new life.

Chapter 53

Monday morning arrived. I waited until Beresford left for work, my mind spinning around in circles. I couldn't stay; another night of making small talk and praying he wouldn't initiate lovemaking was too much; he wouldn't be satisfied with my 'migraine' excuse indefinitely. What was I going to do?

I'm not quite sure how I found myself standing outside Ronald's bookshop. I hadn't planned it; I didn't even have an overnight case – no change of clothes.

"Piper?" He took me inside. I saw Nancy looking at me, her nose in the air. I sensed her disapproval of our friendship as strongly as the smell of the Lilly of the Valley perfume she always wore.

"I've left him," I said, once we were seated in the room behind the shop.

"Where will you go – to your sister's?"

I shook my head. "I don't know. If I go to Serena and Mike's I'm sure they'll try and persuade me to go back. It would seem very odd to them, my suddenly deciding to leave."

"But if you told them the real reason." He reached over took my hand. "Surely they'd understand."

I shook my head and bit my lip hard. "You don't know Serena. As far as she's concerned Beresford can do no wrong. She'd find a way of condoning it – explaining it all away. She'd never understand that I can't bear him to touch me – can't bear to look at him." I wiped away a bitter tear of regret.

"I see."

"I'm sorry to burden you. I really don't know how I got here. I've been walking around the centre of town for ages. But I must let you get on. I'll find somewhere to go."

He stood up and walked to the mantelpiece then circled the room, whilst running his fingers through his hair in concentration. "I've got it. You must stay in my cottage in Saint Abbot's."

"Saint Abbot's?"

"It's an isolated village on the Cornish coast. No one will find you there and it will give you time to assess your situation in peace."

I sighed. "I can't ask you to become involved with my problems."

"You didn't and it's my pleasure. An elderly relative left the cottage to me when I was in my first year at university and I use it to get away from things. No one will disturb you there I can assure you." He came to sit beside me. "I suggest you pop into Kents department store to buy some clothes and things you'll need then I'll drive you down to the cottage and we'll pick up some food at a supermarket on the way.

"This is so kind of you, Ronald. But I'm interfering with your work at the shop."

"Nonsense. Nancy'll see to things here. Best if you leave now and I'll meet you outside Kents in an hour, if that's enough time for you to buy all you'll need? Then I'll tell Nancy I've been called up to London to inspect a consignment of rare books at an auction house. She won't think it's odd – it's something I do occasionally."

"An hour is fine. I'll never be able to repay you for your kindness."

"No repayment required," he said, seeing me to the door.

What happened to Piper Archer?.........K.J.Rabane

I bought underwear, three changes of clothes, toiletries, a pair of trainers, and a small trolley case, cashed up to my limit at the cash machine then met Ronald as arranged and we drove to Cornwall. Throughout the journey I wondered if this was the answer to my predicament but I was so confused I decided, if nothing else, it would give me a chance to think clearly for a while and to get it all straight in my mind.

As we drew nearer to our destination the area became less populated. We passed a supermarket on the edge of a small development and Ronald stopped the car.

"Just sit back and relax," he said. "I'll shop for the essentials, enough for a week or two."

I opened my handbag and began to search in my purse.

"Please, don't even think of it," he said, opening the door.

My first thought was my credit card wouldn't be much use. If Beresford began looking for me, it could be traced very easily. Even then I think I was looking to the long term. Deep down I knew I wouldn't be returning to Lockford anytime soon. But I had the cash in my purse, which would last for a bit. However, every attempt I made to get Ronald to take the money was met with a polite refusal as he closed the car door and walked towards the supermarket entrance.

A while later he returned. "There, you are, all done."

"I don't know how to thank you. What would I have done?"

He leaned across and patted my hand, a reassuring gesture I had come to rely upon. "My pleasure, now please don't mention thanks any more, it's not necessary, just one friend helping another."

What happened to Piper Archer?.........K.J.Rabane

We drove out of the car park, through a small housing development and into the country. After about fifteen minutes Ronald turned left into a small village. Then he continued to drive towards the coast. I could see the headland and the sun shining on the water in front of us. The road soon narrowed and taking another left turn into a lane we continued downwards towards our destination.

The cottage was constructed of stone. From the front it looked like a standard build of a century gone by – a central door, two windows downstairs and two up. The front garden, although slightly overgrown, had been paved, no doubt to make gardening less of a problem. At the side of the cottage stood a garage.

"If you'd like to get out and take a look around," he handed me a key, "I'll put the car in the garage and bring in the groceries and your case."

Opening the door, I smelled a faint odour of disuse, but it wasn't unpleasant; opening a few windows would soon sort that out, I decided. There was a small square hallway with a door on my left, another on my right and one facing me. I chose the one facing me, presuming it to be a kitchen, and found it was relatively well furnished with the most amazing view of the coast. A kettle stood on the worktop, so I filled it from the tap and plugged it in.

"I see you're making yourself at home already," Ronald said, handing me a jar of coffee and a bottle of milk. "No sugar for me, please." He sat down at the table, the bags of groceries at his feet.

"You must be tired, it's been a long drive. Why don't you let me stack the groceries away whilst you drink your coffee?"

What happened to Piper Archer?.........K.J.Rabane

"Thanks. But first I'll take your things up to the bedroom. It's the one on the right at the top of the stairs. I usually keep some essentials in my bedroom so I don't have to bring a case of clothes down every time I come."

When he returned, I said, "Why don't you sit down for a bit and have a rest," then handed him a mug of coffee. "I'll make us something to eat a bit later and give you a shout, shall I?"

He smiled. "I don't want you to wait on me but I am whacked, old age doesn't come alone."

His remark set me thinking. I remembered he'd said he was thirty-one, when we were talking during the trial, but he was a difficult person to age. His thick dark hair showed no sign of grey and his dark eyes were alert but there was an air of antiquity about him, which, I supposed, could have arisen from his background and his love of ancient books. Either way, I couldn't have been more grateful for the kindness he'd shown me in my hour of need.

The sun was sinking on the horizon as we sat at the kitchen table and ate our meal. Orange-yellow streaks coloured the kitchen walls and the sea was transformed into a golden mirror. "What a lovely view. I can understand why you didn't sell the place. Do you get down here often?"

"Not as often as I'd like. It's very isolated, as you must have noticed. But I can assure you. If you want a hideaway, this is just the place. No one bothers me when I'm here. If you need anything there's the shop we passed in the village but it's a bit of a walk." He grinned. "I've just had a thought. My old pushbike is in the garage. It's a fold-up one, small wheels, you know the sort of thing. It will do – better for coming downhill naturally but it means you only have to walk one way and if you want to go further it might be of use. I'll pump up the tyres before I leave tomorrow."

The thought of him leaving made me start to panic. What was I doing? I'd be alone in back of beyond, isolated from my friends and family. Then Beresford's face swam before me and I took a deep breath, knowing I had no choice.

Chapter 54

After Ronald left, the weather changed. Clear skies gave way to dark clouds, heavy rain and morning mists. I knew then how truly isolated the cottage was and how lonely I was likely to become the longer I stayed. However, in the bookcase I found enough books to occupy me and spent my days reading and, when the weather improved, walking along the cliffs at the bottom of the garden. I saw no one except the odd dog walker in the distance.

Ronald rang every evening to see how I was and at the end of the second week, he broke the news. Beresford had contacted the police and my picture was in the newspapers. Now I had a decision to make, either I could go back home and face Beresford with the reason for my leaving or I must make sure no one would recognise me as Piper Archer.

Cutting my hair was not difficult. There was a sharp scissors in the kitchen drawer. I cut my shoulder length hair so that it was short enough to tuck behind my ears and the fringe altered the shape of my face completely. Then wearing a baseball cap, which was hanging on a peg in the passage, I went into the garage, found Ronald's bike, and set off.

The village shop was little more than a converted front room of a cottage. But inside I found a section selling toiletries, another selling cards and a couple of shelves on which were stacked tinned foodstuffs, cereals and loaves of bread. The fridge near the door was crammed full of frozen food and I realised I need never have to move further from the cottage in search of food than this.

What happened to Piper Archer?.........K.J.Rabane

I found the packet of hair colour alongside some bars of soap and paid for my purchases. Thankfully leaving the shop without meeting anyone, other than the sales assistant a young girl more interested in the magazine she was reading than looking at me in any detail, I left and rode back to the cottage.

At the weekend Ronald came down bringing with him more books, food and some winter clothes he thought I might need.

"I must pay you. You can't keep giving me money and buying things. Take my debit card, use it in Lockford that should confuse things."

"It's no bother. I don't mind – it's nothing, really."

"No, Ronald. I insist. I must pay my way."

He looked uncomfortable. "All right if you insist. I'll withdraw money using your card, but out of town, at a supermarket or somewhere quiet, reimburse myself and bring the rest down for you at the weekend. I've also taken the liberty of buying you a new pay-as-you-go mobile phone. If you use yours it can be traced. I know this sounds like something from a spy novel but if you are serious about not being found then it makes sense to take precautions."

I shrugged. "Being untraceable has its own problems I see. Thanks for thinking of everything. I would never have been able to do this alone. Beresford would have found me in the blink of an eye and it's not what I want."

"I understand. Anything you need me to do, just ring the shop on your new mobile. If Nancy answers say you're Debbie from Waterstones."

Watching Ronald leaving the cottage, I realised that I was like a patient convalescing after a long illness. I needed time to heal before I could face the world, face my husband and his negligence, which had changed my life.

Winter set in earlier than usual. Then at the end of November the first snow came. It was little more than a light flurry but the temperature inside the cottage dropped considerably. Unfortunately the central heating was adequate if not exactly efficient. But I found a stack of jumpers in a drawer in Ronald's room and told him I was using them to keep warm, he said I was welcome to use anything I found and once again I thanked him for taking care of me..

Ronald returned on Christmas Eve and stayed until the New Year. He drove to the supermarket and bought our Christmas meal, some wine and enough food to see me through January.

On Boxing Day the snow fell in earnest and after lunch we walked across the cliffs and marvelled at the changing scenery. Never, in all the time we spent together at the cottage did Ronald ever make a pass at me. He was solicitous as to my welfare and supported me when I was going through a particularly bad time, but he never once made me feel uncomfortable. It did cross my mind to wonder if he were gay but I saw no evidence of it, in fact his conversation indicated that he was quite the reverse.

On New Year's Day, the rain came and washed away much of the snow.

"I was beginning to think I was going to be stuck down here until the end of January," Ronald said, packing some things into the boot of his car.

"Don't feel you have to come down at the weekends during the winter months. The weather is bad and the roads are bound to be treacherous, come in the spring. I'll be fine. I've plenty of books, the IPad you brought me, TV, and I can walk around the coast and into the village. I'm OK, honestly."

"We'll see," he replied, kissing my cheek and saying goodbye.

As Ronald's car disappeared at the end of the lane and I was left alone again, I wondered if I was fooling myself – would I ever be fine again?

What happened to Piper Archer?.........K.J.Rabane

Chapter 55

When the warmer weather came, Ronald told me he'd heard that the police had decided I'd probably left with a lover and scaled back the search. I felt numb. To a certain extent it took the pressure off me, I didn't need to hide anymore.

Nevertheless, I did feel bad about Serena. After Christmas I'd even dialled her number on my 'new' phone but when she answered I put the phone down. I didn't know how to begin to explain to her how I felt. Some day, I'd make it up to her, I promised, wondering when that day would arrive.

Spring brought with it a lifting of my spirits. Flowers began to bloom in the cottage garden and I spent long hours cutting back overgrown bushes and weeding the border plants. The days passed quickly, the weekends, when Ronald arrived flew by and summer approached bringing with it the knowledge that I'd been gone from Lockford for over a year.

Time passed pleasurable. I needed the isolation to heal and was almost unaware of the passage of time until one day in September when the weather forecasters were promising an Indian summer I had the overwhelming need to return to Lockford to see my sister. I cycled into the station near the village and caught a connection to a mainline station where I bought a ticket to Lockford. I'd missed the early one and had to get the slow train, which stopped at every station along the way. The journey took ages. I didn't ring Ronald, not then, I just needed to go back - the urge was unrelenting.

I was walking away from the station as evening shadows lengthened and was heading towards the High

What happened to Piper Archer?………K.J.Rabane

Street when I saw them. They were sitting in a restaurant and I knew he'd seen me. I lost my nerve then, and like a frightened rabbit caught in the headlights, hurried back to the station where I took the next train back to Cornwall. I didn't mention it to Ronald. But as the weeks passed I knew at some point I would return to Elm Tree House.

When that day eventually arrived, I travelled by train to Lockford General then took a taxi to Elm Tree House, used my key to open the front door and went inside. Christmas was fast approaching, I suppose that was another reason I felt I had to 'come home' even if I knew it would be a brief visit. It was an attempt to cling on to the intangible.

    The changes since I'd left were obvious. The house was relatively clean but untidier than I was used to and although there was plenty of food in the kitchen it wasn't the sort I would have bought. In our bedroom there was a pair of fluffy slippers in the wardrobe, which weren't mine. The thought that Beresford would have 'moved on' in that direction hadn't occurred to me. Perhaps the slippers belonged to the woman I'd seen him with in the restaurant, I thought. I wasn't sure how I felt about that - it was as if I were numb.

    I can't explain the next bit without realising how odd my actions must seem. Like an automaton, I began to prepare our evening meal, peeling vegetables and putting them in saucepans and when I heard his car in the drive the only way I could control my panic was to act as if I'd never been gone. The shock on his face at seeing me seemed to jolt me into trying to put the whole thing to the back of my mind, to pretend the past had never occurred and I'd never discovered the truth about my infertility.

I suggested he go into the living room and I'd bring him a drink, as I once would have done on his return from work. But suddenly sanity returned and I realised what I was doing was crazy So I left the house, running as fast as I could across the fields, like a phantom in the night.

A cold wind was blowing as I hurried back to the station, running and walking, desperate to get away. The journey took me just over an hour. The night train arrived, I was alone, no ticket collector on the station, no evening commuters, just a woman who had experienced a moment of madness and who was frantic to disappear yet again.

When I reached the cottage, I phoned Ronald and told him what I'd done.

"I'll come down," he said.

"No, honestly, I'm OK now. It was foolish, a sudden need to see my home, to try to be normal. I realise now it was a big mistake. I must move on and forget my other life. I'll have to ring Serena and tell her what's been going on. I should have spoken to her months ago."

I heard him sigh. "Try not to worry. I'll speak to your sister, if that would help."

"You would? Oh, that means everything to me. I don't know how I would start to explain. If you could soften the blow then I'll speak to her later, when I feel more confident about making her understand."

"No problem, leave it all to me. You just relax, enjoy the unseasonably warm weather and I'll be down at the weekend to keep you into the loop, regarding what's happening here."

What happened to Piper Archer?.........K.J.Rabane

Putting down the phone, I breathed a sigh of relief. Serena would understand eventually, especially after I'd explained about Beresford. I was sure she would.

When Ronald arrived at the weekend I could tell straight away something was wrong.

"What is it?" I asked.

"Don't worry now. I'll explain after I've unpacked the food."

I made us a cup of tea and put the groceries away, then insisted he tell me what was bothering him. He was obviously finding it difficult to explain. He bit his lip and left his cup of tea untouched on the kitchen table.

"Um, I rang your sister, as I said I would."

"And?"

He looked down at his hands. "She was furious. She said you were ungrateful, didn't you know how much pain you were causing Berry; he was going out of his mind wondering what had happened to you. Why hadn't you rung instead of leaving it to your lover?"

He didn't look up. "That's what they all think; that I'm your lover. But they think I'm someone called Rowland Green."

I sighed. "It's my fault."

He looked up then. "Your fault?"

"They must have looked at my computer. I kept diary entries – you know the sort of thing – *Meeting Jane for coffee 2pm on Thursday.* Well something stopped me from typing your name – I don't know exactly why – so I arranged the letters in a circle – like an anagram and......."

"Rowland Green?"

I nodded. "I'm sorry. I should ring Serena now, and explain."

He shook his head. "I don't think it's a good idea. She's not in the right frame of mind to accept your explanation. She'd insist you speak to your husband at least. And if you're not ready to do that – well – he could come down here and make things very awkward for you."

"I need to think about it. It's one big mess, whichever way you look at it."

Ronald stood up. "I'll open a bottle of wine, pop the curry in the oven then I suggest we try to forget about our problems and listen to some uplifting music. What d'you say?"

"I say you are very kind. I'm sorry I've dragged you into all this but it's not your problem – it's mine. Perhaps I should leave here and sort out my own mess."

"Nonsense. What are friends for? You must stay as long as you like. Here." He handed me a glass, poured the wine, and clinking his glass against mine, said, "A good time to drown your sorrows?"

I smiled. "As good as any," I replied.

What happened to Piper Archer?.........K.J.Rabane

Chapter 56

The months passed in a similar manner but although the weather remained warmer than usual, the scenery idyllic and my situation comfortable, I began to worry about Serena and how I was going to proceed with my life. Ronald continued to ring every evening and he said nothing had changed, except he believed Beresford had been seeing rather a lot of someone called Isobel. He didn't elaborate but the implication that the relationship was more than platonic was, I felt, an unspoken fact.

To my surprise I felt nothing, no jealousy, no anger, no sorrow and the realisation came, like a flash of sunlight on a cloudy day, that I could never go back to my old life. However, I couldn't stay hidden away in the cottage indefinitely – it was time I took charge of my future.

At the weekend Ronald arrived as usual.

"You look radiant today. All this good weather suits you," he said.

"I've set the table in the back garden, come on through. I know it's getting dark but it's sheltered and warm enough, I think."

He sat in the director's chair I'd found in the garden shed and I went back into the kitchen. "Won't be a mo, just relax."

He'd closed his eyes and was humming softly to himself as I placed two glasses and a bottle on the garden table.

"Champagne?" he said, "What are we celebrating?"

"My new life. I've decided to go back to Lockford on Monday, face the music with Serena, and explain to Beresford why I can no longer be his wife. I've had plenty of time to think about what happened and thanks to you I've come to terms with my situation. It's over two years, Ronald. I can't stay here for ever; I'll wish him well with his new relationship and begin a new life of my own."

His glass was halfway to his lips, his expression unreadable. I'd expected him to be pleased, to say he was thrilled he'd helped, something of the sort. But all he said was, "I see."

"Would you mind driving me back on Sunday evening? I thought I could stay at *The Dolphin* for a bit and after I'd spoken to Serena and Beresford maybe move to London. I've a friend who works in the city."

"I see," he said again, leaving his Champagne untouched on the table. "So you've given this quite a bit of thought."

"I've had plenty of time, don't you think?"

"Yes, I can see you have. So you're sure this is what you want?"

"I am."

"Right."

"A toast, to my new life?"

"Your new life." He raised his glass, took a small sip but left the rest to go flat, the bubbles disappearing like my enthusiasm."

Ronald was quiet throughout dinner and when I suggested a walk he said he was tired and thought he'd have an early night. I sat in the garden after he'd gone to bed and began to wonder what my new life would be like. It was a strange feeling but not an unwelcome one; I couldn't hide away forever, two years had been more than enough time to sort myself out mentally.

When Sunday arrived Ronald seemed to have come to terms with me leaving the cottage. He helped me pack a small suitcase with the belongings I'd acquired and which I didn't wish to leave at the cottage, nothing much just a few clothes, a couple of paperbacks and some toiletries.

"Shall I ring and book a room at *The Dolphin* for you?" he asked, as I was closing my case.

"Oh, yes, please. I'll just close all the windows and I think that's that."

I heard him speaking on the telephone and began to feel nervous at the prospect of returning to the world after so long. Part of me was longing for it and part of me was terrified.

"No problem," he said. "I told them you'd let them know how long you'd be staying when you arrive."

"Thanks so much, Ronald. You know I can never repay you. But I'll never forget your kindness." I kissed his cheek and it felt cold against my lips.

He muttered something unintelligible and I could see he was embarrassed.

"Goodbye cottage, thanks for everything," I said, turning back at the gate. How could I have known that my farewell was premature and like a magnet it would be drawing me back sooner than I could ever have imagined.

Chapter 57

"You are sure?" Ronald asked, as we drove away from the village.

"Certain."

Passing the supermarket, he suddenly slowed down. "I think I should fill her up. The tank is just under a quarter full and we have a long way to go." He drove into the forecourt and attached the car to the petrol pump.

I was listening to Classic FM on the radio when Ronald stepped back into the car and turned on the ignition. We drove the short distance to the dual carriageway and I looked back and saw the curve of the bay and the sea twinkling in the morning sunshine. I felt elated, as if during the past years I had been in a cocoon waiting to emerge. But before we'd driven more than a hundred metres or so the car began to slow down, the engine spluttered and stopped. "What the?.." Ronald pressed the heel of his palm to his forehead. "God, no!"

"What is it?"

"I think I've just put diesel into the car instead of petrol. I'm such an idiot. My mind must have been elsewhere – I used the pump I usually use at the supermarket in Lockford, without really looking."

"What happens now?"

"It's knackered."

"Permanently."

"Absolutely. I think I can safely say we won't be travelling in this anywhere today – perhaps never."

He pulled his mobile out from his pocket and rang the garage we'd just left from the number on his receipt. After a while the pick up truck arrived and drove us back to the village.

What happened to Piper Archer?.........K.J.Rabane

"We'll walk from here, thanks." I heard Ronald say. He turned to me. "I'm so sorry. My mind must have been elsewhere. Tomorrow I'll see about arranging a train ticket for you."

"What about your car?"

"Not sure. I'll ring Nancy, tell her I've decided to take my summer holidays at last and stay around for a bit. The garage should be able to tell me something tomorrow, although the guy in the pick-up truck just shook his head when I told him I thought I'd put diesel into the engine."

"I won't go back tomorrow. You've been so kind to me. I don't mind keeping you company. It doesn't really matter when I go back. I'll ring the hotel and cancel the booking."

To be fair he did try and put me off by saying there was no need but I insisted. So for the rest of the day, I unpacked, opened the windows, made the beds up and generally settled back into the cottage, not knowing exactly how long it would be before I'd return to Lockford.

The following day, I awoke to the sound of a crash and Ronald crying out. He was sitting at the bottom of the stairs holding his foot and wincing in pain.

"What happened?"

"I slipped on the stairs. Don't worry, I'll be fine." His face contorted in pain.

"Let me see," I said, removing his slipper, which had obviously been the cause of his fall. He was wearing a pair he'd taken out of the wardrobe not bothering to unpack his overnight case yesterday.

I gently prodded his ankle and he winced. "Try to stand up," I suggested.

What happened to Piper Archer?.........K.J.Rabane

He held on to my shoulder and attempted to put some weight on his ankle. But it was no use.

"Sprained?" he queried.

"At the very least I should say."

"Right. I'll ring for a taxi to take me to the nearest hospital. Then you must arrange your train ticket. Don't worry about me. I'll get patched up and stay on here until I can get around more easily."

"Nonsense. I won't hear of such a thing. I'll stay and help until you get better."

He shook his head but could see I wouldn't be moved. "Then I must insist you don't think of coming to the hospital. I could be hanging about for hours before I'm seen."

I started to protest but he was adamant. When the taxi arrived, I helped him into the back seat then watched it drive away. Afterwards, I went for a short walk into the village and bought a few items of fresh food to stock up the fridge, as I wasn't sure how long we'd be unable to shop at the supermarket.

Ronald was gone for hours, as he'd anticipated. He returned before teatime and limped out of the taxi. The hospital had provided him with a pair of metal crutches and his foot was encased in a surgical moon boot. I helped him into the cottage.

"A sprain and possible hairline fracture," he explained. "They said to keep off it as much as possible."

"I see. Well start as you mean to go on. Sit here, everything you need in on the side table, your book, the TV remote and I'll pop the kettle on and make us some tea," I said, trying to hide my disappointment with a smile.

"I'm so dreadfully sorry, Piper."

"Nonsense. It's just a setback that's all. Perhaps I can use the extra time to think more clearly about what I'm going to do when I get back to Lockford."

"I'm afraid this might take a while to heal."

"It doesn't matter. Forget it. Think of it as a well-earned rest. You said Nancy was looking forward to being in charge of things, so forget work and try and look on this as that extra holiday."

It was a pep talk. I think we both recognised it as such. I had an early night, after seeing that Ronald was comfortable on the bed-settee in the living room. Fortunately there was a washroom on the ground floor. Apparently it had been installed before the upstairs bathroom had been built. It was little more than a toilet and sink, but adequate under the circumstances.

I undressed and slipped into bed feeling more weary than I thought possible. I wanted to be away from here. I'd made up my mind about picking up the threads of my life and was desperate to begin. But how could I leave Ronald to fend for himself after his kindness to me when I needed someone? All I could hope was that he'd make a speedy recovery and my return to Lockford could proceed as planned.

The cottage, although picturesque, was becoming more and more isolated without a car and with Ronald being unable to walk far. With my only means of transport being the old bicycle, we were effectively cut off from the outside world. In addition to which the weather was turning colder with each day that passed.

Chapter 58

Days turned into weeks. Gradually Ronald's ankle improved but the news from the garage wasn't good. The engine was damaged and in their considered opinion - beyond repair.

"The car's old," Ronald explained. "It's not worth paying for it to be repaired."

"In that case, perhaps I could hire a car to take us back to Lockford. At least now there's not much point in hanging about here, now you know the car is useless. I don't mind doing the driving."

Ronald didn't exactly jump at the idea. I began to wonder if he were enjoying the solitude a little too much. Perhaps he didn't want to go back just yet. Finally he replied, "Good idea."

"But?"

He bit his lip. "Er, I think there's something you need to know. I rang Serena."

"And?"

"And she told me Beresford is in a bad state, mentally. I told her you were thinking of coming back to sort things out and she said she didn't think it was a good idea – not at the moment. She's afraid seeing you will have a detrimental effect. He's bound to think you're coming back to him and she thinks it would just upset him further."

"I see." I didn't of course. I didn't understand any of it. I couldn't just stay here forever. And why had Beresford suddenly had some sort of breakdown? Over two years had passed. We were divorced weeks ago, Ronald told me. OK I must have unnerved him when I turned up at the house a while back but time had moved on again and he must know it was over between us.

What happened to Piper Archer?.........K.J.Rabane

"Maybe it would be better to stay here just until he gets better? You know you can stay as long as you like – there's no hurry." Ronald suggested.

I didn't reply. My thoughts were racing. London. I'd ring Grace. I was sure she'd help. But I didn't tell Ronald just then. I didn't want to upset him, after he'd done nothing but care for my welfare all these months. So I kept quiet.

Two days later I rang Grace. Ronald was sitting in the garden and I was upstairs.

"Hello Grace, it's me - Piper. I wonder, would it be possible for me to come and stay at your place for a day or two?"

"Piper? Are you OK? I haven't heard from you in ages. Last I heard you'd run away from your husband with some guy."

"Don't believe all you hear Grace. Is it OK for me to stay?"

"Of course, come anytime."

I thanked her and was putting the phone down when I heard Ronald on the stairs. I wondered how much of my conversation he'd overheard. I waited until I heard the bathroom door close then went downstairs.

Later, I broached the subject as his walking had improved and I couldn't see any reason why he couldn't return to Lockford, if he wished. "Ronald, I can't thank you enough for the support you've given me but I can't hide away any more. I've decided to go up to London to stay with a friend."

I was shocked by his reaction. "No, that's not such a good idea, Piper, not at all."

"Why ever not?"

What happened to Piper Archer?.........K.J.Rabane

"There's bound to be a fuss. You turning up in London, someone's bound to put two and two together and it would get back to Beresford."

I shook my head. "Forgive me but I don't think it matters anymore. Beresford has moved on with his life and I'm going to do the same."

"What about your sister?"

"I'll ring her – explain it all."

"It won't be easy you know."

"I know. But you mustn't worry about me any more. I'll leave first thing in the morning. Now, if you don't mind, I have some packing to do." I smiled at him as I left the room, hoping to soften the blow.

Taking control of my life once more was liberating, I sang my heart out in the shower, dressed for bed and placed my small suitcase near the window. As I started to draw the curtains I saw the glow from a mobile phone in the garden and realised Ronald was talking to someone. Through the open window I heard the odd word floating up to me. *I know what you said but I can't help it. It's too late for that.* Fragments of conversation are always frustrating as the eavesdropper tries to fill in the gaps. I had no idea who Ronald was talking to, although I suspected it was work related but I didn't mistake the urgency of his tone and it somehow made the hairs on the back of my neck prick up with unease.

What happened to Piper Archer?.........K.J.Rabane

Chapter 59

I kissed his cheek and said goodbye. He seemed resigned to the fact that I was leaving and told me to take care and once again said if I needed help at any time to ring him.

Sitting on the train leading to another life, I decided the time had come to ring Serena. I opened my handbag and searched for my phone. It wasn't there. I knew I'd put it in my bag this morning. I remembered seeing it on the dresser in the kitchen and slipping it inside before I left the house. Ronald had handed me my bag as I'd stepped into the taxi, before he'd put my case in the boot.

My heart began to race. It was a ridiculous reaction to being without my phone, my mother once said that when she was young there were no such things as mobile phones and in an emergency one had to find a phone box. But in today's world things had changed and losing my phone felt like a lifeline drifting away on the tide and I had to take a few deep breaths to stop from panicking.

When the train arrived in the station where I was due to catch my London connection, I stood on the platform and glanced up at the train arrivals on the digital display.

"Oh good, I've caught you." I looked down from the board to see Ronald standing in front of me, holding my mobile. "Thought you might need this," he said.

"I do, thanks, it's so kind of you. Surely you didn't get a taxi?"

"No. I hired a car. My ankle's holding up fine."

"I'm glad. So you're on your way back to Lockford?"

"I am. Look, it's not that much further for me to drive you to your friend's place in London. It seems to be more sensible than buying a train ticket. They're so expensive."

What happened to Piper Archer?.........K.J.Rabane

I hesitated.

"Of course, if you'd rather not." He looked downcast. "To be honest I could do with the company. It's such a boring drive."

He'd been so kind and it was such a little thing to ask. "Thank you, Ronald. I'm grateful but please just drop me on the outskirts and I can take a tube to Grace's flat."

"We'll see," he replied with a smile, as he held out his hand for my case.

The rain started ten minutes after Ronald drove away from the station. I watched it trickle down the side windows then saw the rivulets disperse from the windscreen as the wipers did their work.

"It will be a while before we reach the motorway. Take a look in the back. There's a Thermos of coffee behind my seat. Can you reach it? You might like a drink before we reach the services."

"Thanks. What about you?"

"I'm OK. Best to keep driving for a while."

The coffee was bitter but hot and for that I was grateful, not having drunk anything since breakfast. The rain continued, the wipers swished the water away, the heater began to work, and my eyelids closed.

What happened to Piper Archer?………K.J.Rabane

Beresford

Chapter 60

I put down the phone and pick up my mug of coffee. Upstairs in the shower room I can hear Isobel singing. She has an awful voice but it doesn't stop her trying and in spite of Serena's phone call it brings on a smile.

I suppose I should be upset by the news. However, I've moved on at last. Piper, having spent the past two years with a man who sounds like a bowling green doesn't surprise me. I no longer feel the tug in my chest the heartache, for which there is no cardio-logical explanation. I've agreed with Serena, there is no reason why she should continue to employ Richard Stevens. The facts speak for themselves.

The kitchen door opens and Isobel appears, wet hair curling around her cheeks, wrapped in a white bathrobe.

"Coffee?"

She kisses my mouth and I smell her shampoo. "You read my mind," she says, "Ever thought of transferring to the psychology department?"

I can't take my eyes from her and I realise how much Isobel has come to mean to me. She has supported me when I was at my lowest ebb, never leaving me to my own devices, never asking for something I couldn't give.

"Will you move in, permanently?" I can hear the words and apparently I've said them out loud for she looks up at me over the rim of her coffee cup.

"Beresford? Did you just ask me to move in or am I dreaming?" She was smiling and my heart skipped a beat.

What happened to Piper Archer?.........K.J.Rabane

Darling Isobel, I don't know when I started loving you but it's happened. This time the words stay locked inside and I just nod. She waits for more. "Only if you want to." I give her the option of a refusal without messy explanations. "It's just, I suppose I've got to like having you around." I'm aware it sounds less than an attractive proposition and look down at my hands praying the answer will be yes.

What happened to Piper Archer?.........K.J.Rabane

Piper

Chapter 61

My head hurt. Where was I?

"Ronald?" I croaked.

There was no answer. I began to piece together the events of the day, starting with the loss of my mobile phone and Ronald suddenly arriving at the station. The journey in the car, the rain, the coffee – then it hit me. The coffee – it must have been drugged. But why? It was a question for which I had no credible answer along with where he'd been taking me. All I knew, without any doubt - it wasn't to London.

It was so dark. I put out my hand. I was lying on a sort of camp bed in a room that smelled of something I couldn't identify. I tried not to panic, to keep my breathing at a steady rate.

Then I heard the sound of footsteps outside and a key being turned in a lock. I could just make out the shape of someone tall and thin but I couldn't tell whether it was a man or a woman. A flashlight was turned on and its beam pointed straight at me so that I was blinded, seeing only black shapes. I blinked. "Ronald," I called out but the word came out of my mouth like a whisper. There was no answer.

I could see nothing but I recognised a smell, was it perfume, soap, hairspray, or cologne? I wasn't sure but it lingered in the back of my mind, torturing me to remember.

The place also smelled of disinfectant or bleach like a hospital, but I knew it couldn't be. A tray was placed in my hand the flashlight's beam still playing on my face.

What happened to Piper Archer?.........K.J.Rabane

Then the figure walked away, closed the door and I was left alone once more.

As my eyesight gradually returned to normal I saw a sandwich, an apple and a plastic mug of water on the tray. I put it to one side on a small table, not feeling the need to eat, only the desire to escape from my prison. The room, neither particularly small nor large, housed a camp bed, a chair, side-table and a wardrobe. In one corner was a door, which I discovered led to a toilet and wash hand basin. It smelled of bleach; where on earth was I? It felt like a room, which hadn't been used for sometime. A room in a basement – a room at the top of the house? I had no idea which. In a haze of confusion, I seemed to remember someone forcing me to walk down some stairs and being made to lie on the bed. So the room must be in a basement? Now I was alone I had no doubt that the door was locked. None of this made any sense. Why was I here? Was it to demand money from my family – from Beresford – from Serena? I couldn't in my wildest dreams imagine Ronald blackmailing anyone; he had been so kind and supportive. Surely I couldn't be so wrong about someone? I decided I could. Beresford had been my rock and my saviour and I had made the biggest mistake of my life in marrying him.

I took a deep breath and once more thought there was something familiar about my prison; then it struck me, it was perfume. It was only faint but I knew I'd smelled it somewhere before. However, in spite of my certainty, where was a mystery.

I lay back on the bed and as the darkness of night filled the room, exhausted by my ordeal and still suffering from the effects of the drugged coffee, I somehow managed to sleep.

What happened to Piper Archer?.........K.J.Rabane

Something woke me, a sound, a scraping, I wasn't sure what exactly. All I knew was the light from the window indicated it was morning. I looked around, as hunger pains griped my stomach.

"Hello, someone, help?" I cried out repeatedly.

A short while later I heard a key turning in the lock and the door opened. Someone wearing a navy padded jacket with the hood pulled down, a scarf covering the lower half of the face and wearing sun glasses was standing in the doorway carrying a tray. I wanted to laugh, the figure looked so ridiculous. It looked like someone in fancy dress.

The figure came towards me and handed me a tray, containing a dish of cereal, some fruit and a mug of hot coffee.

"Why are you doing this?" I asked

No answer. Last night's tray was removed from the side table without a word being spoken.

I smelled the perfume I thought I'd recognised last night. It was coming from the padded jacket, I was sure of it. Forcing my memory to produce the face belonging to the fragrance, I inhaled and waited for my brain to do the rest.

Locked in my room again, I waited to make sense of the noises coming from outside. Birds were singing, so it was early morning. I could hear the sound of heels on a pavement, the distant hum of traffic, the ping of a bicycle bell and, nearer still, the slam of a door closing.

I struggled to get to my feet but the muscles in my legs were cramping and I fell into a heap on the floor. The window was too high up and too dirty for me to see clearly into the street, all I could make out were shapes floating by like spectres, indistinct and transitory.

What happened to Piper Archer?.........K.J.Rabane

In the gloom I ate the cereal and the fruit. The coffee was hot and it tasted bitter reminding me of Ronald and his Thermos of drugged coffee. Was he keeping me a prisoner – had he an accomplice?

Gradually, I familiarised myself with my prison, used the washroom and looked around. But, as far as I could make out, there was nothing I could use which would aid my escape.

The sound of a car's horn being angrily pressed repeatedly, followed by raised voices, made me look up to the window. By now I'd decided I was alone in the house and it was pointless calling out, I knew I wouldn't be heard. Sunlight streaked through the grime-covered window and it suddenly occurred to me that if only I could break the glass, I'd have at least a fighting chance of being heard if I shouted loudly enough.

What happened to Piper Archer?.........K.J.Rabane

Ronald

Chapter 62

I couldn't help thinking what I was doing was wrong. The sedative in the coffee was easy enough. I just wanted her to sleep. I didn't feel too bad about it. She was relaxed; in sleep she looked even more beautiful. It was a dreadful day; the rain was making driving more and more difficult. I drove to the services and left her in the car asleep whilst I used the washroom.

When I returned I could see she was gone. I waited, thinking perhaps she'd woken up and was using the washroom. But as the minutes ticked by and she didn't emerge I realised I was alone. She'd left me. But where could she be? She'd been asleep, it was only a mild sedative. If she'd woken up she'd have soon discovered she was at a motorway services and surely would have waited for me to return. She couldn't have walked anywhere. What if she'd been taken, abducted, my thoughts ran riot as my fear increased.

The rain continued until I reached the outskirts of Lockford. I parked in the courtyard at the back of my flat and entered by the rear door. Nancy had been in. I could tell by the faint smell of Lily of the Valley. It was the same perfume as my mother always wore.

The food cupboards were well stocked and in the fridge I found two bottles of lager and a cottage pie. I smiled, Nancy again. Removing a bottle I opened it and took a long drink. I was parched, not daring to stop any longer at the services, as I wanted to be home as quickly as possible and there was no way I could drink from the Thermos.

It was dark outside and a cold wind was whistling around the courtyard, whipping up leaves into a mass of swirling dervishes. I wondered if she was OK. I wondered what she was thinking of me. I hoped she didn't blame me for what I'd done. I hoped she'd realise it was only for her own good.

Nancy rang as I was putting the pie in the oven.

"Everything OK?" she asked.

"Yes thanks. I found the pie. You really shouldn't have bothered."

"No problem, but you know that's not what I meant."

"Yes, everything's OK," I replied, wondering if it was. I couldn't explain to Nancy, not yet.

Would anybody know how much I ached for her? When she sat at my side in the cottage garden and we watched the sun go down together, could she have imagined in her wildest dreams how much I longed to run my fingers through her hair, to stroke her soft skin, to lie at her side and watch morning come?

Never once did I make the mistake of showing my feelings. As far as she was concerned I was a good friend, nothing more. I knew if I couldn't have what I ached for, I'd have to settle for being her friend or risk losing her altogether.

There had been a time, as the first year turned into another and she was still living in the cottage that I believed she might begin to think differently. There were times. After Christmas, when the snow lay in the fields like a duvet, plump and soft, or when the first hot day of summer arrived and she wore shorts and a sun top, or when she'd drunk too much wine and the cottage was filled with her laughter. There were times I dared to think she might have feelings for me.

It never happened and I never pressed it. So we were still friends but she had gone. Would she ever forgive me? The wind whistling around the courtyard had no answers to the questions swirling in my mind and I could only wait and hope.

What happened to Piper Archer?.........K.J.Rabane

Chapter 63

I was trying to forget what happened on the day I drove Piper away from the station. She would never believe that I didn't plan it. It was a spur of the moment thing. I'd like to have had the chance to explain to her. It just got out of hand.

You'd have to have known how it was before to understand. I suppose I was trying to find an excuse but deep down I knew there was none. But how could I have made things right without someone I love getting hurt?

I couldn't go back to work in the shop just then. It wasn't safe – apparently someone had called asking to see me. It was such a mess. I didn't know why I was in this position. Why I had to hide. There had to be something I could do. Nancy was covering for me in the shop, which was an enormous help.

If I hadn't told Piper about her husband then none of this would have happened. If only I could turn back the clock. I'd do things differently. Worrying about her was making me sick.

Mixed emotions churned around in my head. I had no idea where she was. I felt responsible. If I hadn't started it all with a lie none of this would ever have happened. Nancy's been like a mother hen fussing around me. She knew how I felt about Piper. But there's nothing anyone can do now. Even if Richard Stevens found her, she'd never forgive me. I'd never forgive myself. Beside Archer would crucify me if any of this got out.

I tried to find her, to re-trace my steps but it was impossible. I couldn't go to the police. They'd charge me with abduction and God knows what else. What if she was never found? What if she was dead?

What happened to Piper Archer?.........K.J.Rabane

I tried to act normally. After a day or two I tried to go to work as if nothing happened. I didn't talk to Nancy on the phone in the shop anymore. I must admit I was shocked when that woman appeared from behind the new display. I thought I was alone. If she'd heard my conversation, which was more than likely, would she put two and two together? It was two years since Piper Archer was in the news. Some of the papers carried the story for a month or two after she disappeared then other news intervened. I realised I was probably over reacting. I doubt very much if she was even listening. She'd smiled at me and bought a leather bound book of poetry, a collection of *The Romantics*, if I remember rightly. Surely she would have said something or at least given me some sort of an indication that she'd heard my conversation but she'd just smiled, commented on the beautiful binding, and left the shop with her purchase. Funny thing was I thought I'd seen her before – not in the shop – somewhere else - but I couldn't for the life of me remember where.

Waking up in my flat the next morning, I decided I had no alternative but to talk to Richard Stevens. It wasn't as if he was in the police and if I explained it all to him maybe he'd understand. I could always deny I'd said anything, if he decided to report our conversation to the police – it would be his word against mine.

Nancy phoned before I had a chance to get showered. She said it was important that I come into work after lunch. Someone, a Private Investigator, wanted to talk to me. It was obviously something to do with the visit I had from Richard Stevens's PA, asking about Piper, a while back. I couldn't face going into work but Nancy insisted, saying they were handing over their files to the police,

What happened to Piper Archer?.........K.J.Rabane

unless I agreed to speak to them. "You have to speak to them, Ronald," she'd said. " You can make something up to get them off your back. Otherwise you could be in deep trouble. Remember you can't tell them the truth."

They obviously weren't going to leave me alone. Perhaps the time had come to explain. Nancy wouldn't like it but what more could I do? It was eating away at me like a fungus, spreading its spores into every part of me and I didn't know how to stop it.

When I rang Nancy, a while later, I told her of my decision.

"They won't believe you. You'll be in big trouble. They'll think you've done away with her. You know they will, especially after the lies and keeping her in Cornwall all this time."

She had a point and I could feel my heart pounding in my throat at the thought. But I had to explain to someone and Richard Stevens would be waiting for answers.

I agreed to meet them after lunch. Nancy wouldn't like it. I would tell them everything. But I couldn't go on. It was driving me mad. I had to know what had happened to Piper. I was desperately afraid some harm might have come to her.

What if, by chance, her husband had driven into the services whilst I was shopping? What if he was so mad, at having seen her with me he'd waited until I'd left the car and then taken her? What if he was so angry at the fact she'd left him in the first place, that he'd been driven mad with worry over what could have happened to her and he just lost it – attacked her – killed her?

My palms were hot and sticky as the scenarios piled up like fallen leaves rotting into the ground. There was no way out for me, I just had to tell them the truth.

What happened to Piper Archer?.........K.J.Rabane

I couldn't eat lunch. Nancy had left sandwiches in the fridge. She was concerned that I was losing too much weight. I left them untouched. Waiting was the worst part, watching the lunch hour tick away minute by minute. When only five were left, I went into the bathroom, washed my face and hands in cold water, ran a comb through my hair, which I noticed had grown so long it was curling up on my collar then walked the short distance to work, opened the door into the shop and went to face the music.

They were on time. I couldn't stop my hands from shaking as I opened the door and showed them into the back room. Richard Stevens came to the point as soon as we'd sat down.

"I believe you've not been straight with us, Mr Wengren, regarding the whereabouts of Mrs Piper Archer."

There was no softly, softly, approach this time. I could feel the heat rising up to my cheeks and ran a finger around my collar, which had suddenly become chokingly tight. I saw his PA exchange a glance with her boss.

"What do you want to know?" I asked, my voice shaking.

"After the time you and Mrs Archer spent together during your jury service, you said you met her just the once when she called into your shop. But that's not true is it?"

"No".

"Mrs Archer had made computerised diary entries suggesting she was regularly meeting someone called Rowland Green. Miss Smith was soon able to deduce that Rowland Green and Ronald Wengren were one in the same."

My cheeks were burning.

"You agree?"

I nodded.

"So you met on several occasions after the trial?"

Again I nodded.

"And?"

All the fight went out of me. It was a relief in some ways as I explained how we'd become friendly and she'd told me about her marriage problems. I didn't let on that I'd told her about her husband being the cause of her infertility. Some things are better left unsaid, I always think.

"And since then Mrs Archer has been living in your cottage in Cornwall?"

"She wanted to get away, to hide from all the publicity regarding her disappearance; she needed to think about things."

"Why didn't she let her sister know where she was?"

"I don't know. I didn't ask."

"And you didn't think to contact either Mrs Platt or Mr Archer, who were both extremely concerned about her safety?" Richard Stevens was leaning forward in his seat. I thought it a bit intimidating.

"I respected her wishes."

"I'd like you to go over again what happened on the day Mrs Archer decided to go to London to visit a friend and to leave the anonymity of your cottage."

I shivered even though the heating was pumping out hot air. "She was asleep in the front seat of my car when I stopped at a service station and went in to buy something to eat and when I returned she'd disappeared. There was no sign of her."

What happened to Piper Archer?.........K.J.Rabane

"And that's the last you saw of her? No further contact, is that right?"

I nodded.

"What about her handbag, her suitcase, did she take them with her?" Miss Smith, who had been silent throughout Stevens's questioning, looked up from her IPad.

"Her handbag was missing but her case is here. I didn't know what to do with it so I decided to keep it if perhaps she rang and wanted it back. I thought she might call in the shop as she has never visited my flat."

"Can we have a look at the contents?" she asked.

"Certainly. I'll fetch it. It's only a small case."

I watched as the two of them inspected Piper's belongings, opening the wash bag, lifting up the clothes, searching every corner of the case.

"And that's it, after all this time?" Miss Smith asked.

"There are some clothes still left at the cottage but nothing she wanted. She said she'd buy new, once she got to London."

"You do realise that the police are going to find your explanation a little odd, to say the least," Stevens said.

"It's the truth. I promise you."

"They are going to wonder if you had an argument and maybe it got physical. Perhaps you were angry she was leaving you, perhaps it was an accident, perhaps you didn't mean to kill her."

My heart was racing again. I felt as thought I was going to faint. "Kill her? I couldn't...I didn't...I wouldn't do such a thing," I stammered.

"Is that because you were in love with her?" The PA asked, softly.

I hesitated, thought of lying, but the fight went out of me and it was as though a great weight had been lifted from my shoulders. But the words wouldn't come so I hung my head and muttered. "She can't be dead."

"And why are you so sure about that?" Richard Stevens bent forward so his face was close to mine.

"She can't be. I would know," I said with conviction.

What happened to Piper Archer?.........K.J.Rabane

Chapter 64

Afterwards, I decided I had to talk to Nancy. She always took Thursday afternoons off as she'd joined a creative writing class. I usually closed the shop to stocktake and catalogue the contents. Looking around the empty shop I sighed, some of my burden had been lifted but the rest still remained. At least Richard Stevens knew the truth; it was up to him what he did with it, I knew I'd done the right thing this time.

Nancy had been like a mother to me for years. She deserved to know what I'd told them. So later, I drove to Westbourne Avenue but as usual the road was crammed full of cars. It was always hopeless to park in the evenings. The properties had garages but people never seemed to use them. Eventually I managed to back into a space further down the Avenue and walked back to Nancy's place.

Most of the houses I passed were in reasonably good condition but they were large properties and cost a fortune to renovate. An estate agent's representative was busy taking photographs of one of the houses, no doubt trying to get the best out of his shot. The upper floors looked in need of a coat of paint and the basement looked disused, the window coated in a thick layer of grime. A woman was getting out of her car at the kerb. The memory I'd been struggling with suddenly fell into place. This was where I'd seen her before, the woman in the shop, the one who might have overheard my conversation with Nancy. I remembered seeing her when I was visiting Nancy on more than one occasion. She was very striking looking. Tall, broad shouldered, with curly black hair, attractive but a bit intimidating I thought.

What happened to Piper Archer?.........K.J.Rabane

When I opened the gate of number twenty-six, I noticed a slight similarity to the one I'd just passed. The basement looked in a sorry state, weeds grew out of the brickwork and around the grubby window but there the similarity ended for the windows on the upper floors had been replaced with UPVC and the pebble-dashed brickwork had been painted cream.

"Come in, Ronald dear, there's a cold wind today." Nancy said, closing the door behind me. I followed her down the passageway into the living room at the back of the house. "How is Maddie doing?" she asked.

"She's OK. Eager not to make any more mistakes so you needn't worry, sit back and enjoy yourself; take a few days off, we're not busy.

Nancy frowned. "I feel I should come in, what with all this trouble landing on your doorstep. I don't need to take time off. It's not as if I'm going anywhere. I would only be cleaning this place from top to bottom nothing that couldn't wait."

I smelled furniture polish and smiled. There was a faint smell of bleach drifting in from the kitchen and I knew Nancy was as meticulous about housework as she was about making sure the shop ran smoothly.

"Let me just put the kettle on and we'll have a cuppa and a chat."

I followed her into the kitchen and she handed me a cake tin, "Help yourself, dear."

The cakes were the ones I remembered my mother baking from my childhood and Nancy, knowing my fondness for them, had continued with the tradition. I suspected it was just in case I popped in. On the draining board was a bottle of gin, half empty and a plastic bottle of bleach. She saw my eyes resting on it and tapped her stomach. "Helps my indigestion," she said.

What happened to Piper Archer?.........K.J.Rabane

"The gin or the bleach?"

She chuckled. "Get away with you. Come on, let's make ourselves comfortable in the front room and you can tell me what's bothering you."

The front room was in immaculate condition as usual, the furniture polished to a high shine, the piano in the corner devoid of dust and the mirror above the fireplace unsullied by fingerprints.

When we were seated and had finished our first cup of tea I told her about my conversation with Richard Stevens. After I'd finished, she put her cup and saucer down on the table, the cup rattling against the china saucer, and sighed. "Oh, I do wish you hadn't told them."

A sound from beneath my feet made me gasp. "What on earth was that?"

Nancy bit her lip. "Nothing, dear," she said, "Just these old central-heating pipes. I'll have to get them fixed one of these days. Another cup?"

My eyelids felt heavy. I hadn't slept properly for days. I suppose the warm room, the hot drink, and Nancy's gentle voice nudged me towards sleep. The last thing I remember her saying was, "That's it my dear boy. Off you go, it will do you good to have a nice, long, sleep."

Beresford

Chapter 65

It seems an age before she answers my question about moving into Elm Tree house. I've been looking down at my hands wondering what more I can say.

"I want to, of course I want to; it's all I've ever wanted. You must know I've been in love with you for some time. But if you don't feel the same way and this is a convenience thing then I'd rather not," she says in a rush.

Her eyes are sparkling with unshed tears and I feel the return of a sensation I thought I'd lost the day Piper disappeared. I stand up and go to her side, take her hand in mine and kiss her fingertips. "Love is something I never thought I'd feel again but I do love you, Isobel."

She smiles up at me. "Then I'll move in as soon as I'm dressed."

I pull her to her feet and feel her soft body fold into mine as we kiss. I couldn't be happier and tell her so. I want her to understand I'm serious and, in the only way I know how, say, "Will you marry me?" The words are out before the idea has had time to form properly. It's too late to take them back and besides I'm not sure I want to. My divorce from Piper came through weeks ago. Over two years have passed and I think taking the decision to sever the ties was a step in the right direction. I know Serena didn't agree but it had to be done.

She takes a step back.

"I understand you must think it's all a bit hasty but I've spent too much time doing the right thing and I'm old enough to know my own mind, so I can't see the point in waiting," I say, aware that I'm unused to expressing my emotions and hope my proposal doesn't sound too clinical.

"My darling man, of course I'll marry you and as soon as you like."

We are in each other's arms again and it seems the most natural thing in the world to go back to bed, to seal our love in the best way possible before moving some of her possessions into Elm Tree House.

Isobel hesitates when I suggest she arrange for an estate agent to give a valuation on her house and says she will, but not at the moment. She has to make up her mind about which pieces of furniture she wants to keep and which she wants to leave for the house clearance firm to give her a valuation.

"I'm so happy, Beresford. I can't wait to be your wife. I'll move some of my clothes in tomorrow but tonight I have to see to things at my place," she says as we shut the front door.

There's a lot to be done but I've insisted on buying her a ring. It's my way of showing her I'm serious about our relationship.

As we step outside, a cold wind blows down the drive. I click the remote to open the garage doors and Isobel reaches into her handbag and removes a headscarf. Ice forms around my heart as I look at her. The headscarf – it's Piper's I'm sure of it.

What happened to Piper Archer?………K.J.Rabane

Piper

Chapter 66

I counted up the nights and when I reached ten decided I had to try again. Each day my futile attempts to escape frustrated me beyond measure and I'd given up trying. The person in the padded jacket had worn dark glasses, the disguise was complete and I still had no idea whether it was a man or a woman. The voice was deep but there was no conversation on which to pin my assessment, except for the jacket, which looked like something a woman would wear. My food was regularly left near the door and there was a small part of my brain telling me I'd met this person somewhere before but as I was usually blinded by torch light I couldn't be sure.

A pattern had started to evolve. There were times when I was certain I was totally alone in the house at night. The periods when I was sure this was the case were increasing.

There was a strong wind blowing outside. I could hear it howling around the building, rattling the windowpanes. If I had to be thankful for small mercies it was because central heating pipes running along the ceiling warmed the basement room but it was small comfort. If only I could reach the window I could break the glass and call out, but I'd discovered on a daily basis that it was impossible. I'd been eating mostly liquid food for over a week, thin soups, stale bread and water in a plastic bottle, weak tea and breakfast cereal. My strength and determination were faltering when daylight seeped from the sky and the sounds of the night drifted into silence.

What happened to Piper Archer?.........K.J.Rabane

I couldn't sleep. My mind kept searching for answers, not only as to why I was being imprisoned but how I could escape. Then I heard the sound of footsteps outside the door. I knew it was dark outside but had no idea of the time.

"Help, " I called out. "Someone, please.

The door opened and in the darkness I could see the outline of my captor dressed as before in a thick padded jacket with a hood, a bit like a ski coat with a flap, which covered the bottom half of the face. This time I was sure it was a man. There was no blinding torchlight but still it was difficult to make out much more, as the hood hid most of his face and the dark glasses did the rest.

He didn't speak but came towards. I was terrified and backed away, pressing my body into the wall in fear, as a sliver of moonlight sliced through the grubby fanlight window.

There was nothing I could do but wait. He stood in front of me bent forward and from his pocket removed a handkerchief. I could smell a sweet, sickly stench as he came towards me and held it over my mouth. I knew I struggled but as the darkness descended I went to meet it.

The first thing I became aware of, when consciousness returned, was that I was sitting on a bench and a cold wind was blowing through the trees on Lockford Common.

No longer in possession of my handbag or mobile phone I tried to stand but staggered and fell back on the bench until the muscles in my legs stopped cramping. Eventually, I started to walk along the road in the direction of town, hoping that someone would stop to help me.

What happened to Piper Archer?.........K.J.Rabane

I'd been walking for some time when the first fingers of dawn lit the sky and I saw a car approaching. Part of me was terrified that this was a dream and I was still imprisoned in the basement room but as the car drew to a halt a man with a bald head wound down the window, smiled and said, "Need a lift, love?"

Hoping this lived-in face was the face of my saviour, I said, "Cccould you drive me to Lockford Police Station, please?"

What happened to Piper Archer?.........K.J.Rabane

Chapter 67

The wind had brought down the remaining leaves on the trees lining the High Street. Richie closed the office window but continued looking out. He saw early morning shoppers waiting outside Kents department store, unaware that it was staff training day and the store didn't open until ten o'clock. In the distance he heard the scream of a train whistle as the London bound commuter train swept out of Lockford General and saw Sandy peddling furiously down the High Street, her fair hair streaming behind her like a golden wave.

He was smiling when she opened the office door. "What?" she asked, pulling dried leaves from her hair?

"Nothing," he replied, clearing his throat and adding, "Today we find out what's happened to Piper Archer."

"As easy as that?"

"No harm in being optimistic is there? Anyway, someone isn't telling the truth and between us we are going to find out who that person is."

"Still being optimistic then?"

"Pragmatic, Miss Smith."

"Right, Boss, who are we going to visit first?"

"Nancy Smedley."

Sandy bit her bottom lip. "She's suspect number one?"

"I wouldn't go as far as to say that but I have a strong suspicion she hasn't been straight with us and whatever it is she's hiding, I'm certain it concerns Ronald Wengren."

"Does she know we're coming?" Sandy pulled the last remaining leaf from her hair and threw it in the wastepaper basket.

"No. I thought the element of surprise might work in our favour. Ready?"

"Excellent," Sandy replied, following Richie down the stairs and into the basement car park.

What happened to Piper Archer?.........K.J.Rabane

Serena

Chapter 68

Who'd have thought it – Berry and Izzie? I'm really surprised. I said to Mike I didn't know it had gone this far. I thought she was just helping him out of his depression. He looked up from his paper and gave me one of those frowns – you know the kind – the ones that say – you've changed your tune.

Mike thinks I'm only fond of Berry because he's got money but it's not true. Money helps, of course it does, I suppose Izzie will find that out now. If only Piper hadn't run off. If only he'd found her and brought her back.

I should be glad Berry's moved on. I felt bad about what Piper did, he didn't deserve it, neither did I come to think of it – she could at least have phoned me – she must have known I'd be worried sick. Berry never treated her badly, bought her everything anyone could want. She was so lucky to find him, after what happened. I couldn't bear the thought of Berry not being part of our family anymore. Anyway, that's my excuse for what I did.

When I first met Izzie her Mum had just died and she was in the middle of moving into the family house on Westbourne Avenue. Nice houses but much too large for one person. Izzie said it made sense, she was paying rent on her apartment and it was costing her a fortune. She thought she might do up the old house and rent out the basement and attic rooms. Of course she won't need to do that now. She won't have any money problems once she marries Berry. I expect she'll sell the place on

What happened to Piper Archer?.........K.J.Rabane

Westbourne Avenue. I expect she'll know how to spend the money too.

I'll have to find a nice dress and hat. Apparently the wedding is going to be soon. Well you know how it is, why wait she said, when there's no reason to? Mike thinks it's marry in haste, repent at leisure. I'm inclined to agree. I've seen it happen before. I'm the practical one. I can see trouble before it happens, always been able to. I knew Simon Roach was trouble. Piper would have been in a mess if it weren't for me. It was me she came to in the end, me who sorted it all out. Like I'm trying to do now.

Time to clean up this place before I think about going into town to shop for clothes. Mike leaves the Den in such a mess after him and his mates get together. He says I'm putting on airs and graces, calling it the Den when it's only a poky basement. Come to think of it I can't remember the last time he went down there, so I'll give it a miss. What's a couple of cobwebs? I cleaned it out at the end of the summer and as I said, I don't think he's been down there since. Understandable really, Alan Beaston built a bar-room in their back garden during the summer. It's got everything a man could want, Mike said. I doubt if it's got EVERYTHING but I kept my mouth shut. You have to sometimes, to keep the peace.

Izzie's so excited. I couldn't get her off the phone last night. The wedding will be in Lockford Register Office; she knows the registrar apparently, and she'll sort things out, so they don't have to wait too long. Saturday after next, Izzie said. That's why I have to get into town today. What I'm going to wear is a mystery though, I've put on a few pounds during the summer and nothing looks right. But the reception is going to be in Lockford Hall and it's not the sort of place you can get away with a dress from M&S. It will have to be from Kents, the designer section. I won't show Mike the bill. He's bound to have apoplexy.

Not a day goes by when I don't wonder what's happened to Piper. I wish she'd talk to Berry and try and sort out this mess. I'm sure it's not too late. Well not if I can help it. It's been over two years now and still no word.

I don't want to feel angry. She is still my sister. I don't want to think about how she was always a pain in the neck, even when we were young. Not many men would have put up with doing their courting and having their girlfriend's younger sister always on the scene. Johnny Hickson didn't and I loved him to bits. 'Can't stand having that kid around,' he said, when he left me.

At the time I was devastated. Johnny Hickson was handsome, had a great job, plenty of money and a red sports car but Piper ruined my dream of marrying Johnny and then I met Mike. He wasn't in the same league, of course, but we jogged along together and he was kind – he didn't mind Piper – he was one of six kids and was used to always having a younger brother or sister hanging about.

I suppose it was just as well I met Mike but I do sometimes wonder what it would have been like if I'd married Johnny.

Isobel

Chapter 69

So it's done. Beresford has arranged it all. We are to be married next Saturday. I've spoken to Serena and she and Mike will be our witnesses. We want a quiet affair, just the four of us. Beresford said he is relieved I don't want the whole works. He's afraid of unwanted publicity. I don't blame him. When Piper disappeared newspaper reporters invaded his privacy so it's understandable. And it doesn't bother me as long as I end up being Mrs Archer.

I can't sleep I'm so excited. I'll be glad to get rid of this place too. These last few weeks staying at Elm Tree House has made me realise how much I want to get away from here. This house is a mess - too much money needs to be spent on it - money I haven't got. I should have sold it months ago. But perhaps it's just as well I didn't, under the circumstances.

When the telephone rang, I was in the bedroom sorting out some clothes for the charity shop.

"Izzie, have you bought the dress yet?" It was Serena.

"No." I was cautious; I knew what was coming next, a suggested visit to town where my 'new' sister-in-law would help me choose my wedding dress. "I'm not going to buy anything too fancy, Serena. I might even have something in my wardrobe." I hoped she'd get the message.

"I see," she said. "It's not as though you'll have to watch how much you spend in future though. You do know Berry's loaded? You're sure to find something in

Kents. That's where I'll be looking. Berry would like me to make an effort."

There was no way out. She'd smell a rat if I insisted I couldn't make it. It was a shame. I had other plans for today but I said, "Right, perhaps I'll see you there then?"

"If you like."

So for the rest of today I would be with Serena. She means no harm but I could do without hearing about Mike, Ellie and her fruitless existence when I have so much to think about.

All my worries would be over soon. In the shower I started to sing and imagined Beresford smiling at me and telling me I've got a lovely voice, as usual. When he said this we both knew he was lying. Was I in love? I believed I loved him as much as I could love anyone so why would I worry about passion? He was the answer to a prayer; I'd have been a fool to worry about waiting for 'the one'. From the outset I knew this was what I wanted and the rest had been worth it, especially as, at last, I've got what I wanted.

What happened to Piper Archer?.........K.J.Rabane

Chapter 70

From the outside the house looked well cared for. Richie managed to find a parking space in the road as a red Nissan Micra was pulling away from the kerb when they arrived.

"Jammy devil," Sandy said.

"Let's hope our luck doesn't run out then. The element of surprise is what we are after here, Miss Smith. Let's give Nancy Smedley the impression we are near to solving this case."

"So I need to call upon a few redundant acting skills from my murky past?"

"Precisely. I'm counting on you."

Nancy Smedley was holding a yellow duster and wearing a navy and white striped apron when she opened the door. Her hair was pulled into an untidy bun from which grey Gorgon-like tendrils escaped.

"Might we have a word with you?" Richie asked.

"What now? I'm busy."

"No problem. We won't bother you if you're too busy. It was only a courtesy visit before we gave our information to Lockford Police."

Her face lost its colour. She rammed the duster into her apron pocket. "Come in then, if you must," she said, standing aside.

The front room was comfortable and spotless. Richie and Sandy sat opposite each other on two floral patterned armchairs whilst Nancy stood near the fireplace anxiously biting the skin around one finger. Sandy kept her waiting as she slowly withdrew her IPad and a pair of tortoiseshell framed reading glasses from the depths of her handbag.

What happened to Piper Archer?.........K.J.Rabane

"Ready, Miss Smith?" Richie asked.

Sandy nodded, looking over the rim of her glasses at Nancy and frowning.

Richie again admired the way her persona had changed to suit the situation as she read a transcript of their recent interview with Ronald Wengren. His eyes were fixed upon Nancy Smedley as the women listened and became more and more agitated.

When Sandy finished, he said. "So you see, Mrs Smedley, there is no doubt that the police would be very interested to hear about Mr Wengren's association with Mrs Archer and his part in her disappearance."

"He wouldn't do anything to harm her. Not my Ronald. I've known him since he was a baby. Besides he was mad about her. I told him he was a fool to get involved." She started to pace the room and stopped when she heard a sound from below.

"Central heating pipes," she explained, biting her fingernail.

Sandy looked up. "You have a basement."

Richie narrowed his eyes.

"I do, why?"

"Large houses like this usually do," Sandy said, quietly. "How do you manage to clean it all?"

"I don't bother with the basement – it's all shut up."

"Really? I thought I saw a light on the other evening when I was visiting a friend further down the road."

Richie looked on admiringly.

"Ah, well, yes. It's shut up – now, but I had to let the central heating people in recently as there was an air lock in the pipes."

"Strange. Why would you shut up the basement when you need access to the central heating boiler?"

What happened to Piper Archer?………K.J.Rabane

Nancy Smedley was rattled, her face glowed with anger but she managed to cover it – just – only her voice betrayed her annoyance. "What I meant was, I don't clean it. When I said it was shut up, I meant I don't use the place so why would I clean it?"

"I see," Sandy replied. "So you wouldn't mind if we take a look?"

"At my basement? Whatever for?"

Richie had to agree and waited for Sandy's reply with anticipation.

"I told you I was visiting a friend the other evening. Well, she has a basement like yours and she's willing to let me rent it from her as I'm looking for a suitable place to live. The problem is she was out when I called so I have no idea how big it is or whether it will suit me. I wondered, as we are here, whether you'd mind if I take a look at yours? If it's no bother."

Not bad for the spur of the moment, Richie thought.

"Well, if you must, although it's in a mess. But tell me first what you have decided to do about Ronald?"

It was a trade off; Richie could see it a mile away. This woman was no fool. "For the moment we will continue with our investigations and let you know," he said, following them through a door in the hallway leading to the basement.

What happened to Piper Archer?………K.J.Rabane

Serena

Chapter 71

Izzie's hyper. Understandably so, she's over the moon about Saturday. I've never seen her looking so radiant. Mike's going to be best man, although we are both really only witnesses but he says he's going to take pride in performing the duties of the best man at Lockford Hall later. Lockford Hall is posh beyond measure, but Berry knows the owner and he has a private room booked – just for us. I wish it wasn't happening. I wish she'd come back. I've done my best to keep Berry thinking about her although I admit, at first, I thought him meeting Izzie was a good thing but I soon realised what it would mean – I wouldn't be his sister-in-law any longer.

Yesterday, Izzie and I went shopping. I offered to pick her up at her place but she said, no, she'd come for me. She was wearing a scarf I thought I'd seen on Piper, before she went missing. I said, "That's nice. Where did you buy it? I think Piper had one the same."

"Oh this old thing? Really? I'm not sure now. In London I think," she said, driving into the car park behind Kents and then she picked up her mobile. "Sorry, Serena. Just have to make a quick call. You go on in. I'll meet you in the coffee shop."

I found a seat and waited and to be honest she kept me waiting for quite a while, I'd drunk two large Cappuccinos before she returned. I wondered if she and Berry were having a long chat. I remember what it used to be like when Mike and I were first 'in love'. I say I remember but it's all a bit of a blur really.

What happened to Piper Archer?.........K.J.Rabane

She was flustered when she eventually sat down. She was carrying two mugs of black coffee and I didn't have the heart to say I'd had enough coffee to float the Titanic. "Sorry, sorry, call took longer than expected. Right, let's finish our drinks and get shopping, shall we?"

As I said, she was hyper – high as a kite on a windy day. I found it difficult to keep up with her. First she wanted to buy underwear and nightclothes but spent an age in the changing room trying on one set after another. For some reason, as I waited for her to show me what she'd decided upon, I felt a tear roll down my cheek. I remembered how it had been during the week before Piper married Beresford and I desperately wished the past two years had never been.

"What d'you think?" Izzie was standing near the door of the changing room wearing a figure hugging cream dress and a three-quarter cream and black coat of the same material. "I need to buy some shoes with a higher heel but I think it works don't you?"

"It does. You look lovely, Izzie; Berry will be very proud." My smile was a struggle. I did wish her all the best but not necessarily with Berry; I couldn't bear it.

We ate our lunch in the restaurant on the top floor. Through the panoramic windows I could see the Common in the distance and beyond it I knew lay Elm Tree House. Izzie didn't seem at all concerned that she'd be moving into the house Berry had shared with Piper. After we'd clinked our glasses of Pinot Grigio and I'd wished her health and happiness I said, "Will you be content to live in the house, knowing all the furnishings were done by Piper. I don't know if *I* could. I think I'd worry that he'd have all those memories of her floating around the place like ghosts."

She frowned. "Not at all. It's just a house, besides once the dust has settled I'll persuade Beresford to let me employ a firm of interior designers to refurbish the place."

She was so sure of herself. It was something I'd always admired in Izzie but I began to wonder if Berry would be quite so keen to go along with her intended changes especially as it meant wiping away all traces of Piper.

Chapter 72

Nancy Smedley's idea of a mess was what most people would consider to be neat and tidy, Richie thought, casting an eye around the basement. The window was a bit dusty but then it was too high up for her to reach without a stepladder but the camp bed, chair and chest of drawers were dust free as was the rug on the floor, which although a little threadbare was perfectly clean. Through a door beside the chest of drawers there was a washroom and toilet, which smelled of disinfectant and bleach.

"Thank you, Mrs Smedley. At least I now know what to expect," Sandy said. "I'm sorry to have bothered you."

"It's no bother." She followed them up the stairs and turned the key in the lock on the basement door.

They were standing near the front door when Richie said, "I'd advise you to have a word with Mr Wengren. Tell him if he doesn't go to the police and explain his involvement with Mrs Archer then I'll have to pay them a visit."

Nancy Smedley bit the skin on her finger again. Then as if coming to a sudden decision said, "There's something you should know, Mr Stevens. I think perhaps we should all sit down, whilst I explain." She opened the door to the front room and once they were seated she paced the floor. "Ronald is the son of a very dear friend of mine who died a while back. Ever since her death he's become like a son to me. It's as if he was able to cope with his mother's passing by keeping close to me. There's a bond between us."

Richie could see how difficult it was for her to explain the unusual relationship, which existed between them.

What happened to Piper Archer?.........K.J.Rabane

"When he told me how he'd driven Mrs Archer to the cottage I was worried. Her picture was all over the newspapers at the time and I was concerned that someone would discover he'd been involved in her disappearance." She took a deep breath, stopped pacing, and sat down on the edge of the sofa.

"As the months turned into years I was becoming more and more concerned. Although the investigation into her disappearance had stopped months before I couldn't get it out of my head that Ronald would be in trouble, especially as I was beginning to get the impression that Mrs Archer wanted to leave the cottage and he was trying to find all sorts of excuses to keep her there. That was when I decided I had to do something."

Richie ran his fingers through his hair. He wondered what was coming.

"I thought,…" she stopped, hesitated, then continued, "I thought, if I could make Mr Archer think his wife had come back, or at least was in the Lockford area, it would help. At least no one would suspect Ronald of being involved."

"But no one did," Sandy said.

"I know that now. But then, you see I was so worried for him. And worry can lead you to do all sorts of things, Miss Smith."

Sandy nodded.

"I started telephoning Mr Archer and I suppose he was so willing to believe it was his wife I really didn't have to say much, although on one occasion I told him I'd be home soon, something like that."

"How did you get into the house, without a key?"

She hung her head. "I didn't."

"You expect us to believe that?" Sandy asked.

"It's the truth. Telephoning was bad enough, it was all I did, I promise you – I couldn't risk being seen near the house."

"I see." Richie stood up. "Well, I can see why you were reticent to let Mr Wengren go to the police. Both of you could be in deep trouble, especially as Mrs Archer is still missing."

"We had nothing to do with it. Believe me, Ronald is telling the truth. He was distraught when he arrived here. He assured me he'd left her asleep in the car. It was only a light sedative."

Richie heard Sandy's smothered gasp.

"This gets worse. You're now telling me he drugged Mrs Archer?" Richie asked.

She became very agitated, twisting the ties of her apron into a knot. "Not drugged – he wouldn't – he just gave a something to help her sleep on the journey."

Richie could see whatever Ronald Wengren did Nancy Smedley would cover his back and he wondered if he could believe a word either of them said.

"What are you going to do now?" She stopped twisting her apron strings.

Richie sighed. "I suggest you leave it with me, at least for a day or two and I'll get back to you. Tell Mr Wengren to stay put for the moment."

She sighed, as if relieved to have got it all off her chest.

Richie hoped it wasn't misguided relief. He wasn't looking forward to the next few days. First he had to decide how much of this information he should release to the police without putting Piper Archer's life in further danger. He was sure Nancy Smedley's love of her godson would allow her to cover for his actions, whatever he did, but did that include murder?

What happened to Piper Archer?.........K.J.Rabane

He had the strong feeling things were about to get decidedly messy.

What happened to Piper Archer?.........K.J.Rabane

Chapter 73

The call came through from the police station whilst Sandy was busy painting her nails. Richie picked up the phone.

"Detective Inspector Liam Mayes, Lockford Police station; I understand via the grapevine that you've been investigating the disappearance of Mrs Piper Archer."

Richie had heard there was a new inspector on the force. He didn't recognise the name and by his voice he sounded young. "That's right."

"Earlier today we had a visit from a woman who insists she's Piper Archer. She has no identification documents and has some garbled story about being abducted. We have informed her sister, a Mrs Platt, who told us she is your client so I wonder if you could spare the time to come down to the station, Mr Stevens. I'd like to have a word with you regarding your investigation."

"Of course. I'll be there in ten minutes or so," Richie said.

When Sandy heard the reason he'd been summoned to the police station, she blew on her fingertips and looked up expectantly.

"No way," Richie said, with a grin. "Carry on the good work at this end, Miss Smith. I'll let you know all about it when I return."

Her resigned expression spoke volumes as she picked up the nail varnish and applied another coat. Richie was always anxious when work was as sporadic as it was at the moment. It was just the time she might decide to look elsewhere for employment.

What happened to Piper Archer?.........K.J.Rabane

Lockford Police Station was a short walk away at the end of the High Street. Richie turned up the collar of his coat against the bitter wind and walked briskly towards his destination. This latest development was baffling. Piper Archer turning up out of the blue insisting she'd been abducted would surely add weight to Ronald Wengren's story but it was anyone's guess what Inspector Mayes would make of it all.

Reaching the station, Richie hurried up the steps and in through the double doors into the welcoming warmth of the waiting area near the front desk. The desk Sergeant, Bill Turner, recognised Richie and raised an eyebrow. "Boss said to go right in. He's in interview room 3."

"Thanks, Bill. How are the pigeons?"

"Fair to middling, Richie."

Reaching interview room number three Richie smelled disinfectant, a reminder that most of the inmates in the cells this morning were likely to be drunks from the night before. The smell evoked a memory of Nancy Smedley's basement and he wondered if she and Wengren's stories were credible or had they planned the whole thing in order to confuse the issue of who had actually abducted Piper Archer and why. It also occurred to him that with a little ingenuity chloroform could be manufactured from such household ingredients as gin, bleach and disinfectant all of which he'd noticed during their visit to Westbourne Avenue.

His knock on the interview room door was answered by a young WPC and once inside he saw Serena Platt sitting alongside a slight woman with badly cut brown hair, which stuck out in places like the quills of a porcupine, blonde roots showed at intervals giving her a distinctly odd appearance. She was almost unrecognisable as the image in the earlier photographs of Piper Archer. Inspector Liam Mayes was, as Richie had suspected, young. However his fresh face was at odds with his baldhead, which shone in the light from the overhead neon strip-light.

"Take a seat if you would, Mr Stevens," Mayes said, "Now Mrs Archer. If you're ready, then perhaps we can begin. I've asked Mr Stevens to sit in on this interview as he has information which I've no doubt will assist our investigations."

Richie had been wondering why a DI, even one so young, would be so keen to let a Private Investigator sit in on this interview; in general the two didn't always rub alongside together, the former being of the opinion that the latter were usually a pain in the proverbial. But now daylight dawned, as soon as Mayes began to speak he could see Norm's expression as clearly as if his old friend DCI Norman Freeman of the Metropolitan Police force, were sitting in front of him. Mayes must be Norm's sister's boy. He'd forgotten her first husband's name was Mayes. It was beginning to look as if Lockford had suddenly become a haven for the offshoots of the Freeman family, it being within commuter distance of London and Norm no doubt having passed on the news that it was a great place to live.

Richie cleared his throat and waited for the interview to begin.

What happened to Piper Archer?.........K.J.Rabane

Serena

Chapter 74

I'd just put the phone down to Mike, who was visiting an old friend of his in London, when it rang again. When the policeman told me Piper was at the station and could I come down, I thought I was dreaming.

I don't even remember driving into town. They'd asked me not to inform Berry. Not at the moment, they'd said. That was the difficult bit for me, especially as I was feeling guilty about the way I'd acted prior to his forthcoming marriage to Izzie and the part I'd played in trying to stop it.

I was thrilled Piper had turned up, of coarse I was, but I did think Berry needed to know. This was what I'd wanted all along. I didn't want him to forget her. I didn't want him to marry Isobel. I liked having him as a brother-in-law, and whatever Mike said, it wasn't just to impress my friends. He thought I was obsessed with Berry, his job, his friends, the fact he was married to my sister. But it wasn't like that - I thought he was good for Piper, and under the circumstances, she was a lucky girl. None of this was fair, but then when had Piper ever thought of anyone but herself. It was why she was in this mess in the first place. Happy though I was at the thought of seeing her again, I couldn't help but feel aggrieved at her not contacting me and I was determined to let her know at the earliest opportunity.

At the police station I was shown into a room where a woman was sitting alongside a female police officer. At first I didn't recognise her and then all my anger at her behaviour disappeared. Piper looked awful and I couldn't begin to think what could have happened to her since I'd last seen her, which would account for her being in this state.

She began to cry when she saw me. I went towards her and cradled her in my arms like a baby. "It's alright, I'm here, and you're safe. Berry will be so pleased to see you." As I said it I thought of Izzie and the wedding and the words stuck in my throat. What a mess this was.

"Don't call Beresford. I don't want to speak to him. Not now."

I patted her hand reassuringly, "Don't worry, anything you say. I'll take you home, once we can leave here."

She sighed, wiped her eyes with my handkerchief and gave the ghost of a smile. The face I hadn't recognised when I first saw it became Piper's once more.

I held her hand in the interview room and when Richard Stevens arrived I felt at last we might get to the truth.

Chapter 75

DI Mayes stood up. "Thank you, Mrs Archer. I think perhaps it's time Mrs Platt took you home. I'll be in touch when we have more news for you."

Serena Platt nodded to Richie and helped her sister from the room. Both women looked exhausted.

"How's Uncle Norm then, Liam?" Richie asked.

The inspector grinned. "I wondered how long it would take for you to recognise me. The hair, I suppose?"

"Yes, well, that of course and my failing memory. I didn't equate little Liam with Inspector Mayes. Why didn't Norm ring me, tell me you were in Lockford?"

"I asked him not to. I wanted to plant my size tens under the table first. Besides, I knew you'd want to help but I had to fit in under my own steam."

"Inspector eh? Sounds as if you've had no trouble in that direction."

"I'm not as young as you might think, Richie."

"Anyone under forty's young to me, lad."

Liam smiled. "You're not that much older than me, Richie, don't try to kid yourself. Now. I think it's time we asked Ronald Wengren and Nancy Smedley to pay us a visit, don't you?"

"Right I'll leave you to it then. Nice to see you again, Liam."

"You too. I'll be in touch. Let you know how Wengren and Smedley perform."

"If it's any help. I believe them." Richie winked as he left the room.

What happened to Piper Archer?………K.J.Rabane

Sandy was waiting for him and before he could take off his coat she said, "Well? Is that it? She's come back. End of?"

"Coffee first, Miss Smith. I think you are going to need a strong black one. It's a long story."

Afterwards, Sandy sat back in her chair. "So? Do we have any ideas about who abducted her?"

Richie stood up and walked to the window. Looking down on the High Street, he watched the shoppers hurrying by, heads bent against the strengthening wind. "I'm not sure but I think we need to pay Beresford Archer a visit. It will be a bit difficult to bring up the suggestion that he might have been the cause of his wife's infertility though. But we do need answers before we can proceed."

"More unpaid work then?"

With his back to her, Richie closed his eyes, dreading the moment she would say, 'well, thanks but I'm off' or words to that effect. However she phrased it the effect would be just as devastating. "'Fraid so. But you'll get your wages as usual, Miss Smith, never fear."

He hadn't heard her approach. She was standing behind him, looking over his shoulder.

In a soft voice she said, "You know it's never been about the money with me, Boss."

He was afraid to turn around in case she'd see how her words had affected him. She must have sensed his mood though, as she turned away. "It's the pleasure of your company and the luxurious office space that keeps me getting up and making my way here, every morning."

"Glad you've got your priorities right, Miss Smith," he replied, thankful for the chance to mask his emotions. So, give Beresford Archer a ring please and arrange a suitable time when we can call on him."

"Will do."

Sitting at his desk in the inner office, Richie wondered whether Beresford Archer would be able to shed some light on his wife's assertion that she'd been abducted or whether he would dismiss it out of hand. There were so many questions that still required answers, Richie thought. He believed Beresford Archer might be just the tip of the iceberg.

Beresford

Chapter 76

Isobel has explained about the scarf. I ask her where she's bought it. She looks bewildered for a moment, frowns and says, "This? Not sure, let me think. Oh yes. I picked it up at a charity shop event in Lerbury a week or so ago. I liked the colours."

I have no doubt it had once belonged to Piper. I remember buying it in Rome, on our honeymoon. It cost the earth, some designer or other, she'd made a fuss and said it was far too much to pay but I could see how much she liked it and told her it was only money. There was a wrinkle at the hem, which was so faint it was almost impossible to see. But I remember her distress when, one Christmas Eve, some candle wax had dropped on it as she'd bent over to set the table.

When Serena phones to tell me Piper has turned up at the police station I don't know what to think. I've already come to terms with the fact that she must be disturbed mentally. Whether I believe her story about abduction or not I'm not sure. In view of the fact she's been harassing me for months by playing stupid games I tend to think this is just one more. Although the logical part of my brain is convinced she needs psychiatric help, I no longer want to see her. I've moved on with my life and Piper is in the past. Isobel is my future and at the weekend I'd make her my wife.

She arrives just after I've dressed and I'm in the kitchen drinking my second cup of coffee of the day.

What happened to Piper Archer?.........K.J.Rabane

She kisses me and says, breathlessly, "You've heard then? How are you feeling?"

"Fine. Serena will sort her out. We have a wedding to think about."

She sighs, kisses me again then pours coffee into a mug and sits opposite me.

"I couldn't believe it when I heard Piper had returned," she says. "And ever since I've been so worried."

"Worried?"

"Afraid you'd call off the wedding, want to be with her, oh I don't know, any number of scenarios have been keeping me awake this morning."

I reach across the table and take her hand. "You don't have to worry any more. Piper is history and you are my future. By the way, Richard Stevens and his PA are coming over this morning."

"The Private Investigator?"

"Yes. He wants to talk to me about something."

She frowns, two deep furrows appear between her eyes. "I don't like the sound of that."

"Nonsense. I've told you – you've nothing to worry about. I'll take them into the conservatory, you don't even have to see them."

"It's not that. I don't mind; if I can be of any help, of course I will. It's just that I didn't really know your wife, except for the odd occasion I met her at Serena's."

"I understand. If they need to speak to you, I'll give you a shout. In the meantime, sit back, there are those magazines you left in the living room, perhaps even at this late stage you'll find some little piece of advice regarding our wedding arrangements which will require your attention."

What happened to Piper Archer?.........K.J.Rabane

The doorbell rings as I finish my coffee and watch Isobel walking towards the living room. I open the front door and show my visitors into the conservatory. Richard Stevens apologises for disturbing me then explains the reason for his visit.

"No doubt you've heard from your sister-in-law about Ronald Wengren's involvement with your wife?"

I can't stop an involuntary response, my breath hisses between my teeth in disgust and I nod.

"Well I've had a recent conversation with Mr Wengren during which he explained why your wife left you."

"Is this important?" I ask, not wishing to go over old ground, which brings back painful memories.

"I think it is, Mr Archer. I'm sorry to have to ask you this but I need to hear the truth and I believe only you are in possession of the full facts."

"Oh well, if you must," I reply, wishing the whole thing to be over as quickly as possible.

"You are aware that Mr Wengren served as a juror on the same case as Mrs Archer before she disappeared. It was how they met and it was he, whom she later visited on several occasions."

"Rowland Green."

"Exactly. It was her way of keeping his identity a secret."

"The details of her illicit affair don't concern me, Mr Stevens."

"There was no affair."

"I don't understand."

"The reason your wife left you was not because she was having an affair. It was because Wengren told her it was you who was responsible for her infertility."

What happened to Piper Archer?.........K.J.Rabane

I'm lost for words. What on earth is he talking about? He continues but none of it makes any sense, "Apparently, he told your wife he knew someone on the staff of the Princess Royal Teaching Hospital who, when asked, had said there was a cover up over a botched operation in the Obstetric Department around the time Mrs Archer was admitted for her termination. He told her the surgeon responsible for her operation was you."

"What? That's rubbish."

As I listen to the details Wengren has erroneously fed Piper, I feel my world tilting. What must she have thought? I should try to make her understand. But guilt, like a locked box, is stopping me from explaining to Richard Stevens exactly why revisiting the events of my surgical training at The Princess Royal is so difficult, especially as I now know it concerns Piper.

What happened to Piper Archer?.........K.J.Rabane

Chapter 77

"He had a women there," Sandy said, as Richie turned the key in the ignition. "I could smell her perfume."

"Astute as ever, Miss Smith."

"Isobel Myers?"

"I should think so."

"I wonder if we might have a word?"

"Why?"

Sandy bit her lip. "I would like to know how she's feeling about wife number one turning up. It's a bit like a film I saw once about a woman who got lost on a desert island and after a few years her husband, thinking her dead, remarried. Then the first wife re-appeared and havoc ensued. It was an old film – Doris Day or someone, played one of the wives."

"Mm, A comedy?"

"Yeah."

"This is no comedy, that's for certain. But I think you might have a point. Perhaps we *should* have a chat with Miss Myers."

Richie stopped the car. "In fact I think the sooner the better – Saturday is their wedding day – so it must be now or never."

Beresford Archer answered the door. His smile slid from his face when he saw them. "Forget something?"

Richie looked apologetic as he said, "We did. I'd like a word, with Miss Myers if possible."

"Um, I don't know. I'd have to ask her. Wait a moment."

He left them standing on the step and, a short while later, returned. "You'd better come in. Isobel is in the living room. Straight ahead and to your right."

What happened to Piper Archer?.........K.J.Rabane

The room was furnished in shades of beige with cream walls, the design minimalist; the effect was relaxing. Isobel Myers was reading a magazine and she stood up when they entered the room. She was tall, slender and fashionably dressed. Richie thought she wasn't pretty in the conventional sense, nothing like as pretty as Piper Archer but there was something attractive about her, sex appeal was too strong a description, it was indefinable.

"Please sit down. Beresford said you wanted to speak to me about something?" Her voice was low pitched.

Sandy was the first to speak. "First, let us wish you all the best for Saturday. It must very traumatic for you, having the first Mrs Archer suddenly appear out of nowhere."

Richie watched Isobel Myers trying to sound unconcerned. She almost got away with it, if it wasn't for the constant finger stretching of her left hand, the thumb seeking out the band of her engagement ring and stroking it.

"It's far worse for Beresford. It's something we have to get over together."

"Have either you or Mr Archer any intention of seeing Piper Archer before the wedding? I understand her sister and her husband are witnesses."

"Well, I suppose it's inevitable that we will meet, as Piper is staying with Serena and Mike."

"How do you feel about that?" Sandy was doing all the questioning giving Richie time to see her reaction.

"I won't lie and tell you I'm happy about it but as I said it's something we have to get over."

Her left hand tightened into a fist and the diamonds sparkled in a sudden shaft of sunlight shooting through the windows like an arrow.

Richie stood up. "I see. Thanks for giving us your time, Miss Myers. That's all we wanted to know. We'll leave you in peace now."

"That's it?"

"Just tying up some loose ends," Sandy said, with a smile. "I hope it's a sunny day for you on Saturday."

They left the house, each of them wondering if their conversation with Isobel Myers had been worthwhile or not. Eventually, Sandy said, "Is it just me, or is there something not quite right about her?"

"It's not just you," Richie replied, putting his foot firmly down on the accelerator and driving down the lane in the direction of Lockford.

What happened to Piper Archer?.........K.J.Rabane

Isobel

Chapter 78

I'm not a bad person. It's not as if I've committed murder. He might understand. But I know that's rubbish, he won't and who can blame him? Would I? I have my reasons and they stem from my childhood - the middle child of a family where you had to fight your corner to get anywhere.

I can almost hear Beresford saying, 'that's no excuse'. My first husband was a user, a selfish pig of a man with a handsome face but no money. It was years ago and ended when the brute put me in hospital with a broken jaw. Again it's no excuse – it's an explanation.

Moving to London was the best thing I did, far enough away from him. I worked hard, made some money and some good friends. When the chance came to work in Lockford, I jumped at it especially as my mother had died and left me the house. It was no surprise as my brother and sister lived abroad and could have bought three houses each on Westbourne Avenue without turning a hair.

I knew the manager of the Atlas Insurance Company Company, Kenneth Barnes, as I'd worked with him in London. He was easy going; we'd had a no strings affair once, a long time ago and remained friends.

It was through him I met Serena; he was a friend of Mike's. She used to go on about her sister and her wealthy husband as if they were royalty. I was intrigued, so encouraged our friendship. We used to meet up every week in town during my lunch hour. Bit by bit I got to know about Piper and her enviable lifestyle – a lifestyle I wanted. When she disappeared, I saw an opportunity and I took it, it was as simple as that. I followed Beresford Archer until managing to create a situation whereby we would meet and the rest is history.

I never expected her to return before I could complete my plan to hook him. The phone calls, the things left around the place suggesting Piper was coming back, unnerved both of us. He began pushing me away bit by bit but I stuck with it, determined not to let her come back into his life.

We were nearly there. I was sure he'd forgotten about her, put the whole marriage thing in the past where it belonged. His divorce came through and we'd named the day. Then my mobile rang and all my plans vanished like the new life I knew would never happen.

Serena

Chapter 79

It took a day or two, before I stopped pinching myself, believe me. It had all happened so quickly – the phone call from the police – seeing her – helping her to settle in to our spare bedroom. Piper spent most of the day, following her return, in bed and I waited on her hand, foot and finger. Mike left us to it. Privately I thought she should go back to Beresford and sort out her life, pick up the threads, make things right between them but she refused, so what could I do, she was my sister? But I could tell Mike wasn't happy about it, not by a long chalk.

On the Thursday, she was up and in the kitchen before me. "I thought I'd make you and Mike breakfast in bed," she said, putting a couple of slices of bread in the toaster.

"Mike had an early start love, he went ages ago. But thanks for the thought. You feeling better?"

"I am. And I can't thank you both enough for looking after me. But it's time I went to see Beresford. I can't hide here forever. He needs some sort of explanation."

"Want me to come?"

"Would you?"

"Of course."

"Then thanks. I'm not looking forward to seeing him one bit. I could do with some support." She took the wind right out of my sails then and no mistake. She came towards me and gave me a great big hug. "You've always been there for me, Sis," she said.

Before I knew it I was feeling angry. "Then why didn't you phone me – let me know you were OK?"

She looked confused. "Ronald said he'd spoken to you and you didn't want me to ring. I asked him several times and he said he was keeping you in the picture but that you didn't want to speak to me as it would be too upsetting."

"And you believed him?"

She sat down and pulled the sleeve of my dressing gown over her hands. "I did. You mean to say it was a lie?"

The fight went out of me. Anyone could see she was telling the truth. "I've not seen or heard anything from or about you for over two years, Pip."

The tears were genuine, they slid down her cheeks and she let them fall. Her head sank to her arms resting on the table and she sobbed uncontrollably. I cradled her as I'd done when she'd told me she was pregnant all those years ago.

Eventually, she shuddered and in a hoarse voice whispered, "Perhaps he was always lying. Perhaps none of it was true. Oh God I've been such a fool. I have to see Beresford. I have to explain."

"Berry's getting married in two days time; he might not want to see you, love"

She shook her head. "I can't leave it, Serena. For once I have to sort this out and on second thoughts, although I know you mean well and have always had my best interests at heart, I think perhaps this is something I have to do alone."

I stood up and stretched my cramped muscles. "OK. Let's get you ready then. This will be an ordeal. You've both been through the mill one way and another."

What happened to Piper Archer?………K.J.Rabane

Before she went into shower, she kissed my cheek. "I'm sorry all this has happened, Serena. I'm sorry I didn't phone. I'm sorry about so many things. "

She gave a weak smile and I hugged her. "No more apologies – let's move on, eh?"

She was still my sister after all, whatever Mike said. He was only thinking about me, afraid I'd be hurt. But what Berry was going to say about it all I dreaded to think.

Beresford

Chapter 80

I'm glad I decided to take a few days off before the wedding. Isobel suggested it might be wise and although it's going to be a very small affair I have been quite busy. I try not to think about Piper. Isobel said I must forget her now, as we have a life together to think of, and to stop looking back to the past.

She's as excited as a dog with two tails. This morning she's gone up to London. I think she's got a surprise up her sleeve and I find her spontaneity very appealing.

In my dressing room I'm looking for the tie I bought for Saturday when I hear the doorbell ring. I'm humming a chorus from La Bohème when I open the door.

My face must have registered shock at seeing her standing on the step.

"Can I come in, Beresford," she says; her voice is lower than I remember, her hair darker and badly cut. But I would have recognised those eyes anywhere.

"I'm afraid I'm busy at the moment," I sound sharper than I'd intended. The hurt is still there.

"Please. I understand why you don't want to speak to me but I must explain."

She looks so pathetic I capitulate. "If you must then." I stand aside and she passes me. I feel distinctly uncomfortable.

She makes for the kitchen and for some reason I feel annoyed. It's no longer her home.

"In here, please." I open the door into the conservatory.

What happened to Piper Archer?.........K.J.Rabane

The room is warm. The sun shines in through the glass walls and the residual heat from the central heating lingers. She sits on the chair, upright as if afraid to rest back on the cushions. I can see she's upset and the fight goes out of me. She meant so much to me once and I'm sorry it's come to this.

"Would you like a drink?"

"No, thank you. I need to say this. Then I'll let you get on."

I wait as she pulls the sleeve of her jacket down and looks up at the ceiling as if seeking inspiration. "I was told you operated on me when I was a teenager. I was told you were negligent. I was told it was why I wasn't able to have children." A single tear runs down her cheek and she wipes it away with the back of her hand and at last her eyes meet mine and I can see the depth of sorrow there.

I go to her and touch her hand. "It wasn't me."

She looks as if she hasn't heard properly. "I….." She shakes her head as if to clear her mind, "what d'you mean……I don't understand. You did work in obstetrics at the Princess Royal at the time. I've had it confirmed."

"I did. I was a Senior House Officer working on Aneurin Davies's team."

"So I *was* right. I was booked under him. But he didn't do the operation. It was someone else. I wasn't sure who at the time, as it was all such a nightmare one way and other. Serena and I hadn't told our mother and when they said the outcome of my termination was that I was unlikely to have children in the future, all I could think of was getting out of there and forgetting the whole thing."

What happened to Piper Archer?.........K.J.Rabane

I stand up and pace the floor, memories flooding back like an unstoppable tide. I have to tell her. There's no hiding the truth. I sit beside her and take her hand.

"During my time as an SHO I worked under Aneurin and his Senior Registrar, a man called Vernon Shackleton. Shackleton had the reputation of being a drinker and I'd often heard rumours that his failure rate was unacceptable. I was aware that the outcomes of some of his operations were lamentable and I suspect he was the one who performed your termination. The way his negligence was covered up by Aneurin Davies was one of the reasons I left the Princess Royal. It's always been something I regret – that I was too much of a coward to make a fuss – to blow the whistle on what was happening. If I had then maybe you, and people like you, wouldn't be in this position."

She shakes her head and sighs. "It's not your fault." She gets to her feet. "I should have told you before we were married then none of this would have happened."

"I'm sorry, Piper. Sorry you've had to live with this and sorry you couldn't confide in me. It must have been hell for you. And maybe, indirectly, I was to blame after all."

She shakes her head again. " No. That's not true. It wasn't your fault and I wish we could wipe it all away."

She looks so sad. The very least I can do is to comfort her. We hug. It's awkward at first but neither of us is willing to break away, knowing it will be the last contact we will have.

I'm aware we are no longer alone. I smell Isobel's perfume. "Darling, I've a surprise for you." She's standing in the doorway holding a package wrapped in wedding paper. Piper has broken away from my embrace. She rushes towards Isobel, lifts up her hand and strikes her across the face.

What happened to Piper Archer?………K.J.Rabane

Piper

Chapter 81

I knew it was her straight away. I could smell her perfume, heavy, cloying; I'd been trying to get it out of my nostrils for days. It was the woman I'd met at Serena's on several occasions before I'd been called for jury service. It was the scent I'd been trying to identify during the days I was locked in the basement room.

Anger welled up inside me, I broke free of Beresford's comforting arms and before I knew what I was doing I'd slapped her full across her face.

"Piper? What on earth are you doing?" Beresford caught my arm before I could slap her again. He could see I wasn't about to stop my assault on his fiancée.

"It's her," I spat at him. "She's the one who's been keeping me a prisoner for the past two weeks."

The woman put a hand up to her cheek where a red mark was growing larger by the minute. It was small satisfaction to see it, a payback, however slight, was definitely deserved.

"I don't know what she's talking about. She's making it up. I've been staying here for weeks – tell her, darling. Surely you don't believe her, Beresford?"

He looked confused. "I er, no of course not." He shook his head then walked into the hall and came back carrying my scarf. He held it up.

"I was wearing it when I came back from Cornwall," I said.

He didn't say a word just took his mobile from his pocket and I heard him say, "Could you come over to the house? There's a situation arisen and I need your advice."

"Sit down, both of you," he said.

The woman, I can't bring myself to say her name, tried to protest, but he was firm. I was content to wait. I was sure he'd called the police. They would sort things out, once I explained."

But I was mistaken; he hadn't called the police.

Chapter 82

They arrived at the house and parked the car in the drive, as a shaft of sunlight broke through the clouds swiftly followed by a shower of rain. Sandy looked up.

"Look, Boss, a rainbow; what d'you think - an omen?"

Richie pressed the doorbell. "We are about to find out, Miss Smith," he said, shaking raindrops from his hair.

They were assembled in the conservatory, the fading rainbow arcing above them. Beresford Archer indicated a two-seater sofa and Richie and Sandy sat down awkwardly perching on the soft cushions as if waiting outside the headmaster's study.

"I've asked you both to come here, instead of involving the police, as this is a very delicate matter and you are aware of the history behind this case," Beresford Archer was pacing the floor and addressing them as if giving a lecture.

He outlined the events preceding their arrival and, when he'd finished, sat in a chair well removed from either of the two women.

"As far as I can see you are faced with two possibilities here," Richie said, "Either you tell the police what you've told me and Miss Myers is charged with abducting Mrs Archer or Mrs Archer agrees not to press charges. But either way I will have to inform Lockford police; it can't be avoided.

Isobel Myers wrung her hands as her eyes filled with tears. "It wasn't my idea," she said. "I didn't abduct her. I just helped a friend. I didn't know why he wanted my basement I thought perhaps he'd had a row with his wife." She turned to Beresford. "Please believe me. I gave him a spare key, I thought he needed a place for a friend to stay in a hurry and, as I was staying here, I couldn't see a problem."

Piper Archer's reaction was more difficult to read. Eventually she shrugged and stood up. "I've had enough of it." She turned to her ex-husband. "If you want her, you can have her. I'm only sorry for doubting you in the first place. If it wasn't for me leaving you'd never had met her. I'll be staying at Serena's for while until I sort out where I'm going to live." She looked at Richie "If the police want to talk to me, tell them where to find me. I have no interest in pursuing this any further. I just want to forget the whole thing."

After she left the room, Richie and Sandy soon followed, leaving a visibly shaken man and his distraught future wife alone.

As they drove away from Elm Tree House, Sandy said, "Do you think they'll get married?"

Richie frowned. "Never in a million years."

Ronald

Chapter 83

Nancy thought she was doing the right thing. I had no doubt my best interests lay at the bottom of it. Although why she'd acted as she did was beyond me. After I'd explained about my conversation with Richard Stevens, I'd woken up to see her bending over me.

"What is it?" I asked.

"Oh thank goodness. I thought you'd taken something. You've been asleep for ages."

"I was shattered." I rubbed my eyes.

She sat down at my side and sighed. "It got out of hand, that's all. I never meant….she was no good for you, Ronald."

"Piper?"

"When you first mentioned she was leaving and you were determined to bring her back to Lockford, I was worried sick. I knew it would all come out, about you and her, and I was afraid the police would think you had taken her against her will."

"That would never have happened, Piper wouldn't let it," I said, indignantly.

"She could have caused trouble for you. First, I tried ringing Mr Archer pretending to be his wife. I hoped he'd start looking for her again and eventually they'd be reunited. Remember, I had no idea you'd lied to her about her husband."

I couldn't believe it. "Nancy? You rang pretending to be his wife?" I was incredulous. "Surely he would know her voice?"

What happened to Piper Archer?.........K.J.Rabane

"I've always had a good ear for mimicry but just to be sure I didn't say too much. He wanted to believe I was her you see? I just had to keep you safe, dear. But then you said she was planning to go to London after she'd sorted things out with her husband and I could see that perhaps it was better that he did marry Isobel after all."

I was confused. "Isobel? Who is Isobel?"

"Isobel Myers, dear. She lives further down the Avenue. We have the odd cup of coffee now and again, and she told me all about her forthcoming marriage. But then I saw her."

"You saw Piper?"

"She looked as if she was drunk and a man was helping her up the steps of Isobel's house. He opened the door and they both went inside."

"And you didn't think to tell me? All the time I was worried sick about what had happened to her and you didn't say a word?"

She was shaking her head, her eyes brimming with tears. "I know it was wrong of me but I was glad she was no longer your problem and I thought if I kept my mouth shut until after Isobel and Mr Archer were married it would solve a problem for both of us."

I stood up and walked to the window. The trees in the avenue were now devoid of leaves; they stood like sentries guarding the houses on either side of the road. Piper had been here all the time, in a house a stone's throw away from Nancy's.

"I'm so sorry, Ronald. I should have said something."

There was nothing more to say. She cared about me. She was the only one, it seemed.

"See you tomorrow then," I said, not looking at her.

What happened to Piper Archer?.........K.J.Rabane

"I'll be there, nine on the dot, as usual," she replied, straightening up and blowing her nose into a clean white handkerchief.

What happened to Piper Archer?………K.J.Rabane

Serena

Chapter 84

It was time I cleaned out Mike's Den. All this fuss with Piper had drained me. I needed to do something normal. She was staying with a friend in London for a week or two. Berry and Isobel had cancelled their wedding – well not cancelled exactly – postponed I supposed would be a better word, although I really can't see them getting together after all that's happened.

Carrying the cleaning materials downstairs, I smiled. Mike always said if I needed to sort things out I was like someone with cleaning mania. He was in London for a day or two, training, he said. I told him all this training at his age couldn't be good for him.

I don't know what's going to happen to Piper. Now she knows the truth she must think differently about Berry. She must still love him. At least he's still a member of our family for a bit longer, even if they are divorced – at least he hasn't got a new wife and I'm glad of that. Whatever Mike says, he's good for my sister, always has been. But it's anyone's guess how this mess is going to turn out.

The Den smelled musty. I opened the window with the pole Mike had made for me and let in some fresh air. It was a bit dark, as the sun hadn't come round to that side of the house yet. The dartboard looked dusty also the billiard table. I put on the radio. I never liked working without some music in the background. After dusting, I set about tidying the room. In one corner I picked up a pile of magazines and old newspapers and put them into a black plastic binbag along with a computer print out on how to make chloroform using household materials, although what Mike wanted that for was anyone's guess. I shook my head and sighed, there were a couple of empty cans of lager on the desk alongside a paperback and some emails about work.

I cleared the desk of rubbish, humming along to an old Rick Astley hit and opened the bottom drawer to put the paperback and emails away. That was when I had the shock of my life. Piper's handbag, the one she'd sworn was with her when she'd been abducted was there, half hidden by the brown paper folder Mike keeps for his work emails.

My heart began to race. Why was my sister's handbag hidden in my husband's desk drawer?

Chapter 85

Sandy was filing her nails when Richie arrived at the office.

"Nice haircut," she said, with a grin.

"Yeah, I know, scissor-happy Sid has taken over Bert's appointments, something about Bert coming down with gall-stones. At least I think that's what he said, you can never quite tell when Sid's got his mouth full mint humbugs."

"We might have a new client on our books. A man with a Welsh accent said he'd like to make an appointment to see THE BOSS. So I booked him in for Monday afternoon."

"Not tomorrow?"

Sandy put down the nail file. "Er, no. I thought we might have a few loose ends to tie up regarding the Archer case."

"Did you indeed?" Richie tried to look cross but failed as usual. "And to what 'loose ends' would you be referring?"

"Who is the man who Isobel Myers said abducted Piper Archer?"

"You don't think she was making it up to save herself? Remember Piper Archer seemed pretty sure it was her."

"Perhaps, but it doesn't make much sense How could she have been in two places at the same time?"

"I'm not with you."

"Archer confirmed that she had been staying at Elm Tree house during the time his wife insists she was kept locked up in a basement somewhere. At the very least Isobel Myers must have had an accomplice."

What happened to Piper Archer?.........K.J.Rabane

Richie paced the floor. "Who is in the frame? Ronald Wengren is the only one I can think of. Why would anyone bother to hide her for a couple of weeks only to release her later – there was no talk of a ransom."

"I doubt if we'll ever find out," Sandy said, despondently, whilst continuing to file her nails.

"Don't be disheartened, Miss Smith. We'll get to the bottom of this. I suggest we talk to the one person who knows the identity of Piper Archer's abductor."

"Isobel Myers?"

"Precisely."

"And you think she'll talk to us?"

"I think there's a reason she was reluctant to disclose the identity of this so called friend of hers. I think it's because either Piper or Archer know him."

Richie drove past Nancy Smedley's house and continued down Westbourne Avenue until he reached Isobel Myers property. It was a dark, dismal day and a light was on in a downstairs window.

"So she's not spending today at Elm Tree then," Sandy said.

"Looks like we're in luck." Richie parked further down the Avenue and they walked back to the house.

It was obvious that she'd been crying. Her face was pale and there were dark circles under her eyes. She was wearing an unflattering grey woollen cardigan and jeans.

"Miss Myers?"

She tried to close the door but Richie put his foot inside. "We won't keep you a moment. But we do need to speak to you. I suggest you let us in, otherwise you'll be having a visit from Inspector Mayes of Lockford Police."

What happened to Piper Archer?.........K.J.Rabane

She stood back and allowed them into the hall. "In here then," she said.

The room was sparsely furnished. The whole place looked shabby, an air of transition hung around the walls and lingered over the furniture.

"Well. Get it over with." Sitting on an upright chair facing them she shifted uncomfortably and nervously bit the skin around her thumb.

"We need to know the identity of the person who you said had access to your basement room."

"I don't see why. Piper Archer's convinced it's me and she doesn't intend to pursue it any further."

Richie stood up. "I see. Well I would just like to point out that your reluctance to give us a name will not go down so easily with Lockford Police. A crime has been committed and they will consider you are withholding evidence."

He could see Sandy was impressed. So he must have sounded convincing even though he thought it highly unlikely the police would pursue the matter as neither Piper nor Beresford Archer seemed in a mood to prosecute.

Isobel Myers stood up and placed a hand on his arm.

"Mr Stevens, my reluctance to give you a name is because this will only cause more trouble for the family."

"I see. However, would you be happy to divulge his identity were I to tell you this information will be kept in our files and not disclosed to the police or anyone else? Of course if the police decide to follow up the matter it will be up to you and your conscience how to proceed. However, Miss Smith and I need to close our case files and would be grateful for your co-operation."

What happened to Piper Archer?.........K.J.Rabane

She sighed "Very well. I can see you are not going to let this rest until I tell you. So, I will have to rely upon your discretion.

What happened to Piper Archer?.........K.J.Rabane

Serena

Chapter 86

I was waiting for him to come home. I'd been at sixes and sevens all day, ever since I'd found Piper's handbag. I was so distraught I couldn't even finish the cleaning. I'd lost count of how many cups of coffee I'd drunk.

The handbag was sitting on the coffee table in front of me when I heard him turn the key in the lock.

"Serena, love. I'm home."

My hands were shaking and I knew he'd come looking for me, after he'd seen I wasn't chained to the stove cooking his tea, as usual.

"What are you doing in here, love?" He came towards me and bent to kiss my cheek. "Are you OK? You're shaking. What on earth's the matter?"

He saw it then and I felt him stiffen.

"Explain that, Mr Platt!" I spat at him.

He slumped in the chair opposite me.

"I can, I promise. Just give me a second."

"Time to make up a story, is it? Time to think up a tale to explain why you would have my sister's handbag in your desk drawer. The one she had with her when she was abducted."

He put his hands up to his face and rested his head on them, closed his eyes and sighed. "OK. Time to come clean. I admit it."

I almost felt sorry for him he looked so dejected then I remembered what he'd done. He'd locked my sister up for nearly two weeks before releasing her. "Go on then – let's hear it – every last bit of it."

What happened to Piper Archer?........K.J.Rabane

Mike said he'd stopped at the services a short distance from home. He'd been visiting a friend in London, the one who'd had the heart attack on the golf course. He'd parked alongside a dark blue Ford and was about to go into the service station for something to eat when he saw her asleep in the front seat.

He said it made him insanely angry when he thought about all the worry she'd given me. Then he decided she must be on her way back to Beresford. He was sure it would all start again, the worry, Izzie's marriage plans failing, Berry being upset. Mike was desperate to see that the marriage happened so that I'd be free of Beresford Archer and his problems. He said he didn't know what came over him.

He said she didn't wake up even when he opened the car door and called to her. It was as if she were drugged. Before he knew what he was doing, he'd hauled her out of the seat. She was so light it was like carrying a bag of feathers, he said. He didn't actually carry her of course, that would have looked suspicious. He placed his arm around her shoulder and opening the passenger door to his car, which was only a short step away from the blue Ford, slid her into the front seat. Then he anchored her seatbelt and drove off as quickly as he could. Once on the motorway, he began to think about where he could take her and the only place he could think of was Izzie's. He was sure she wouldn't want Piper turning up either, until she was safely married.

To tell you the truth I still can't believe he did it. He did say it was like a madness had come over him and once he'd started he couldn't stop, especially as he soon found out that Izzie was willing to go along with it all. He didn't want to hurt Piper, not for a second, just keep her out of sight until the marriage was over. He told me

What happened to Piper Archer?.........K.J.Rabane

he was fed up of me hero worshipping Berry and making him feel inadequate. I told him that was stuff and nonsense but I can see how he might have thought so, that's why I think I might stick by him.

Anyway, the next thing that happened was Mike found a parking space outside Izzie's front gate. It was getting dark and Piper was still drowsy but as luck would have it Izzie was just leaving the house with a suitcase. She was off to stay at Elm Tree for a while. To cut a long story short, together they managed to help Piper inside, Izzie opened the basement door, Piper's scarf floated to the floor and he remembered Izzie picking it up as he guided Piper down the steps. It was like controlling the strings of a gigantic puppet, he said, she swayed and faltered and at one point he thought she was going to topple forward down the steps. But she wasn't heavy. She fell on top of the bed and drifted off to sleep and by now he was certain she'd been drugged and knew that someone else had also been determined to keep Piper away from Elm Tree house.

He knew keeping her locked up in the basement was wrong, he knows he shouldn't have done it; it just came over him. He hated the whole business but once he'd started it, he couldn't see a way out. Letting her go before Berry married Izzie was because he couldn't bear leaving her there a moment longer, every day that passed he regretted what he'd done.

When he'd finished telling me it all, he took my hand. "I'm sorry, love. I'll never be able to make it up to you. Please say it's not the end for us," he said.

"It should be," I replied, but didn't take my hand away from his. I could see he was sorry – it was a mistake and we all make mistakes after all – we're only human.

What happened to Piper Archer?.........K.J.Rabane

"Isobel promised she would't tell anyone it was me, unless the police put the blame on her. But she's told me that neither Piper nor Beresford want to go on with the case. They just want to forget it ever happened," Mike said, stroking my hand.

"Piper said as much before she went up to London but I had no idea there was anyone else involved. She said Izzie made up some tale but she was sure it was a lie. But if they can forget it then I suggest we do the same. Get rid of that though. I don't want to see it in my house again.' I thrust the handbag at him. 'And if there is anything else you haven't told me, you can take a hike. By the way what about her suitcase?"

"There's nothing, Serena, I promise. I didn't see a suitcase."

I was furious with Izzie It was her fault this had happened. If she'd refused to help Mike hide my sister he'd have brought her home, I know he would. So it was she who was to blame really. Mike just made a mistake. And I know how that feels better than anyone. When Berry told me Piper had returned, cooked a meal then left whilst he was having a shower, I was sure he was imagining it. But the more I thought about it and the closer he got to Izzie I decided it would do no harm to keep him thinking Piper was about to come back. I feel ashamed of what I did now, making him think she'd had a shower, letting him believe I'd arrived to find evidence that she'd been to Elm Tree house, when all the time, it was me, planting hair in the shower, leaving food in the kitchen and on the table in the garden – so you see I could understand how bad Mike was feeling about his part in it all.

I did feel sorry for Piper, she was the innocent one, but she's OK now, isn't she? I know they say blood is

What happened to Piper Archer?.........K.J.Rabane

thicker than water but I've always looked out for her even when she was little. It's time I supported Mike now. He is my husband after all and I'm not comfortable about the part I played in all this. As the bible says – he who has no sin cast the first stone – or something of the kind.

Beresford

Chapter 87

The wedding day has come and gone and so much has happened since the day Piper accused Isobel of keeping her locked up in her basement.

I've managed to come to terms with it now. I knew it, immediately Piper came to the house that day, I couldn't go through with my marriage to Isobel. I'd been fooling myself all along. Even with her badly cut hair and after all that had happened I knew there was something still there and consequently it was over between Isobel and me. Unable to forget her part in Piper's abduction, whatever her motivation had been, we agreed to call it a day. Isobel has moved back to London and I think it's for the best for all concerned.

I've decided to retire from medicine. I don't need the money; I need peace to work on my novel. It started with my diary entries about what happened to Piper and I found I liked the solitude writing gives me. The book I'm working on is a fictional account based on comic recollection of incidents during my career. My agent likes the finished draft and sees no reason why it shouldn't be a success. I intend to publish under a pseudonym; having experienced more than my fair share of publicity it suits me to write incognito. Anonymity is far preferable to the alternative.

As for my relationship with Piper, I believe we can at least be friends for the moment. We are no longer husband and wife and I've long since come to terms with any regrets I've had regarding my marital status. Whatever lengths Isobel went to are for her to wrestle with her conscience over; I will always be grateful that she helped me steer a steady course when my mind was in turmoil. She still insists she was just helping out a friend during the time Piper was locked in her basement. I'm not sure I believe her but she shows no signs of divulging that friend's identity, so I suppose it's a lie. Piper and I decided not to pursue the matter with the police or Richard Stevens but to let sleeping dogs lie. The harm was done to our relationship long before Isobel intervened. It happened with a lie told by a man who was in love with my wife.

Piper shows no immediate urgency to live elsewhere and Serena says she's welcome to stay as long as she wishes. She enjoys the company since she and Mike split up. I don't think anyone saw that one coming. I always thought they were happy. Maybe the ripples in the stream caused by Piper's disappearance reached them and grew into something more destructive.

I meet Piper once a week for a meal and a chat and neither of us is looking for more, but it's early days. There has to be time to heal, time to grieve over our past life together and see if we can build a new one.

However, in my experience, life has a way of complicating matters, just when you thought you were quite safe it creeps up behind you like a thieving jackdaw stealing away the bright jewel of certainty.

THE END

What happened to Piper Archer?.........K.J.Rabane

If you enjoyed reading this book please don't keep it to yourself and if you have a spare moment let me know by reviewing your purchase on www.amazon.co.uk.

If you are looking to read more from me, visit www.kjrabane.com.

Many thanks, K.J.Rabane

What happened to Piper Archer?.........K.J.Rabane

K.J.Rabane has written short stories for magazines and an anthology of crime fiction, in addition to which she's written television scripts for an on-going drama series, which is ready for submission. She is also a commissioned writer for the Food & Drink Guide and works as a freelance supporting artist ('extra') for film and television productions.

Her main interest is in writing crime fiction and psychological thrillers but her novel *According to Olwen* falls into neither category. All her books are full of idiosyncratic characters and her crime fiction novels are plot driven.

Her poem *Luminous socks* reached the final of the 2012 All Wales Poetry Competition and her novel *Who is Sarah Lawson?* reached the Quarter Finals of the Amazon Breakthrough Novel Award 2013 Competition. To check out a comprehensive list of reviews on all of K.J.Rabane's books visit www.amazon.co.uk.

Follow K.J.Rabane on Facebook and Twitter.

Printed in Great Britain
by Amazon.co.uk, Ltd.,
Marston Gate.